Fireflies
in the
Field
a birch harbor novel

ELIZABETH
BROMKE

PUBLISHING IN THE PINES

White Mountains, Arizona

✿ Created with Vellum

PROLOGUE

Nora

Some years earlier.

Boats bobbed against their slips, drifting up and down over the soft evening waves of Lake Huron.

Nora stood at the piling and held herself against it. A gentle breeze slid inside her chiffon shawl, cooling her skin and sending a shiver down her spine.

The dock lamps glowed softly above and around them. Just hours before, boat shoes and flip-flops tromped up the wooden planks and into Birch Harbor. Just hours before, he'd arrived. His weekly trip. His forever promise.

This time, however, was different. Not all different. For, Nora's response never had changed. *No*, she wasn't interested. *No*, she wouldn't go with him. *No. No. No.*

It was Gene who'd turned over a new leaf.

Earlier that day, they had bumped into each other at the Village. Where else?

That's when she found everything changed. The game of cat and mouse. The unending history. Their secret. It was over.

They locked eyes outside of the Harbor Deli, where he stood ordering on behalf of a wisp of a woman. Icy blonde like Nora. Fewer grays. Better root coverage, maybe. Firmer skin. More expensive sunglasses. All of it. She was Nora if Nora had aged better. Or Nora ten years earlier. Or ten pounds lighter and six inches cuter. Still, a fierceness about their dynamic assaulted Nora. Eased her but irritated her, irrationally.

Gene nodded at Nora, lifting his paper cup of midday margarita in a distant toast. Nora turned to her girlfriend and ignored the gesture entirely.

But moments later, she looked back and caught the woman watching her. That's when Nora knew. It was time.

Time to say goodbye for good. Time to tell him that she was so happy for him and that it gave her peace to know that Gene could move on.

Yes, Gene could move on from her, if not Birch Harbor; and it was apparent that he wouldn't be doing the latter. It was painfully apparent that she'd have to share the small town, *her* small town, with this man who was once a boy who found himself wrapped inside of the worst thing that could happen on the heels of a summer fling. And he didn't even run from it. He'd clung to it. To their shared drama.

But Nora wouldn't. She pushed ahead, of course. She pushed past the whole horrid thing with a passion. And then, there was that second wave of shame and humiliation. The one that Nora could *not* move on from. Ever. Ever. Ever.

"Gene," she called into his boat.

She had followed him there carefully. Once the little blonde tucked herself inland in some weekend vacation rental (at least, that's what happened in Nora's mind's eye), Gene, always the gentleman, had wandered past the house on the harbor, in full view of Nora as she sat smoking a cigar. *A cigar! For goodness' sake! What was wrong with her?*

She sat there, in a weather-worn deck chair, her gaze following the steady flow of traffic, local and tourist alike, her eyes homing in on any gray-haired six-footer with a bright polo and khakis. There were many, in fact. Some cooler than others. Some more handsome. None emitting the distinctiveness that Gene Carmichael always seemed to.

Eventually darkness fell. Late. Too late. After the vast majority of foot traffic ebbed, she caught him waving goodbye to someone or some ones, she wasn't sure. Nora kept her gaze on him. Just a hundred yards or so away, she confirmed it was Gene when he found his way to the third berth, *The Carmichael Berth*, as she called it to herself, although Gene was the only Carmichael who drifted in and out on any given weekend.

The Carmichaels visited Birch Harbor when Gene was a senior in high school. Eventually, he'd gone off for college, returning soon after and taking up with the school district, pinching Nora out to the lake. Crowding her. Pressuring her.

After some years teaching then running Birch Harbor

High, his time rounded out to a split in some city down the shore and far inland and weekends in Birch Harbor, where Nora had the displeasure of watching him cavort as some sort of half-tourist-half-local hybrid. A charming phenomenon who came into town wearing polos and left wearing Hawaiian shirts.

She glanced briefly inside to ensure Clara wasn't watching. Clara, her bored little helpmate who had no idea how much Nora treasured her. Never would, probably.

With the coast clear, Nora dipped down off her back porch and picked through her yard, then down onto the sand.

Gene had long disappeared into his vessel, but she forged ahead, jogging lightly toward the dock, pulling her shawl around her shoulders as her short hair bounced off her neck. She felt young again, with new energy to confront this man who haunted her. Asking her always to come back to him, especially after Wendell left.

Seeing him like that, earlier, at the deli, should have been confirmation enough that he'd finally leave her alone. Let her *be*.

But Nora wanted confirmation. She wanted it over with. She wanted to know that he was done pestering her, done hoping. That she could well and truly settle into her golden years without the threat of this man always begging, always nagging her to be his.

He wasn't a predator. He wasn't a bad man. He was a bothersome, meddlesome man who tied Nora to a bad memory. Sometimes, though, a person like that—a person with whom one shared a bad memory—became bad by virtue of the commonality. He was made worse, of course, when he wouldn't just leave her *alone.*

And now she would go to him. She would *go to him* and see to it that he was done. That they were done. That they could bury the past and that Nora could take whatever time she had left on the earth and know that this threat—this threat of her secret surfacing or her connection to the wealthy summer tourist named Gene Carmichael... Nora could know that it was over.

"Gene!" she cried, this time shielding her call with her hand and glancing back up to the marina, fearful of drawing attention.

A shadowy figure appeared in the sunken doorway of the boat.

Nora waited, and when she saw that it was Gene, glassy-eyed and dark in the night, she began to unleash. "The woman," she began with no hello, no easy slide into a calm adult conversation.

Gene frowned, but Nora had no patience for that game.

"Listen, it looks like you're happy, but I just want to make sure—"

He interrupted her. "You want to know if I've moved on?" An eerie grin took shape on his mouth as he moved, hand over hand on the side of the boat, toward her.

Tugging her shawl over her like a blanket, she nodded and frowned. "Listen Gene. I'm happy for you. This is a very good thing. It means we can let bygones be bygones. Right?" Nora dipped her chin. He was just in front of her now, near the piling she'd pushed off of as soon as he emerged from the bowels of his vessel. It was his turn to grab it, hold himself there. She took one step back, but they were still within just feet of each other.

Gene's expression was hard to make out even with the lamplight overhead. It was his voice that gave her reassurance, though.

"Yes. Bygones. Nora," he went on. His boat rocked beneath him and grabbed the piling with his second hand. The feebleness took her by surprise. Gene was a seafaring tourist with pocketsful of money and every summer to spend on the harbor. And here he was, unsteady on his feet. As he pulled himself more upright, new light spread over his face and she saw up close the soft wrinkles. The shaven jawline and sparse eyebrows. The shell of the man who she more often than not had, unreasonably perhaps, *feared*.

And in that moment, Nora was no longer frightened. Everything about their dynamic flipped itself like a scaly trout, flopping across the wet wood of the dock.

Just when Nora was about to thank him and leave and feel that her entire quest was a success... that she could go home, smoke another cigar, sip a glass of wine, and chat with Clara and be *free*, a second figure emerged from the inside of the Carmichael houseboat. A small figure. Frightening and threatening Nora all over again. It was the woman from the deli, and there was a wide, strained smile plastered across her glowing white teeth.

At first, Nora tried for decency, offering a small wave. But then, a look about Gene's petite companion told Nora that no good would come of even the briefest and sweetest of introductions.

Gene, apparently, agreed. When Nora glanced at him, his face grew red and he fumbled over some explanation about an *old schoolmate* and something about planning a *high school reunion* as if Nora wasn't the *mother* of his *child* who he had *refused to leave alone* all those years.

There, just in front of her, he *lied*. He told this beautiful, miniature version of Nora some *lie* about their history. A distortion. A twist of the truth so far removed from her sense of reality, that Nora had to grab at the piling herself just in time for Wendell to release it and move to the woman.

The dock gave way beneath her feet. Maybe it was bucking over a heavy wave, but then Gene's boat wasn't rocking. The lady wasn't rocking. Gene wasn't. Just Nora. Unmoored by the strange disconnect between how Gene had veritably chased her for so long, moving into her town and planting himself there like some sort of king of the lake and how he was framing their connection, undermining the truth to this tourist. This strange *tourist*.

And then Nora knew that nothing was over. It had only just begun. And she wondered where this would go. How it would end. *If* it ever would.

"A schoolmate?" the woman asked, nearing Nora and lacing her fingers across crisp white shorts, entirely steady on the water. "But Gene isn't from Birch Harbor?"

Inexplicably, Nora found herself adding to his lie, to the story. Her own spin, stringing out from her mouth on floaty notes as if she was always in on it. "Right. He spent a semester here. He taught my girls. The reunion, um, is for them. Gene was like a father to my daughters."

Surprise stretched across the woman's face. "How bizarre," she murmured as silence swept across the dock. "I'm afraid I'm not quite sewn into the fabric of this place yet." She lifted a smooth, tanned, manicured hand up toward the Village.

Gene cut in, saving them all. Or condemning them, perhaps. "Judith, this is Nora. Nora, this is Judith Banks."

There was no handshake. Not across the turbulent distance between the Carmichael houseboat and Nora's refuge at the piling. But a crafty smile curled across Judith's mouth.

"Nora," she said, the name sounding strange on the woman's lips. "Nora...?"

Frowning, Nora flicked a glance to Gene.

He answered his friend. "Hannigan. Nora Hannigan." Then, with a foolish grin, he added, as if on accident, "They call her the Queen of Birch Harbor."

And it was the wrong thing to say. Nora knew in an instant. It was the wrong thing to say.

1

MEGAN

Heat prickled along her skin as Megan Stevenson leaned over a sun-bleached patio chair. Pinching the corners of the little waterproof pillow, she frowned.

Her backyard had never looked so good. It was a shame, really, that one's house was at its absolute finest on the precipice of the end.

Megan and Brian had agreed to list.

Just to see, she'd said, hemming and hawing over price point and what concessions they ought to make (spoiler: none). *Maybe we'll get a nibble*, she'd said, knowing full well in her heart that even if they got a full-priced offer, she'd chew on the tips of her nails, little black bits of polish flaking off until she couldn't take it anymore and she'd say, *Brian, you just decide. I can't* do *this*.

And he did decide, for the both of them. They had no choice, really. It was inevitable.

In the interim, the seemingly endless expanse of time

between when the house *might* sell and whatever happened next... well, who knew *what* they would do.

Okay, that was unnecessarily dramatic.

They *did* have a loose plan in terms of living arrangements.

Brian had found a townhome closer to the city. Closer to new opportunities. More affordable. He'd even shown Megan the listing. She'd responded to him ambiguously. *That* could *work*. And *Right. Maybe*. She knew it maddened him to be free floating. No commitment. Other than to their tenuous marriage, of course.

Did such a thing exist? Commitment during the threat of divorce? Megan wondered. It would appear that, yes, they were still committed. Delicate though the bonds of that commitment may be.

For her part, well, Megan had all of Birch Harbor. She had a room at the Heirloom Inn. Or an apartment at The Bungalows. Her sister, Amelia, may even have an extra futon in the lighthouse, if Megan needed it. If worse came to worse, then she could stay in the cottage, too.

Then, there was the land. Out off of the main drag, less than a mile from the shore. Acres of it. A wood-encircled plot that once could have been a cherry orchard or a dairy farm, grassy and lush with a pond at the far corner. If Megan knew how to pop up a tent, it was hers for the taking. Brian could bring a tent, too. If they got cold overnight, she'd tiptoe barefoot across the dew-damp grass and unzip his little tent door, slip inside, wiggle her way into his sleeping bag as he snored, and...

And Sarah? Well, even more of Birch Harbor belonged to their seventeen-year-old daughter. She had all of the above and then some. Her aunts would happily welcome their sweet niece. Her new townie friends, made quickly and over the summer as teenage friendships often are, were already begging for Sarah to stay over. To *move* there. To become a local.

Hah. Megan had laughed at that one. *You can never be a local, even if we move there,* she'd chided. Sarah pouted in reply. Brian had smirked. Megan liked that. The small agreement. The ounce of hope.

Now, Megan pushed her fingers into her temples and massaged tight circles.

"Kate, what if it sells right away?"

Megan's older sister (and newly appointed realtor) lifted her eyebrows. "Wouldn't that be a good thing?"

Shrugging, Megan left the patio in favor of a blast of air conditioning. Kate followed. The open house was set to begin in just minutes. Inside, Megan fiddled with the short stack of spec sheets, pages hot off the printer from Brian's in-home office.

"Listen, Meg. You have a plan. Once it sells, you come to Birch Harbor. Brian rents the townhouse. You two figure it out from there. Easy."

It did sound easy when Kate said it. Like a firm set of guidelines for "How to Navigate A Fledgling Separation." However, Megan knew what Kate did not know. The ugly sadness of things. The state of the union and the people inside of it.

Kate's plan and the hidden truth were a far cry from Megan's twilight vision of how things *could* go in her fantasy, the one that played out over a wine-tipsy dinner when Sarah was gone and they had the house uncomfortably, tantalizingly, to themselves for once.

That was the dinner where previous momentum, the

momentum of lawyer-speak and paperwork and dissolution this and division-of-assets that... it crashed to a stop.

That draining momentum had picked up on the heels of a marriage that got caught in a cove of craggy rocks and just stuck there, like seaweed, gooey and lifeless and useless. And all over what? Her wish to find a great job? His drive to carry on like usual, whistling as he worked? Their mutual silence about the fact that Megan was floundering. Floundering in a sea of self-doubt and the sorts of regrets only homemakers can know. The ones their husbands cannot fathom. The kinds of things that drive Virginia Woolf types to do Virginia Woolf things.

Megan was no Virginia Woolf, though. She'd watch documentaries about the woman. Read books if she was *really* bored. But ultimately, Megan was happy.

Anyway, it was at that private, tentative dinner, just weeks before, on the tails of discovering the lighthouse and Nora's diary entries and in the wake of Kate's reunion with Matt... it was there that angry energy turned soft. Megan and Brian shelved the legal pages that had been so carefully curated by their two separate lawyers. She'd clapped the ick from her hands and smiled at him over the table. He smiled back. They shoveled mint chocolate chip ice cream into their mouths.

And then, he murmured an apology.

No.

No divorce yet. That part of things remained the same. By now, the paperwork was likely expired. Did divorce paperwork expire? Was there a best-by date when someone said they wanted to quit love?

She hoped so.

Still, the grand fantasy fizzled in a matter of days.

June wore into July. Megan and Brian's alone time, the time away from Sarah, who stayed in Birch Harbor to help her aunts, began to feel less like alone time and more like *together time*. And in a wobbly marriage, *together time* was generally a bad thing.

The Fourth of July, Megan's second favorite holiday after Halloween, had presented a fresh opportunity. She and Brian ambled down to the local parade, a Who's Who of Suburbia.

But that year the floats lacked the magical patriotism that Independence was meant for. Instead of hope, each coasting trailer blared out messages of disruption. And those were the better ones. Others were decorated commercials, touting garish sponsorships out of Detroit. Then, the school's marching band passed them *in between* its rotations of "America the Beautiful" and "This Land is Your Land," so all Megan and Brian had were the tired drummers, fumbling along to a beat, weak and out of tune, ready to shed their itchy uniforms and chug a pop before the cherry pit spitting contest.

Then, later, Megan and Brian returned home to what might have been an intimate barbecue. But the burgers Brian cooked were too charred. Megan's lemonade too sour. Finally, the fireworks, the part she anticipated so fiercely that there was no way they could have lived up to her dreams... well, those fireworks started too late. So, after the parade and crispy burgers and acrid lemonade, Megan and her almost-ex fell into bed.

The same one, yes.

But sleep came too quickly for one or the other. Neither knew which since both were pretending.

Now, Megan folded one of the real estate spec sheets

into a tight square and shoved it into her back pocket. A memento or scratch paper for some undetermined future use, she didn't know which.

The doorbell rang. Megan stirred back to life. No one liked a sulky attitude. Least of all potential homebuyers. Of course, they also didn't like the home seller to be around, peeking over their shoulder as they inspected the drawers for signs of errant hair ties. Or as they criticized the distinct lack of storage space—storage space, of all things!

"I'm out of here," Megan whispered to her sister, as the latter strode towards the front door.

Slipping back out onto the patio, she cinched her dark ponytail tighter and tiptoed through the backyard and around to the front of the house in time for the first arrivals to step into Kate's warm, realtor-y greeting.

Once in her car, Megan let out a sigh of relief. She turned the ignition and punched the air on, then checked her mirrors, ready to take a few lazy loops throughout the neighborhood.

The gear stayed in park, though, and soon enough Megan found herself on the phone, her fingers navigating to him, the familiar name and the familiar digits... hitting Send. Waiting as it rang. Once. Twice. His voice came on.

As he answered, another call came in. Kate. Megan let it go to voicemail. Soon enough, she'd hear about the open house. The interested party with the hefty down payment and a taste for pillows on patio furniture.

It was all but irrelevant because as Megan heard his voice, something occurred to her. Something more important than a house in the suburbs with its lack of storage space and close proximity to the school.

The burgers weren't that burned. The lemonade was more tart than sour, really. The fireworks weren't too late... the bed was just too comfy. And Megan knew for a *fact* that when she thought he'd fallen asleep, finally, long after the finale of stars and stripes had petered out... Brian's hand had brushed hers. Beneath their covers. Just days before.

Maybe the Fourth wasn't a bust. Maybe it was a beginning.

"So, what's the plan?" Kate flashed a grin at her sister and Brian. "You'll both move into the Heirloom Inn? With me?"

Previously, she'd been under the impression Brian was going his separate way. To an apartment or something. But then, a day after the offer came in on the Stevensons' house, he decided to join Megan on the lake for the day. And Megan had whispered something to Kate about hope. A reunion. New plan.

Kate was confused.

Sure enough, there they were, back in Birch Harbor, sipping iced tea at Birch Village. Shore birds barked just yards off, at the edges of the dock, as tourists and locals came and went, striding in steady measure up and down the wooden planks, laughing and flushed in the Michigan summer sun.

Megan held Kate's gaze, slowly nodding her head. "As long as you're sure we aren't taking income from you. And as long as Sarah has a comfortable place somewhere. Until we make permanent arrangements. For *everyone*."

They'd been over this. It was the only option now that the offer on the house was in. Things were moving fast. Too fast, perhaps, for Megan and Brian, who weren't as cemented in their plan as Kate thought.

"Sarah can keep staying with Clara. Or Amelia. She's the least of your concerns." Kate said. "You can stay with me. Both of you. For however long you need." She lifted a brow to them. "We reserved my old room for family. It's empty. It's *yours*." She smiled at Brian, who shifted in his seat, uncomfortable.

Megan's eyes flicked to her husband before returning to her iced tea. "Does that work for you?" She frowned, running her finger up the side of the glass.

Brian's hands flew up. "Listen, this is awkward. I didn't think the place would go fast. When Megan called me before I left town, I panicked. I... I stopped by that townhouse and signed. The lease, I mean." He shook his head to himself and lowered his gaze, pushing his fingers into his eyes and rubbing them.

"You *what*?" Megan replied, her voice cold. Kate's anticipation turned to dread. No way did she wish to be a party to drama. Megan kept her cool, but her face and voice filled with hurt. "Why didn't you tell me?"

Kate sat, quiet, trying to pretend she wasn't even there. Just another patron at a different table minding her own business. Someone wasn't telling the truth. Megan, probably. Or, even worse, she wasn't *facing* the truth.

"Just a month-to-month. I didn't want to take a chance." His answer came out under his breath, like he was ashamed to admit it.

Megan's tone softened. "Oh. Okay." Then her eyes flashed back to Kate. "I'll stay with you. That'll be fine. I can help. At least until..."

Surprised at how quickly the building squabble halted into resolution, Kate simply lifted her gaze. "Until?"

Brian reached a hand to the back of Megan's chair then started to recoil, then settled it on the edge. The smallest hint of how tenuous their dynamic really was. Still, he left it, and Kate thought he was trying to watch Megan from the corner of his eye. It was fascinating to behold: that subtle game of cat and mouse wherein the roles continually flipped back and forth. Brian cleared his throat and Megan finally met his stare. Kate thought her sister's face reddened. Maybe it was July playing across her cheeks. Maybe something else. "Until we have a place," he said, his voice low.

Megan's eyes grew wide, and Kate wanted to grin like a fool. Instead, she followed Megan's cue, simply smiling and sipping from her tea.

"Yeah," Megan managed, choking a little on her tea. "Good idea."

With the matter settled, they commenced eating their sandwiches. The afternoon stretched before them, and Kate's to-do list, which previously felt miles long and thicker than a stack of Bibles, turned into mindless fodder for the remainder of the trio's lunch. Having odds-and-ends to discuss apparently relaxed Brian, who chimed in on occasion, going as far as to make frequent eye contact with both Kate and his wife. His hand settled further along Megan's chair back, and from Kate's position, it looked like he'd wrapped it around his wife's shoulders.

It was no wonder the divorce ended up rockier than the marriage, Kate thought. Those two were meant to be together. It's why they lost the paperwork. It's why Brian returned to town with Megan, like a forlorn puppy dog. But it didn't explain why they put their house on the market. If a couple wasn't quite certain about parting ways, why add another monkey wrench and give up the only stable force in their life?

No matter how sweet his nervous hand or easy agreement, or how quick Megan was to smile at him... it was clear to Kate that they still needed *out* of something.

Maybe that was why they listed.

A fresh start. Someplace new. Even if the someplace was no place and they weren't together, anyway.

BRIAN COVERED THE CHECK, shuffling between a couple different credit cards before settling on one, thanking the women for their company, then leaving to head back into the city. He needed to see about the townhome and settle some other paperwork.

Megan sighed deeply after he strode from the table. Her eyes never left him.

Once it was just the two sisters again, Kate suggested they stroll down to the lake and walk off lunch.

"Do you think it'll close quickly?" Megan asked, as they slid out of their shoes and plucked them up by the heels, stepping onto the warm beach on the north end of the dock.

Kate wiggled her toes until crunchy grains of sand pushed up between them. "You mean your house? Yes, I do."

Megan looked thoughtful.

"Is that what you want?"

"Yes. I think so."

"Can you bring me into the loop, here?" Kate's face hardened, but Megan didn't return the stare and instead darted closer to the water. Following her, Kate asked again, "Why did you two want to rush to sell? Don't get me wrong. I thought it was because you were going to see through the separation. Give each other some space. And, Megan, I am happy to help however you need. I'm glad you're making a fresh start of things, but I'm confused. One minute you're not together, then the next you're talking about a 'permanent arrangement.' You want to list, then you don't. Now you're both here, but Brian signed a lease *there*..." Kate's voice trailed off.

"We *were* getting a divorce."

A gull swooped low, just missing its chance at a broadsided fish of some order. Kate didn't know much about fish or fishing or any of the marine life on Lake Huron or any other. In truth, she didn't know much about life, period. But she knew when her younger—*youngest*—sister was holding back. "It's okay if you don't know," Kate said at last. "But you need to be careful about making big decisions *while* you're uncertain. Does that make sense?" It was the best advice she could offer. For them to slow down. Look at the big picture. Not rush into divorce or selling a house or getting back together... and especially not all three at once. Even if they were edging toward a fresh start.

"I know," Megan whispered back. "I feel like..." she hesitated, lifting water from the edge of the lake on her toe and flinging it out. "I feel like I need someone else to make decisions for me. The house thing just happened fast. I mean, that was the plan in May, right? Then in June. And then things sort of improved, but we'd already decided. And Sarah wants to be here." The last sentence came out weakly, and Kate recalled that Megan had all but laughed at the notion of uprooting her daughter the year before she graduated.

"Sarah had one more year of high school. Did she really want to miss that?" Something didn't add up.

Megan drew her hands to her face and shook her head, a sound like a sob preceding what she said next. "Brian lost his job."

Kate gasped and immediately regretted it, covering her mouth in her hands to shield her sister from her reaction. It was too late, of course. "Megan," she hissed in sympathetic accusation. "Why didn't you tell me?"

Taking a deep breath and letting it out slowly, Megan then cinched her dark ponytail and dropped her arms. Her hands clapped her thighs. The sob that had caught in her throat must have fallen back down to her chest, settling there. Megan was good at that. Holding back tears. Kate, less so.

Above them, the sun started its earthward descent, drawing short shadows on the sand. At length, Megan replied, "I wasn't sure it would affect me."

"How could it not affect you?" They stopped along the wet line where water crept in slow rhythm, nearing their feet. Sometimes it met them, a cool pull of beach tugging them nearer to the lake. Sometimes it didn't, teasing instead.

"We weren't going to be together, remember?" Megan's tone was acid. "Maybe we still won't. I don't know. Every day feels different. Every moment, even. When he told me, he was so crushed. Humiliated even. He lashed out. Then he got better. I just didn't think it would matter. I figured... oh, hell, Kate. I don't know why I didn't tell you. Maybe I was humiliated, too."

Swallowing, Kate reached a hand to Megan, who took it.

They stood like that and stared across the water for some moments, the noise from the dock pulsing across them like a shock wave, leaving them in an odd silence against background buzzing. Like they were at a party, having some drama in a room upstairs while everyone else was laughing and enjoying life.

Finally, Kate broke the quiet. "Is he working now?"

Megan nodded. "He has another week. We found out two weeks ago. He wasn't *fired,*" she added quickly. "The company had budget cuts. His position was eliminated."

Wide-eyed, Kate frowned. "A week ago? That's when you called me. To list the house. You were so... *adamant.*"

A weak smile lifted the corners of Megan's mouth. "We figured it was a sign. That mortgage is insane. And I have nothing to contribute. It felt like the safe move. For him and for me. For *us.*" Megan's eyes flashed at Kate. "You can't say anything. We were going to keep it quiet. Even Sarah doesn't know. She's already struggling with... well, you know. And anyway, Brian has a few interviews this week. He'll be fine. *We'll* be fine. And if the house sale goes through, then we'll really be fine."

Kate nodded, assuring Megan she'd keep the secret. Another thought came. "Do you have savings? I mean, I will help however I can. But if you have something to tide you over, maybe you don't have to sell? I don't know. I don't know what I'm saying. Oh, Megan, I'm sorry." She blinked and pushed the heel of her hand to her head, Megan's stress welling there inside, forming a headache. "I shouldn't pry."

"It's fine. And yes. We have a little. It'll get him set up, I guess. It's another reason the divorce is on hold, frankly." Megan blinked and kicked at a lump of sand. "He'll find something. I'll find something. And I'll help at the Inn, okay?" Megan narrowed her eyes on Kate, the little ruddy attitude breaking through Megan's sadness. It was the same face she'd made as an edgy teenager. Her eyes lit up, her cheeks blazed red, and her hair even turned darker. Like a tantrum. Kate sometimes couldn't see her sisters as grownups. Didn't want to, maybe.

Without answering, Kate grabbed Megan and pulled her out of the lip of water and into a deep hug.

And they kept walking. For a long, quiet time.

"You know what?" Kate said once they'd passed the spread of shops and eateries and started to round back.

"What?" Megan asked.

"I think you were right." Kate smiled. "I think it was a sign."

3

AMELIA

"You told me that Brian thought you should start a business," Amelia pointed out. "Why don't you?"

It was late afternoon, and the sun had already crept down below the third floor of the house on the harbor, casting the backyard and the cove beyond in a long shadow, cooling that slice of waterfront space just enough to enjoy an early wine on the deck. The four Hannigans and Megan's daughter, Sarah, had settled there together, in game-plan mode. The mission? Help Megan figure out what in the world she was going to do with her life.

Sarah and Clara lounged in bikinis, towels tied around their waists. They'd spent the afternoon laying out, despite Kate's nagging about sunscreen and UV rays and skin cancer. Amelia could see clearly that Clara had started to change. She was different that summer. Outside more. With others more. A good change. A change that trumped an hour in the sun, probably.

Amelia, Megan, and Kate sipped on their wine at the

patio table, feet away from the younger two. Amelia's eyebrows pinched together at her revelation. *Younger* two. Clara was falling back in time a little. That's what having a younger niece (or, rather, *cousin*) did. It reversed the aging process. Amelia should really get her hands on a younger cousin. Maybe she could wipe away the crow's lines she'd worked so hard to erase.

"He did say that," Megan answered. Her speech was a little slower than when Amelia first showed up at the Inn after a long day up the shore.

The lighthouse project was coming along nicely. By Labor Day, she and Michael expected to be open for business, hosting day tours. Her evenings were already consumed. It had taken only weeks for Amelia to ingratiate herself with the Birch Harbor Players. And she took on the role of full-time property manager for The Bungalows. It was funny to her, now, that she thought she was so busy in New York. Life was slow, then, by comparison.

"Why did he?" Amelia prompted her sister.

Megan sighed. "We had this weird moment back at the start of summer. It was when I didn't get that job with Mistletoe."

"*Mistletoe*," Amelia scoffed. "Really, Megan? *Mistletoe*." Amelia glanced at Kate and caught quiet agreement in her eyes. Still, she braced for Megan to retaliate with some equally snarky remark.

Instead, Megan laughed. A full-bellied, echoing laugh that produced tears at the corner of her eyes.

Amelia giggled along. Kate, too. Clara and Sarah smiled, unsure what to make of the older three and their wine-induced cackling.

But it wasn't the wine. It was the truth.

Megan wiped her eyes with the backs of her fingers. "You're right, I guess. I'm more *Ghost Adventures* than *The Bachelor*. I love them both equally, though."

Rolling her eyes at the comparison, Amelia replied, "You don't have to define yourself by your favorite TV shows. I get it. You like the matchmaking thing. The drama. The ups and downs."

"It's more than that," Megan cut in. All laughter had died out. A serious expression darkened Megan's face. "I've thought a lot about this. Why matchmaking? Or a dating app or whatever that company was. Who even knows?" She threw up her hands before going on. "I've thought about what I want to do. And why I want to do it, you know?"

Amelia took a sip of wine, her gaze settling past Megan and on Sarah, who sat quiet, waiting for her poor mother to spill her guts about dream jobs and dashed hopes.

But Megan surprised them all. "I know I wear black and like ghost stories. I know I'm not into musicals, *Amelia*," she punched all four syllables of Amelia's name. "But I've always been into setting people up. Ever since you two." Megan tipped her wine glass toward Kate.

"What do you mean?" Kate asked, skeptical.

"You and Matt. And that party. I knew you two were going to be together. It's when I fell in love with love."

"Too much wine, Mom!" Sarah spat across the porch, rolling her eyes.

Amelia laughed. "Let the woman speak. She's onto something here. I think we're making progress."

Megan shook her head. "This has never changed. This hasn't come about from my *divorce*." She choked over the word, flashed a glance back at her daughter then refocused on Amelia and Kate. "I do like the drama of it. I like the puppet master thing. You know, sort of conducting something. That power. I've set people up, and when it works out, it's so..." Her eyes fluttered shut as she searched for a word.

"She's a control freak!" Sarah interjected.

Megan squeezed her eyes shut harder, ignoring the teenage joke.

A control freak is exactly what Megan sounded like. But Amelia knew her sister better than that. If anything, she was the opposite. She was casual and fun. Sarcastic sometimes. She liked camping out on the couch with popcorn and a glass of red and making bets about how a movie would end. She liked entertainment and she liked her black nail polish. The one thing Megan didn't like, though, was not having a *thing*. It was a common complaint. Amelia remembered when Kate started working as a real estate agent, Megan was awed at the shift from being a stay-at-home-mom, peppering the oldest sister with questions over Christmas dinner.

And Megan had been the only one who had ever traveled more than once to see Amelia in productions, making the drive to New York or Chicago for a long weekend just to see Amelia in a maid's uniform or hidden in the chorus, never with a speaking part. After, Megan would ask her sister to spill all the details. She was less interested in the behind-the-scenes theater stuff, however, than in the little details of how Amelia navigated the gigs. How long it took to get ready. Was Amelia exhausted after? Elated? Did she love her job? Megan wanted to hear the humanity about it. Like Amelia's *life* was the show, rather than the performance being the show.

Amelia could read her sister like a book. "You're not a control freak. You're passionate. You people watch and you dissect it all like a scientist."

Megan opened her eyes and peered at Amelia with suspicion.

Grinning, Amelia launched into her speech. One that had been percolating ever since she caught wind of unrest in the Stevenson home.

"You're a mom first. That's been a hard thing for you, because you thought you were supposed to be a wife first. Mom taught you well." Amelia winked at Megan. "Then when you were both, you loved it. Like Kate," Amelia nodded in the eldest's direction, "you're organized. You put together neat schedules and you volunteered at school. You made perfect meals and indulged in your favorite shows at night. No work to take home. Just a husband to cuddle with."

Megan's frown deepened, but Amelia pressed on.

"Your life was in place for a long time. You'd met your soulmate, you had your kid, and things were good. Orderly. You had friends who didn't have it as good as you. On the weekends, you'd hire a babysitter and have fun with setting up those single friends. You did it to me, even. Remember?"

Kate and Megan both laughed at that particular debacle. Amelia had threatened never to talk to Megan again after the double-date from hell.

"He took his toupee off at the dinner table as a party trick!" Megan roared. "I can admit that one was a bust."

"Why did a twenty-five-year-old have a toupee? That's

what I want to know," Kate added, laughing so hard she was crying. It wasn't quite a shared memory for all of them, but Kate and Clara and even Sarah knew the story well.

Amelia's own giggles died away and she took another sip before holding up her hands. "Okay, so, you played matchmaker for a little personal entertainment. At people's expense, I might add, rather than for their *benefit*." More giggles. "Then your kid grew up. Volunteering flew out the window, because, well, *teenagers*," Amelia grinned at Sarah who accepted the lighthearted dig. "And your friends got married. Divorced. You saw it all happen, and none of it was a reality show. It was, well, actual reality."

The women fell quiet.

Still, Amelia went on. "And then, even when you yourself were faced with the threat of an empty nest and a dying marriage, you applied to work for a dating app. A *matchmaking* company."

"You're right," Megan breathed the words, set her wine glass on the table and pressed her back into her chair, staring at Amelia coolly. Her voice dripped with sarcasm. "What was I thinking? *Mistletoe*."

"You're missing my point," Amelia answered evenly.

Caught off guard, Megan's eyes flickered. Her brows fell low. "What?"

"A social media foot soldier for an online dating app." Amelia set her glass down and folded her arms across her chest.

Megan shrugged and glanced at the others who were also waiting for Amelia to elaborate.

"That's not what you want to do. You don't want to

post ads and gimmicky polls for some app. You'd be totally removed from the very process you believe in." Realization slowly crept across Megan's face, but Amelia continued. "You need to *be* the matchmaker. And, you need to *see* it. You need to see the love play out. You need to meet the people. See them. Know them. Talk to them." Amelia uncrossed her arms and took a sip of wine. "Megan, Brian was right. You should start your own company. Your own matchmaking company."

4

CLARA

After dinner and another round of wine, it was time for the women to turn in.

Amelia called Michael for a ride to the lighthouse (her new home).

As dutiful a boyfriend as ever (or, *man friend*, as Amelia had taken to calling him), he'd schlep her to the moon and back if that's what she wanted. When she clicked off the call, she did a twirl in the foyer for her sisters. "He's *literally perfect*."

A gag formed in Clara's throat, and it had nothing to do with wine, which she'd unsurprisingly abstained from. She even went so far as to declare that she was not spending another evening at the Inn if they were going to go through an entire bottle of wine in one fell swoop then act like giddy sorority girls.

Amelia had scoffed, arguing that two bottles between three adults was little more than a tasting.

"*Two*?" Clara glared at Amelia, who shrugged.

"Maybe it was three?" the would-be actress replied, her eyes glassy.

"It was one-and-a-half, and the problem is that none of us ever usually have more than one," Kate cut in, her voice tired and low. "And keep the volume down. We have two rooms booked." She pointed upstairs.

The guests had tucked away into bed an hour earlier, after arriving back from a day on the lake and poking their heads onto the back deck. Previous to Kate opening the Heirloom Inn, Clara was generally irritated with summer visitors. But seeing them now, as both revenue and innocent travelers softened her opinion. Hospitality suited Kate, and Clara liked to see her happy.

Giggling, Amelia stumbled onto the wooden bench by the front door, then launched into a series of slippery-tongued *see-you-tomorrows* despite the fact that Michael wouldn't be there for at least ten minutes.

The others ignored the swoony sister and started to peel away. Kate went back to the kitchen to clean up for the morning. Clara dipped behind the front desk to grab her purse. Sarah started to join her hostess on the bench, but Megan stopped her in the center of the foyer, lifting a hand to her daughter's cheek. "Sweetheart, make sure you lock the doors at the lighthouse. I don't trust Amelia to be the adult tonight."

From her inferior seated position, Amelia glared at her younger sister. "Rude," she remarked, shaking her head then taking a long swig of water from an aluminum bottle covered in faded stickers.

Clara raised her hand and gave a small wave from the desk. "Maybe it would be best for Sarah to stay with me tonight. I think Amelia is worn out. After all, not only did she overindulge, but she also spent the majority of the night psychoanalyzing our love lives."

That much was true. After dissecting Megan's journey through life and love, Amelia had turned to the others, noting Kate's long-lost passion and search for true romance, Clara's unwillingness to let loose and enjoy life, and Amelia's own final realization of happiness. Everyone was happy for Amelia, who really did glow with contentment. And her rambling assertions on their circumstances was further proof of her new beginning. She was like a young woman, fresh on the heels of a honeymoon, brimming with new knowledge and wisdom and bubbling over with the urge to cry from the rooftops *Look at me! I'm in love! You should do it, too!*

And besides Amelia's wine-coated exuberance, there was another reason for Sarah to forgo a night at the lighthouse. She and Clara had bonded. With their new relationship underway, it was as if Clara had never known the girl. Now, they were more like friends than aunt and niece. They really were cousins, in fact.

It'd be nice to connect with someone other than Kate or Amelia or Megan. Clara needed that new bit of friendship, even if it was in the form of a teenager. Ever since learning about her true place in the Hannigan family, Clara had been free-floating. Summer was a bad time for someone like Clara to be free-floating. She needed structure. She needed stability.

Plus, she could use a little help at the cottage, her new home. Anyway, spending time with teenagers *was* Clara's forte. She wasn't as drained of energy after a day with the younger set like she was with adults. Her peers exhausted her. Younger folks energized her.

If only she were a mother by now, maybe her need for isolation would be balanced with the joy that came in fits and spurts during her day job.

That was the problem with teaching: summer vacation.

As much as Clara needed the break, she hated it. After all, it was her only true source of social interaction.

This stark reality felt at once like a slap in the face.

Clara was still, even in her late twenties, getting to know herself. Some parts of who she was, she realized, didn't make her an embittered recluse, mysterious and eccentric. They made her lonely. She didn't feel lonely around Sarah.

"That's a great idea," Megan agreed. "What do you think, Sar?"

TURNS OUT, Clara and Sarah had more in common than their ancestors and the sound of their names.

After two hours of chatting on the sofa in the cottage, Clara learned that Sarah was a reader, devouring everything from Harlequins to horror on a continual basis. Even as they trekked to the back bedrooms, Sarah stalled at the hallway bookshelf, the one thing that had been accomplished in the weeks since Clara officially moved in.

"See anything you like?"

Her fingers ran along paperback spines and hardcovers until she stopped at *Great Expectations*. "My AP Language teacher said we were going to read this one next year. In Lit. I guess I'll miss out."

Nodding, Clara crossed in front and reached for the book, tugging it loose and passing it over. "What do you mean you'll miss out?"

Sarah bit her lower lip and grinned. "You know. I might be staying in Birch Harbor. I mean, me and my mom. *We* might."

Unsure whether to court the speculation—Clara did realize there was a very good chance they'd stick around —she simply nodded. "That'd be so cool if you did move. You'd have Beitermeyer for AP Lit at the high school. He's good. I don't think he does Dickens, though." A thought occurred to her. "Oh, shoot. I think he's retiring, actually."

Taking the book, Sarah turned it over in her hands. "Guess I could read it either way."

"Of course you can. It's one of my favorites, anyway. Start tonight, and we can have a little book club over breakfast, okay?"

With that, Clara grabbed a spare set of pajamas and got her little niece situated in Nora's old room. "You're sure you won't mind?" she pressed as she turned down the covers.

Sarah knew Nora as a distant, enigmatic grandmother. They'd shared Christmas dinners and the odd mass or special event, but Clara was fairly certain that the bond was less of a tether. More like a memory for the girl.

Anyway, if Sarah couldn't stay in Nora's room, Clara would let her stay in her bed and just sleep on the sofa. No way could Clara stay in her dead mother's room. She'd worked hard to stay in the house at all, overcoming heartbreaking flashbacks by exposure therapy alone. But to sleep in the same bed? In the same room...? "Maybe I'll just stay on the sofa, actually." Clara looked up.

"I can stay in here. It's no problem." Steely-eyed, Sarah's jaw was set, her book gripped in her hands over her chest like a shield against night terrors. "Really. I don't mind. I wasn't as close to her."

Blinking and frowning, Clara just nodded.

That night, she didn't sleep a wink. With every creak or rustle of sheets, she jolted awake, sweaty or freezing and unable to get back to the drifting lull of exhaustion. Having company unmoored her. Especially when that company slept in Nora's room.

By morning, Clara dragged herself to the kitchen and brewed a pot of coffee. Never having cooked much, she vacillated between the untouched pack of eggs in the fridge and the dusty box of pancake mix in the pantry.

She shuffled to her mother's old room then stopped at the door and held her ear close to it before shaking her head and leaning away. It's the same thing she did once her mother got bad. She'd linger by the door, make sure everything sounded *right* before traipsing down the hall to a fitful, urgent night's sleep, as if she needed to sleep to take her away from the waking nightmare of her life.

A life she'd *chosen*, ridiculously. One she'd accepted as her older sisters moved on with theirs, happy as a set of clams to be away and aloof, unseeing and unhearing.

Then again, Clara did not begrudge them those months of blissful ignorance. Clara was a true Catholic, in that way. Caring for her mother in the woman's darkest hours was a penance. Had she not done it, she couldn't live with herself. She wondered how Kate, Amelia, and Megan lived with themselves. The guilt had to be crushing.

But they sure didn't seem to bear the weight with any

degree of pain. In fact, they seemed happier than ever. Kate with *Matt*, the mystery man behind Clara's origins. Amelia with serious Michael-the-Lawyer. Clara couldn't help but admit she liked him. And then Megan, who Clara felt she was getting to know for the first time ever. Megan, the sarcastic one. Funny like Amelia but sharp-witted and thoughtful like Kate. Kate with her openness and desire to bring people in rather than push them away.

Clara didn't see herself in any of the women in her life.

Except for maybe Sarah (less a woman than a girl), who had the reading bug. But a love of good books was hardly passed down through blood.

So, where did Clara come from?

Maybe Kate was right. Maybe Clara did need to spend a little time with that Matt character.

AFTER SETTLING FOR CEREAL, Clara and her houseguest took their coffees to the front porch where Sarah folded herself up on the porch swing. They'd agreed that sleep was a bust for both and promised to make each other take a nap at midday. Maybe on the beach. With lots of sunscreen and wide-brimmed hats and sunglasses.

Two cups in, Clara tested the waters of deeper conversation. "So, how's your dad doing? Kate said things are a little rough right now."

Sarah shrugged. "What do you mean? Like, with the divorce?"

"No," Clara replied. "I mean with his job."

Lowering the cup of coffee, Sarah cocked her head. "What are you talking about?"

Clara narrowed her eyes on the girl. A sinking feeling welled in her stomach. The repercussion of always snapping at her sisters to stop gossiping had left her sorely out of the loop. It was clear now. Clara could kick herself. "Oh, um. Never mind." She frowned and shook her head, mentally backpedaling. "I just thought that since your parents are selling the house, and..." she searched for something else, but Sarah interrupted her.

"Is that why they're selling?" Her eyes grew wide. The cup of coffee tilted precariously forward, about to spill onto the wooden deck. Sarah's eyes seemed to follow Clara's down to her mug, and the teenager over-corrected, splashing black liquid onto her borrowed pajama shorts. "Oh, I'm so sorry Aunt Clara."

"It's fine! It's my fault. I was rattling off rumors or something. Here, let's get you changed into something fresh."

Once they were inside, rummaging through Clara's wardrobe, Sarah prodded again. "Aunt Clara, why were you asking about my dad's job?"

Clara sighed and passed over a pink sundress. "Here. I'll drive you up to the lighthouse, and you can get your swimming suit. And you don't have to call me Aunt, you know."

"It feels weird not to."

"It feels weirder to me if you do. Technically, I'm not your aunt."

Sarah, who was well informed on the recent revelations, argued back. "All of my life you've been my aunt. Just like Grandma has been your mom, right?"

A small smile crept across Clara's face. "Well, if you really move to Birch Harbor, then it won't matter anymore."

"What do you mean?" Sarah frowned as she took the dress and headed for Nora's old room.

"You'll be a student in my district. You'll have to call me Miss Hannigan!" Clara laughed at her little joke, but Sarah's eyes just grew wide in realization.

"Oh my gosh, like *Miss Havisham!*"

"What?" The laughter died off. "You started the book?"

Sarah grinned. "It's slow. And a little hard. Not harder than Shakespeare, but yeah. You're like Miss Havisham. Up here in the cottage all alone, angry and scorned."

Clara was wrong. She was not like Sarah at all. There was a deep divide between them. Sarah didn't know how to read, and worse, she didn't know how to apply what she read. They were *not* going to get along. They were *not* going to be bubbly summertime friends. Or *cousins*. Teenagers were awful. That's exactly why Clara didn't have friends growing up and it's exactly why she didn't have friends currently. People were *awful*.

"Get dressed. I'll drive you to Amelia's."

5

MEGAN

Megan hadn't seen the lighthouse since Amelia, Michael, and Sarah had fixed it up. They had more to do before the opening, but gone were the old cobwebs and rust stains. Amelia lived there now. And Sarah was staying with her, at the very north side of Birch Harbor, in the little home where Megan's grandparents had raised her father, Wendell Acton.

The same man who'd gone missing years and years before, never to be heard from again. The one Amelia was now actively searching for.

Kate drove, and Megan tapped her daughter's contact info into the phone as they pulled onto Harbor Ave and headed north, toward the edge of town. The sun was just starting to set over the lake, turning the sky a warm red and casting long shadows ahead of them on the road toward the lighthouse.

Sarah's voice came on the line with an edge to it. "Hi, Mom."

"Hey, how was your day?" Megan braced for more of the unpredictable attitude that seemed indelible in a teenage girl. Maybe she didn't want to talk to her mom, preferring instead her cooler, younger aunt who was technically a cousin... a cooler, *older* cousin. Probably, though, the lake was calling Sarah. Along with it, the new friends she'd made. Perhaps a boy.

Instead, her daughter's tone turned weepy. "Long day. I came back to the lighthouse to help Aunt Amelia."

"I thought you were staying with Clara and doing the lake thing today?" Megan asked as she and Kate passed the Village and on toward the lighthouse for a late family dinner.

Megan had spent the whole day with Kate, helping turn a room, check in a new set of guests, put out breakfast and prepare afternoon snacks. It was busy and, honestly, delightful. The Heirloom Inn had turned the house on the harbor into a lively, happy place. A place Megan could stay for a while, if she needed to.

"I was, but I changed my mind. I didn't sleep well last night. Aunt Clara made me stay in Grandma's room."

"What?" Megan glanced at Kate, her brow furrowed. "What do you mean *made* you?"

Kate looked over, shaking her head and squinting. Megan put Sarah on speaker.

"Well, she didn't *make* me, but, like, that was the only other bed. If I didn't sleep in Grandma's room, then I'd have to take the couch or kick Aunt Clara out of her bedroom, so, I just tried to be easygoing."

Exchanging a frown with Kate, Megan tried to keep her response light, but it was hard. Typical Clara, making things awkward. She liked to stir the pot. Always had. It was a baby-of-the-family thing. Plus, she was young. Maybe she wasn't thinking? Maybe it was no big deal to her? "So, are you two getting along, or...?" Megan tugged her seatbelt tighter across her chest and prepared for a mini drama.

"Yeah, it's whatever. I'll do the lake tomorrow. My friends get it."

"*Friends?*" Kate mouthed from the driver's seat.

Megan held up a finger, finished her call then shot a quick text to Clara, apologizing if Sarah was being a brat and inquiring about how things went. She needed both sides to make a judgment call.

"She met a group of girls here," Megan said, answering Kate's question. "I think one of them is Vivi, if you haven't heard."

Kate lifted an eyebrow. "*Matt's* Vivi?"

Matt Fiorillo hadn't brought his daughter around much, favoring to keep her sheltered from his budding reunion with Kate. Still, Megan and her sisters had seen the girl out and about. You couldn't miss her. White-blonde hair to her waist and sea glass eyes glowed against Vivi's summer tan, the one that she probably maintained year-round. The look paired with an islander attitude (she and her father lived on Heirloom) was a sight to behold, especially for Sarah, who'd been entranced by the ethereal teen, in spite of herself. Megan had witnessed all this in brief snippets. A text here. A social media post there. But she thought nothing of it. She herself had been there, done that. As kids, Megan and her sisters were the Vivis of Birch Harbor, not as striking, perhaps, but to outsiders, the allure of the local teen was forceful. Lake-smart and knowledgeable, those born and raised in Birch Harbor were less like people to tourists. More like attractions.

"Yes. *Viviana*." Megan pronounced each syllable with crisp attention then dropped the passenger vanity to apply a quick smear of lip gloss.

"I didn't realize they were hanging out. Isn't Vivi a freshman? Sarah's a lot older than her."

Megan's eyes darted to Kate. "Well, I mean, they're both in high school."

"Incoming freshman. Outgoing senior?"

"Sarah's *about* to be a senior. Anyway, if we stay in town, it'll be nice for her to know girls from the school." A line of sweat crept up Megan's spine. She punched the AC. "Aren't you burning up?"

Kate shrugged. "Yeah, I guess." Then she shook her head, pushing the topic away for something more relevant. "Okay, so let me bring you up to speed on the lighthouse before we get there."

Megan listened as Kate went over each recent renovation or project, noting the new paint job, freshly planted flowers, and carefully chosen furniture, most of it culled from the basement at the Inn, some from the cottage, and some from garage sales. They weren't done with that part, yet. The hunt for local artwork and artifacts would be a drawn-out process. Still, their progress should be notable to Megan. "And don't forget to compliment the new doorbell. It took them forever to install it for some reason. Matt did mine in like five minutes." A smug smile formed on Kate's mouth.

"So, let's be real for a minute," Megan said, stopping Kate. "This whole museum thing. Is it legit? Do the people of Birch Harbor really want a museum?" Megan hid her envy beneath a thin layer of skepticism. It didn't work, and Kate gave her an older-sister look. Megan rolled her eyes playfully. "I know. I know. But really. Of all the businesses or... *diversions* that your guests ask about, is museum ever on the list?"

"Yes, Megan. Come on, now. Do you live under a rock? Quirky hidden historical gems are all the rage. Almost every single guest I get asks about local museums or tours. And since the historical society went defunct, Amelia's really found an underserved industry here."

"*Industry*?" Megan asked, trying to free a fine hair from her sticky bottom lip. "That's actually pretty cool, then. And, seriously, I'm happy for her." Sighing, Megan smiled at the thought of Amelia running a museum. And managing the apartments and playing resident ingenue for the Birch Harbor Players. If anyone deserved to have it all, it was Amelia Ann. She'd spent her entire life searching for something. It was about time she found it. "What other *industries* are underserved here, anyway?" Megan curled the word in her mouth, testing it out. If her funky, offbeat sister could pull off small-business owner-ship... then maybe Megan could, too.

Kate shrugged. "Anything you can think of. Summer here is crazy, as you know. Seeing it like I do now, from a hospitality perspective, well, it's pretty interesting. People who come here for a couple of days want more than an hour on a kayak. Or a good meal. They want an experi-ence. Something to photograph. Something different and memorable. Quaint and cool."

Megan stared out the window as the SUV whizzed past clapboard shore homes on the right, to the east. A blur of green farmland on the left, to the west.

Spurts of the sinking sun peeked through trees, dipping steadily into dusk. "Remember when we were teenagers—before you met Matt, I mean—and we'd hang around the marina looking for tourists our age?"

"You and Amelia were so boy crazy. The guy didn't even have to be cute, and you were all over him, fighting over who'd go out on the lake." Kate smiled at the memory, too. "You didn't even realize the power you had, as a local. That you were just as alluring."

Megan smiled. "Well, there is one thing teenagers want this time of year."

Kate glanced Megan's way. "What's that?"

"Summer love."

Kate chuckled. "That's true. If only they knew it didn't last, though." A shadow crossed her face.

Just as Megan was about to argue that yes, summer love *could* last, for townies and tourists alike, her older sister slowed the SUV.

"Look, Megan, there's your land."

Megan followed Kate's finger to the pretty pasture embedded in a circle of wood. Megan's inheritance. The thing she accepted when posed with the chance to negotiate for every property Nora Hannigan owned. Had she gotten a raw deal? Not when one considered the potential. Acres and acres of green meadow. A pond at the far side. Trees for days.

"Let's stop." Kate didn't wait for an answer and instead turned onto the pebble lane past a rickety wooden sign that used to read *Hannigan Field* before time faded the letters down to a shadow.

"Has that sign always been there?" Megan pointed

back towards the sun-bleached wood as Kate put the SUV in park just beyond the entrance.

Kate lifted her shoulders and unbuckled herself. "I hate to say it, but I don't know."

There wasn't much to explore. For being unmaintained, the meadow wasn't in too poor of shape. No bald spots. The space within the forest must have spanned at least three or four acres. It would have taken them a while to walk across it and find the little pond that was detailed in the deed. The deed also mentioned a cherry orchard or potential for one on some far-off corner of the space.

A beady light flickered in front of Megan. "A firefly!" she gasped, holding her hand out as if the little bug would land there. It bobbed around in front of her, blinking on and off, its sparks pulsing, charging her with fresh energy.

As a girl, the *best* thing about summer were the fireflies. On one hand, she hated that they only came out past sunset and for such a brief season. But even as a girl, she appreciated their rarity. Their specialness.

Kate strode to her, squinting. "I see it! There's another." Two flashes danced against the dusky night sky. It was getting dark. Late. The bugs flashed again. Then Megan turned to Kate. "Too bad we didn't have this place when we were little. We'd have been out here every night with mason jars. We'd have had a firefly farm. Can you imagine?"

Smiling, Kate pulled Megan into a side hug. "Yes, I can. It'd have been a whole business. You'd be mating them. Amelia would be using them to light a stage or something. I'd bring in the customers with a poster board at the Village. Mom and Dad would beam about our entrepreneurial spirits. Eventually, though, they'd get sick of it. We would, too."

"No." Megan shook her head. "I never got tired of fireflies." She watched the little lights drift away until she couldn't see them anymore. With the growing dark, she'd be able to spy many more, but Amelia was waiting for them. "Why did Mom and Dad own this?" Megan asked, picking along the pebble path and back toward the SUV.

"When we went to Arizona that one summer, Mom was freaked out about where we'd live when we came back. She wanted complete privacy. She wanted to hide me."

Megan frowned at the difficult memory.

"Remember? That's when she told Dad to build us the cottage. I think she also had him find some land as another back-up. It was panic, probably." Kate followed Megan to the SUV.

Nodding the memory back to life, Megan added, "That's when they were riding high financially. They could have afforded to buy the whole town if they wanted to. Didn't Mom consider that their social rank would have protected you—or, I guess, *her*?"

Kate opened the door to the SUV and hopped in. "They had money, but they didn't have respect. Not back then. It took Mom a long time to grow that. The Hannigans weren't well-liked. There were feuds, generations old and deeply tangled. Grandma and Grandpa Hannigan fought to keep the house on the harbor, you know. The other Hannigans, the ones who left, were not happy about how everything happened, and they smeared our name before bailing out of here. I'm not sure that Mom ever did overcome it."

Megan shook her head and buckled herself in. It sounded like some old-timey settler drama. Far removed from the modern age where land disputes had more to do with big box stores wiping out mom-and-pop shops. "What were they going to do with this? Build a house? Bury a body?"

"Like I said, I'm not totally sure. I think Mom just wanted an insurance policy, of sorts. A back-up plan. She really thought, I think, that my pregnancy would be her downfall."

"I guess in a way it was." Megan looked at Kate, whose expression remained impassive. "I mean, not because you were pregnant or because of Clara... I mean because when she came back, Dad was gone. And she just never recovered."

Kate nodded slowly. "It would make a good cemetery," she said at last, starting the engine.

Megan laughed. She was right. "It would make a great venue, actually."

Agreeing, Kate pulled back out onto the road, giving Megan the view of both sides of Birch Harbor again. East of the main drag and west. West was known as inland. Scornfully, sometimes. And the east was known as the shore. The road that ran between Shoreline Birch Harbor and Inland Birch Harbor was like a fissure. A divorce between the coveted properties and everything else. Older cottages, forgotten businesses, and empty farmland.

"You know," Megan added, once they were far past Hannigan Field and nearing the lighthouse. "I don't think this town needs a place for the dead. I think it needs a place for the living."

"Tourists or locals?" Kate asked, catching on quickly and throwing Megan a knowing smile.

"Both. *Both.* A place to bring everyone together. Inland people. Marina people. Out-of-towners."

"All ages? Retirees? Families?"

"The old and the young," Megan replied, finding purchase in her mind. An idea.

Kate slowed to a stop at the lighthouse. "You're going to pair off tourists with locals, huh? Sounds like match-making for vacation. Like a cruise or something."

Megan nodded solemnly. "Summer love."

6

KATE

Kate, Megan, Sarah, and Amelia sat around a restored picnic table that nestled in the cove between Amelia's living quarters and the lighthouse.

Though night had officially fallen, Michael ran up to the cupola in the lighthouse to turn on the interior lights there, allowing a soft glow from the lantern pane high above. Along the sides of the lighthouse, Amelia flipped on service bulbs. The resulting radiance was at once romantic and industrial. A unique combination befitting Kate's younger sister and her new beau.

Kate made a mental note to look into those pretty string lights that had become all the rage in exterior design. The Inn could use some backyard illumination. So far, she'd spent her energy on the front and interior. It was time to expand to the back, especially before summer was over. After all, wouldn't it be delightful to host an end-of-summer party? Or gala? *Something.* Something to close out the season with a bang. Draw new attention to help tide her over on the off-season months? Maybe she could pull in local crowds to help spread the good word about the Heirloom Inn.

Her sisters never did host that Grand Opening they'd all talked about. Maybe Kate and the B&B could collaborate with Amelia's opening of the lighthouse. It could be a Hannigan family bonanza of events. Labor Day weekend, perhaps. Or sooner, to avoid any conflict with other local blow-outs.

Forcing herself to refocus on dinner—grilled steak, corn on the cob, and thick, succulent triangles of watermelon, Kate took a long pull from her iced tea, savoring the moment of having a little family reunion. A few important people were missing. Matt, who had an early project to attend to. Kate's two sons, Ben and Will, off in their college towns getting ready for the new semester. And... the youngest Hannigan sister, Clara. Kate's *daughter*. The introvert of the family, continually slipping out during functions, leaving early, excusing herself for other, quieter pursuits.

Kate blinked and tried to laugh along as Amelia regaled them over a tale of stripping gummy stain from a set of old built-in cabinets.

"Every couple of minutes I kept hearing little curses. *Crap. Crap, crap, crap!*" Amelia's imitation of Michael was good fun, and he laughed, too, adding just how painful it was to feel the searing drip on his skin.

"Why didn't you just put long sleeves on?" Kate asked. She was long familiar with the agony of accidently falling victim to a DIY job.

"I *had* them on," he replied, his face red from laughter. It was a new look on Michael, at least to Kate. All she had seen of him lately was his serious lawyer side. Amelia was good for him, maybe. And he, probably, was good for her. "God forbid I push one sleeve up for a moment. It was certain death for my skin." He pulled Amelia into him and playfully nuzzled her neck for a brief moment before remembering they had an audience.

The conversation moved on to how helpful Sarah was. How much work the lighthouse was. How little they had found left behind from the Actons.

"Have you been in touch with Liesel?" Kate asked the question with a degree of hesitation. It was still a soft spot for all of them. Spongy and tender.

Amelia sniffed and dabbed a paper napkin across her lips. "No. Well, yes and no. We've spoken once or twice. Just what I already told you. How she signed over the deed. All that."

"Is she curious?" Megan asked, her tone darker than Kate's.

Frowning now, Amelia replied, "What do you mean?"

Learning about Liesel Hart had rocked their worlds, sent them reeling. Some of them. Not Kate, really. Being at the center of the Hannigan family's deepest shame, she'd always sensed that other, deeper secrets lay in her ancestral line. And while she had never considered how close those secrets might be, the matter of a family scandal was the fabric of her being. She *was* a scandal for so long. Learning of a second, older scandal was nothing short of relief. Not a shock. Not a letdown. A relief.

It was Amelia who appeared to struggle the most with the revelation that they had an older sister. Someone unfamiliar and strange, floating around in the world. For the second oldest Hannigan, Liesel would answer their questions and solve all their problems. That's just how Amelia was. Optimistic and dreaming and so certain in the opportunities of all things *uncertain*.

Kate often wondered to herself and aloud if she even *wanted* to know this woman. After all, just her mere existence was good enough for Kate. *Oh, you were entangled in a teenage pregnancy, too? Sorry about that. Have a good life anyway!*

Then there was Megan, cynical, questioning Megan who rarely accepted the face value of a situation. She was of the opinion that A. Biology or not, this *Liesel* woman was a total stranger, and B. The truth was so muddled that who knew if Liesel was Nora's mystery baby? Would they really spend all their energy nailing down the facts about some stranger when they had a more pressing mystery to solve?

Kate's sister's points were valid. Maybe falling into the black hole that was the Acton lighthouse and Liesel Hart and Gene Carmichael was a risk not worth taking. Instead of learning more, they might realize they would only understand *less*.

"Is this Liesel person *curious* about us? I mean, she held the deed to our father's inheritance—*our* inheritance, then gave it up like that." Megan snapped her fingers and shook her head. "Is she going to come to Birch Harbor? To meet us?" Her eyebrows knitted themselves together, and Megan leaned away from the table.

Amelia's face fell. "I don't think so. I mean, maybe one day, when we've gotten to know her better?" Shaking her head, she glanced at Michael. "She was a little thrown off by the news about Gene and all."

Megan laughed derisively. "Yeah, I'd be thrown off,

too, if I found out the man I pinned for my dad was someone else's dad. Oh, and he had four daughters who wanted the property that I finagled my way into." She rolled her eyes.

A chill crept along Kate's spine. She shook it. Not only had Liesel's mere existence called into question ghosts from their pasts, but it had also dragged out just how convoluted their father's disappearance really was.

Kate held her hands up. "Let's talk about something else for once, please?"

Megan shrugged. Amelia lifted an eyebrow.

"Megan and I stopped at the so-called Hannigan Field on the way here." She threw it out there like a piece of rubbery bait and waited for someone to take it.

Amelia took a long swig of wine, apparently bored. Michael's head turned in interest. Megan, for her part, pressed her lips into a thin smile, expectant. Like Kate was going to make something happen. Magic, maybe.

It was Sarah, though, who chimed in. "What's the point of that place?"

"What do you mean?" Kate frowned at the girl.

"Like, what's the point of having empty land? I don't get it." She set down her half-gnawed-on cob and folded her arms over her chest, picking up on the shift in the meal and running away with it.

Kate persevered, steering them back toward a more pleasant avenue. "Well, having land is like having the world, in case you didn't know."

Sarah twisted her mouth into a sideways pout. "Vivi said the only thing useful on the inland side of Harbor Ave is the high school."

At that, Kate choked on her tea, laughing and coughing together.

Megan hissed at her daughter. "That's exactly what a private school islander *would* say. She doesn't know a thing about Birch Harbor."

Kate hated to agree that her boyfriend's daughter was something of a brat, so she tried to ignore Sarah's snide comment.

"What's that supposed to mean?" Sarah shot back as the conversation further devolved beneath a layer of irritation.

Raising her hand, Kate decided to try once more. After all, Megan's daughter wasn't a local. Not yet. She needed a little lakeside lesson. "Okay, okay. Hang on. I've got this." She threw a look to Megan, willing her sister to be quiet and allow for a calm, clear conversation on one of the most volatile aspects of growing up in their hamlet of Lake Huron. "Heirloom Island is *way* different than Birch Harbor. It's sort of like a miniature Martha's Vineyard. Or Nantucket. A lot of big money goes to the island. That's where the Catholic school is. That's where Vivi was raised. Birch Harbor is a little more down home. More casual. Easy-breezy, you know? So, naturally Vivi only thinks about what she hears at the marina and on the island. She doesn't know the bigger picture. We have lots going on inland here, I assure you. It's where the cottage is. It's where the entire *school* district is. Michael, your office is west of the Ave, right?" She knew full well it was, but pulling in an objective third party could only help.

The lawyer nodded, sagely. "And we have old money in Birch Harbor, both shoreside and inland. Settler money, remember?"

Amelia jumped in. "That's true. The Hannigans, for example, Sarah. Your very own grandparents came from a bit of the green stuff."

"Mom always said that all you did growing up was work. That they weren't rich until later."

Kate chewed the side of her lip, searching for a response. "Well, that's true. But *our* grandparents, Nora's parents, I mean, did have some money. They also had several kids and ended up taking that money elsewhere."

"Where?"

"Some moved closer to Detroit. Some out to Arizona."

"Why did they move if they had money and family here?" Sarah asked.

Her questions, though tiresome, were honest. Kate took a deep sigh before diving into her version of an answer. "I suppose it goes back to some deep-seated small-town grudge or something. Our grandparents owned the house on the harbor which was passed on to them from the original Hannigans who settled the area. Other locals wanted that place to become something else, something to serve the community. That's where they wanted to develop Birch Village or maybe make a little port to drive commercial traffic through here rather than elsewhere. But Birch Harbor never became a city or a big place. It always stayed small. Our mother told us other locals blamed the Hannigans for refusing to develop and squirreling away money from their various enterprises. Some thought they were selfish and greedy. That they didn't give back." Kate glanced at Megan and Amelia, who were listening with as much interest as Sarah, like they didn't know the full story. Or didn't remember it. Maybe they didn't.

"Sounds complicated," Sarah answered. Gone was her condescension. In its place, somber curiosity. "So, Grandma and Grandpa got rich again, after working hard? And locals started to like them again?"

"Yes and no. They weren't making money from the house on the harbor, not like Grandma's parents had with running a boating service out from the cove. Nora and Wendell had to find other ways to bring in money, so they bought The Bungalows for income property. I don't know what locals thought about that. Things were a little crazy around that time in our lives." Kate's memories of high school rushed into her mind, meeting Matt, enjoying her time with him. It was a distraction from her mother's various quests to re-integrate into Birch Harbor society. The woman couldn't seem to find the right balance between making money and gaining respect that way and serving the community and gaining even more admiration *that* way.

"So why the cottage and the farmland? Were they going to start a farm with cows and stuff? Is that what *we're* going to do with it?" Sarah frowned at her mother.

Megan cackled. "*No*, we're not opening a farm. I don't know the first thing about cows. But we *are* going to do something with that land."

"So, we're staying?" Sarah cocked an eyebrow high on her forehead, and Kate saw what the girl had been getting at that whole time.

Kate swallowed and shifted her gaze to Megan, waiting for the answer, too.

Clearing her voice, Megan replied, "Why not?"

7

MEGAN

Things had to move fast if she was really going to make a go of it. After all, the sale of her house was going through, Brian was now in his apartment, and Sarah had started to forge friendships with Birch Harbor's (and Heirloom Island's) most elite clique.

Plus, school registration was underway. Sarah's schooling became the biggest deciding factor in what Megan would do: go back to their old neighborhood and find cheaper digs or make the big move home.

And she couldn't make the choice alone. After all, she was still married to Brian. There was no formal custody arrangement. Technically, they were doing everything together. Including deciding where Sarah would be for her senior year of high school.

Regret had set in. Serious regret. They never should have sold the house. She could have started working at Target during the day. Waiting tables at night. Megan hadn't tried hard enough. Brian hadn't either. He could have done the same. The local grocery store was always hiring after all. They allowed full-on panic and financial fear to cloud their better judgment. But now August was closing in, and school would begin in September.

Even Sarah started mentioning her own worries about the future, wondering if she should move in with a friend from her old school. Maybe Birch Harbor was too weird for her. Maybe colleges would frown on a mid-high-school-career transfer?

It had been just a couple of days since Megan joined Sarah on the lake but almost two months since Sarah had been staying with Amelia at the lighthouse as some sort of apprentice. And four months since talk of a divorce cracked open. The Stevenson family was fractured. They needed stability and they needed it now.

So, she called the only other person on earth who could help her shake her indecision and settle on an answer.

Her almost-ex.

"Hey," Megan said when his voice came on the phone. She sat on the back deck at the Inn. Kate, Amelia, Sarah, and Clara were inside, hatching plans for a summer gala. The plan was to set up an end-of-summer event to draw new attention to the Heirloom Inn and officially open the Birch Harbor Lighthouse all in one fell swoop. Amelia was juggling her new positions across the shoreline with resurrecting the lighthouse *and* forging ahead with the search for Wendell.

Meanwhile the other Hannigans were starting to lose interest. After all, it was hard to care much about a man who left in the darkest hour of the girls' young lives. The grand idea of tracking him down and shaking the truth out of him was losing steam for Kate, Megan, and certainly Clara. That's how things worked on the lake. Water washed ideas in and out on the gentle current. Sure, the facts surrounding Wendell's disappearance would reappear. Just not as a tidal wave or a riptide, but instead as a soft seeping flow, pulling the sand out from beneath their feet once they were certain they had finally found a dry spot to stand.

"Hey," Brian replied. Traffic sounds buzzed in behind his voice. If her timing was right, he'd be stepping out of an interview right about then. She could kill two birds with just one phone call. Get back to her sisters. Take a deep breath. Function again, this time with a game plan.

A smile pricked at her mouth. "How did it go?"

"I have good news and bad news," he said.

She stilled herself. In the new normal of their separation, their free-floating, never-ending separation, the good news could be bad and the bad news could be good. It was all very jumbled. "Okay. Start with the bad, I guess."

"The bad news is I didn't get the job."

Her heart sank. That *was* bad news. He needed a job. He needed money. He needed both more than Megan did. It was a slap to them both, because if Brian couldn't get a job, then Megan had no hope. Brian was *employable*. He had a degree and over a decade with his recent company. In good standing, too. Very good standing, in fact, and if he'd been a little more passionate about the software, he might have been promoted rather than let go. Then again, cuts were cuts, and Brian's competency *should* have saved him. Wasn't that all that mattered anymore? Competency? The ability to perform a job regardless of how interested you were?

Megan was not employable and her applications to various dating apps (the *only* thing she thought she wanted to do) had ground to a halt. Instead, she was now toying with the misery of dropping her bare-bones resume at every shop front and eatery in Birch Village. "Oh, Brian," she replied. "I'm sorry."

"It's okay. It's really okay," he went on, "because the good news is that I have an idea."

"An idea?"

He spoke fast, almost tripping over his words like a kid who just hatched a plan for his next great adventure. "I can develop my *own* app. This is my chance, Meg. This could jolt me back to life a little. I can do what *I* want to do. I know the tech. I just need to find an avenue. An underserved industry that needs easy mobile access."

Underserved industry. The expression stuck in her ear, slogging its way into her brain then hanging there. Megan frowned, racking her brain. *Where had she just heard that phrase?* She snapped her fingers. Kate. The Inn. Birch Harbor's small-town businesses that cater to tourists and townies alike... quirky, off-beat ventures that offer an *experience.*

She shook her head. The connection was irrelevant.

Brian's excitement, even if it was devoid of the greater context of their family's difficult circumstances, *did* produce an opportunity. This was Megan's chance to extend an olive branch to the man in the form of a little support. Yes, support. The thing she'd longed for in much of their marriage but had been too busy with her own lack of it to really put effort into offering it. The thing that got them where they were. Angry nights flashed in her mind. Heated words. Accusations. *You've never supported me!* and *Where's your support?* All those times had turned her against the whole concept, as though it was psychobabble or something.

But here she was now, with her own agenda and needs (and Sarah's, to be fair), and she could go one of two ways: remind him that his dream job mattered several degrees less than their living situation... or encourage him. What was there to lose? Another dead-end argument?

She swallowed. "Brian, that's fantastic. It's a great way to look at a crummy situation. I think you should go for it." Through the very act of quelling her irritation, Megan's words landed with sincerity. "I mean every word."

"Really?" His smile was audible over the phone.

"Really. Whatever you think of will be fantastic."

"Thanks, Megan. That means a lot to me. I know it's going to keep our situation a little fluid. I might have to pull from savings. The townhouse has two bedrooms, though. If you don't want to stay in Birch Harbor longer—"

"Actually," she cut in, taking a deep breath. "I wanted to talk about that." She let out a quiet sigh, a tentatively happy one. It worked. She gave, and now he was giving. Emotionally, at least.

"You want to leave?" he asked, his tone falling deeper.

"No, I want to stay. I think Sarah does, too. Most days, at least." She picked at a fingernail, clearing away the last flake of black polish. Her nails were nearly bare now. She needed a fresh coat. Maybe a different color. Maybe a break from dark.

"That's okay. We can get together on weekends. Sarah can stay here whenever. Or, wait a minute..."

Brian wasn't totally over-focused on his career. She fully expected the lightbulb to click on in his head. And it had.

"Oh. School. It's almost August," he added weakly.

"Right," Megan agreed. "It's time to *really* decide, Brian. It's her senior year." Megan folded her lips between her teeth, bracing for his response. All of a sudden, it seemed absolutely crazy that they hadn't already committed to something. Was it that there *was* a loose commitment? An assumption? That Sarah would just go to Birch Harbor High like they'd sort of, kind of agreed upon one day in early June? The day Sarah declared that nothing would make her happier than to have a year on the lake. *It'd be like studying abroad*, she'd urged her parents against their skepticism. Megan continued, "I mean, a third option is renting something small near home." Even as she said the word, *home*, it felt false. Awkward on her tongue. Their suburbia bliss was no longer home. Hadn't been in forever. Wasn't just as soon as Brian lost his job and they settled on selling the overpriced ranch-style four bedroom. The one on a sprawling acre of crisp green grass with uniform hedges and morning joggers smiling, full of breath and stay-at-home-mom energy...

"You said you want to stay in Birch Harbor. And Sarah does, too. So, that's what we do, then," he answered.

The presentation of it smacked her in the face. Was she *positive* Sarah wanted to stay? Should *Megan* be the one to decide this? It was better for their daughter to finish at her old high school. There was no getting around that. So, then, what were the benefits that outweighed traditionally good judgment?

Having a place to live.

"But," she began, her voice a whine that she couldn't turn off. "We don't really have a place here." The truth had been buried deep. Deep beneath the fact that they didn't have a place in their old neighborhood, either. They didn't have a place in Brian's townhome. Or anywhere. They just didn't have a place.

"Well," Brian answered, smooth and easy and reliable and assured, "what if, since I'm going to work from home, what if I come to Birch Harbor? What if we get something there? It's where your sisters are. It's become Sarah's second home. I think we just need to pick a place and do it, Megs."

We. Her heart throbbed against her chest wall. *We. We. We.*

"Okay." Her whine broke. "Okay." Options shuffled through her mind. Not the Inn, of course. Or the cottage or the lighthouse. They *could* take up Clara's old two-bedroom in The Bungalows. It sat empty, awaiting its next tenant. No, no. If she wasn't going to live in a two-bedroom townhome on the outskirts of Detroit, then she'd be a hypocrite to move into one in Birch Harbor, even if it was rent-free. Even if it was her family's. They were back to square one. They had no place. Her question was the exact same as it had been since they caved to financial duress and put their house on the market. "But where will we live?"

"What about the land Nora left you?"

"It's just land." Sarah's voice crept into her head. What was the point of empty land? "And we don't have any income," she added, angry with him and herself for giving into the pull of pessimism.

"You just told me to take a leap of faith like two minutes ago," he reasoned. "What about that apartment complex where Clara lived? Amelia's running it, right? Are there any vacancies?"

She shrugged to herself. "I don't want to live there forever, Brian. And, besides, why would you want to come cram in with us? You could just stay in your town-house." Doubt pooled along her heart, drowning any hope and turning into a belligerent monster.

"You said you wanted a plan, Megan. And if there's any question about what we should do, then we can at least remove the question of where. For all of us. For you, and for me."

The question of where. The question of what. The question of who. It could be a dream come true. Her fantasy of a reunion. But in a two-bedroom in The Bungalows?

"Maybe you're right. Maybe this is crazy. Maybe we should wait a year. In the meantime, you and Sarah can stay at the Inn or wherever," Brian said, his voice hollow now. "Or move back to the old house. Stay there and keep her there. Like things were. We have the savings. I can use that for your rent and just keep looking for a job somewhere." He could have sighed loudly or tsked or tutted or added a thick coat of sarcasm to everything he said. But he didn't. He just said. He just gave her the alternative. The plain, realistic alternative.

And it was exactly what she needed. "No. Let's do it. We can live in The Bungalows. We'll figure it out. Sarah can stay in the lighthouse if she wants. It can be her *semester abroad*."

Brian's laugh fell across the line, warm and familiar. "Let's ask her first."

"Okay, we'll ask her. And if she says yes?" Megan asked, flirtation spilling across her question.

"Then it'll be just us," he answered, the depth returning to his voice, the word heavy with innuendo.

Megan smiled. "Just us."

8

CLARA

Tired of holing up in her cottage, Clara had finally agreed to come help at the Inn.

The sisters' plans for a summer gala took on a new angle, though. Amelia admitted that opening the lighthouse and doing it right would have to wait. She and Michael were still knee deep in figuring out how, exactly, to run a museum, after all. And they kept growing distracted with any discovery, no matter how small. When she found a button in a windowsill, the day was shot in favor of a silly quest down a long, dead-end road that culminated with an email to the producers of *Antiques Roadshow*. Another time, when they were scraping old paint from the interior of the tower, she thought she detected a love note carved into the metal stairs. No amount of Michael's convincing that it was errant graffiti could refocus Amelia.

And while they had the basics well underway, nothing she alighted upon seemed relevant and very little really was left behind from the Actons. Anything that was became immediate fodder for speculation surrounding Wendell or, conversely, an item that might lend itself to curation.

Clara wished for her sister to have some closure, but it seemed that wherever Wendell went, he intended for no clues to fall into his wake. She even suggested they'd have better luck digging through Nora's room at the cottage, but Amelia had swatted that idea swiftly away like an irksome gnat. Clara just shrugged it off, pleased to keep everyone out of her home.

Kate, for her part, agreed that the summer gala idea might be better planned as a smaller scale event, like a backyard tea party for guests or a rate drop for Labor Day Weekend, rather than a full-blown party. After all, the Inn could only host so many at once, and to have to turn away droves of guests may do more harm than good. Still, she bemoaned the fact that they'd miss the chance to have a blow-out summer bash, something, apparently, Kate had longed for since returning to town. Clara privately suspected it was the remnants of Kate's youth knocking at the door. That, paired with Kate and Matt's budding reunion, likely massaged a good dose of nostalgia into them. Summer love was a real disease.

Anyway, with the decision to move forward with a Labor Day Inn-Warming Party, as Kate started calling it, they still had work to do, some of it unrelated to the Inn or the lighthouse as locales at all. For Amelia's habit of stumbling across small, seemingly meaningful trinkets was catching. Soon enough, reminiscences took over every clean-out session.

It was with that limited momentum, all four sisters (and the added help of the occasional man friend and

Sarah) worked on clearing the attic at the Inn. On days they needed a break from the Inn, they turned their focus to cracking into boxes Amelia had found in the bowels of the lighthouse. The end goal? Progress. Progress toward settling back home and progress toward learning more about Wendell, if possible.

Things were going as well as they could. Clara's feelings toward Kate were softening each day. Small glances, little smiles, and a light touch on the arm here or there started to resume its old meaning. Sisterhood. Now, though, with something a little deeper. Something maternal. Something Clara, to be sure, had missed out on under her tutelage with Nora.

But the relationship, if you could even call it that, with her newfound father still sat icy, like a heap of ice cubes frozen together in a misshapen lump, impossible to crack apart without the added benefit of warmth and time—both of which Clara and Kate and Matt had, in abundance. But still...

Each time Matt came around to drill a hole here or patch a section of drywall there, Clara excused herself.

She wasn't ready. Not to reconnect with her dad. Especially when the dad she thought was hers for the past three decades had still dominated the greater part of their group's conversations.

Spending the summer with Kate, Amelia, and Megan had been Clara's dream for so long, and now that it was here, she realized that a reunion wasn't all butterflies and tulips. It was hard work to get to know people you thought you knew. At least, for someone like Clara, who'd never been very good at making or keeping friends.

Bonding with Sarah was equally treacherous.

Teenage girls, it turned out (in their daily lives, at least) were just as bad as the bullying reports that drifted on rumors through the teacher's lounge and across the front office, curling like wisps of gossip, never quite believable or grave to those adults who were so disconnected from their own traumatic youth. Coming face to face with one such perpetrator changed Clara's opinion on a dime.

She learned quickly that Sarah was not a bully, necessarily, but her mood swings rivaled Nora's. Part of the conflict was the cruel little flippant remark Sarah had left at the cottage just days before.

Miss Havisham.

On the one hand, it *could* be construed as a compliment. Miss Havisham was an elusive, enigmatic enchantress in *Great Expectations.* In some readings, that was.

On the other, Sarah's comparison landed as a slight. Something derogatory and demeaning. Or, could it be that Clara was being sensitive? Did her *cousin* even know what she was saying? Probably not. In all likelihood, Sarah had enjoyed Miss Havisham as much as Clara had as a high schooler. And how could Sarah know just how close to home the accusation hit? That Clara was just like old Miss Havisham, wrapped in lace at the top of a hill, out-of-reach and cruel.

She couldn't. She couldn't know that Clara held a grudge against her mother or resented her so-called sisters or floundered in the summertime when she secretly, *so* secretly, longed for a laughing group of girlfriends to walk the beach with. Or a hot summer date to treat her to a dripping ice cream cone, which she needed help to shape up with a few flirty licks.

Sarah knew none of that.

And she never would have to know any of it, either. Because Clara was making a change.

THEY BROKE FOR LUNCH, having spent all morning pulling weeds. Normally, Clara might stay for the food part and leave for the lingering part. The part that happened after they ate, when her sisters stretched back in their bistro chairs and churned new topics into the conversation like they were folding salt into a heap of dough.

It was just the five of them, there, at an outside table of Fiorillo's. Clara strategically positioned herself so that she faced the marina with all its midsummer bustling. After all, her plan had less to do with her sisters and lingering on the far side of their conversation and more to do with, well, *really* putting herself out there.

Together they sat and sipped iced teas. Amelia asked Kate how things were going with Matt. Kate politely kept mum, for Clara's benefit, no doubt. Megan asked Amelia how things were going with Michael. Amelia launched into a TMI monologue, elaborating on everything from how weird it was to date someone with a mortgage and a bookshelf all the way to their kissing adventures.

"What in the hell are *kissing adventures*?" Megan asked, her eyes wild. "Wait a minute, don't answer that," she added quickly, gripping her daughter's arm protectively. "Impressionable minds."

The others laughed, and Clara did too as she scanned the marina office. No sign of him.

"What about you two?" Kate questioned Megan.

Running her fingers through her dark hair, Megan raked her salad with the other hand. "Sarah and me?"

"I mean Brian and you," Kate replied. Clara glanced at Sarah, sympathetically. She understood the bizarre dynamic of parents whose romantic life was, well, complicated, if not totally non-existent.

Megan's gaze fell to her salad, but a small smile curled her lips, her famous cheekbones lifting above her mouth. Cheekbones were one of those things that you only really appreciated north of thirty. Did Clara have them? She pressed a hand to either side of her face then shook the thought away and again glanced toward the dock. A new throng of tourists deboarded *Harbor Queen,* a small day cruise ship that toured Lake Huron. White bodies glowed beneath broad hats. Beach bags and flip-flops shuffled with confusion up toward the Village.

"Well?" Amelia pressed Megan.

Sarah cleared her throat and asked to be excused.

"Where are you going?" Megan snapped to attention, forgetting for the moment the question at hand. Or, perhaps, conveniently pushing it aside. Clara couldn't quite read her older, brooding sister. Especially when the brooding was overshadowed by... what was this new emotion playing out on Megan? *Joy*?

Sarah pointed a finger to the marina office, and Clara followed it, studying the object of her niece-cousin's focus. Amidst the chaos of the encroaching sightseers bobbed an under-clothed circle of teenage girls. One of the faces was familiar to Clara.

No, *two.*

Vivi, Matt's daughter. Tall, thin, and impossibly blonde. She was Clara if someone strung Clara in a stretching machine and soaked her hair in peroxide. Maybe that was wishful thinking.

The other girl, Mercy Hennings.

Clara narrowed her eyes on the girls. Two others joined them at the back of the office. Beach towels wedged beneath their arms. Their hands gripping chunky beach bags. Mercy's dad was nowhere to be seen, but why else would the group congregate at the office?

"Are you friends with them?" Clara asked Sarah, knowing the answer already. It was more judgment than curiosity.

Sarah ignored Clara's question and directed her question-in-the-form-of-a-sentence at her mother. "Mom, I was going to meet them later, anyway. I'm just going to go now. Okay?"

Megan hesitated, shielding her eyes from the sun. "Why don't you invite them up here, Sar?"

"What." Again, Sarah didn't quite ask. Her flat tone cut across the table.

It was Amelia who shook loose the tension, rising from her chair and holding her hands to her mouth before calling across the cobblestone walk over the hundred-or-so yards of expanse between their position on Fiorillo's patio and the marina office. "Viv! Girls! Over here!" She waved enthusiastically, and Sarah sank in her chair.

Maybe, Clara thought snidely, it *did* make sense that Sarah befriended younger girls. Her maturity was such that she might as well be entering her freshman year of high school rather than her senior year.

But when the girls neared, Clara saw that the two less-familiar faces were, in fact, her former students.

From years back. One had to be a junior. The other, a senior, at least, if not a recent grad.

The chattering girls flip-flopped their way up the uneven path to the other side of the short brick wall that separated the patio from the flow of traffic inland.

With Amelia's confidence setting the tone, Sarah sat back up and flashed a cool smile at her friends.

As they neared, Mercy, who lagged behind the group, peered around them, locking eyes with Clara.

It was peculiar that Clara's most asocial student was now tucked among this flamboyant bunch of would-be beach babes.

Still, Clara smiled at Mercy and was about to greet her especially until a louder, valley-girl voice broke across their closing distance. "Oh my *gosh*, Miss Hannigan!" one of the older two squealed.

Clara's eyes flashed to her. "Paige!" she returned, putting on her teacher cheer. "And Chloe! Girls, how are you?"

In many cities across America, Clara knew from memes and social media, crossing a teacher in public was an awkward, uncomfortable experience. In small towns, though, it was a common occurrence. Except, not for Clara, who basically did not have public outings very regularly. When she did, however, her students fawned over her like a sweet dumpling. Especially her female students who'd moved on to greener pastures, like high school, for example.

She felt Sarah's eyes on her as the other girls bantered away, commenting on Clara's sunglasses and overalls —*so hip!*

"We were doing yard work," Clara answered lamely, feeling all of ten-years-old under their scrutiny.

"So, Miss Hannigan, you know this one," Chloe hooked a finger at Sarah.

Clara and her niece-cousin exchanged uncomfortable glances. "Yep. Sarah is my..."

"Niece," Kate cut in severely. "Clara is her aunt." She smiled at Clara, lifting her sunglasses so her eyes could fully pierce Clara straight down into her heart.

"Girls," Amelia cut in, her voice supplicant, ever the peace-maker, "*So* great to see you. Why don't you steal Sarah away and go have fun on the shore? I could have sworn that I saw a pack of board shorts heading north." She winked at Clara.

"Okay, Sarah, call me before dinner so I know what your plans are," Megan added as the lithe young woman rose and rounded the table, traipsing off with her new, bouncing hodge-podge of girlfriends.

Clara watched them leave, and just before their feet hit the sand on the far side of the village, she saw Mercy's head whip back toward the marina office.

Darting her eyes back that way, Clara saw him.

The object of her new focus. The man who might act as a sweet distraction during what felt like the unending tumult of her parentage.

Jake Hennings. Birch Harbor Marina Manager and former biology researcher. Someone who knew the water better than locals. A handsome single dad. Clara's *favorite student's* dad, to be exact.

Bolstering herself up, she took a long swig of tea and declared to her sisters, who'd begun needlessly gossiping about the younger set, "I'll be right back."

"Clara, wait."

Clara looked down to see Kate's hand on her arm. "What?"

"The whole thing about you being Sarah's aunt or cousin or whatever..." Pain streaked across her face, and Kate flashed her eyes at the other two.

It was a stillborn conversation. Each time they were all together and alone from others, the idea of whether to make some small-town pronouncement butted its way into the conversation. And each time, they'd agreed that for the time being, it should sit. After all, in a small-town, reputation was more fragile than a brittle seashell. And since Kate was back, sliding beneath Nora's crown, she clearly thought she still had something to lose.

"What if Matt already told Vivi?" Clara protested, glancing toward the office, she saw that Jake had disappeared amongst the crowd.

She looked back at Kate, sulking now.

"I asked him not to. And he's discrete, so I think it'll be fine," Kate answered, lowering her sunglasses onto her nose. "It'll be just fine. One day, we can sort of, come out. If you want, that is."

Clara ignored the pandering question and turned her attention to Megan. "What about Sarah? What if *she* tells?" Megan may be the teenager's mother, but Clara knew young women better.

Megan reached for her iced tea and shrugged. "We don't have to worry about Sarah. She is sort of over it, anyway."

Tears pricked at the corners of Clara's eyes. She willed herself not to care either.

Her sisters moved back into their conversation,

commenting mildly about *bikinis these days* and *See, Megan? Summer is full of business opportunities.*

It occurred to Clara that, actually, it *was* better to keep the secret. If the whole town was in the dark, then she wouldn't have to be Matt Fiorillo's long-lost daughter.

And the best thing about that was that she would never have to be Viviana Fiorillo's long-lost sister.

9

AMELIA

"Welcome home, you two." Amelia lifted her coffee mug over the kitchen table in Megan and Brian's new unit at The Bungalows. It was meant to be an early morning toast. Michael had joined them on that Saturday morning, at Amelia's behest. It was always a good idea to have an outsider at family events.

As their mother often said, *If you bring a stranger, then everyone has to behave.*

So far, the advice was working. Brian stood by the bar, one hand shoved into one pocket, the other thumbing along his phone screen. Megan set out coffees. Amelia and Michael brought the bagels.

It was day one: which Amelia had taken to calling The Re-Merging. Sarah had stolen away to help Kate at the Inn. They had an influx of check-ins the night before and *someone* had to help with pancakes.

Kate had offered up Matt to come by and move any furniture, but no heavy lifting was required. Brian's townhome, which he still had three weeks in, had come furnished. Their shared marital furniture and everything else from the house they were selling was now neatly tucked away in a storage unit in some desolate neighborhood outside of Detroit. Plus, Clara had left behind her apartment furniture when she moved to the cottage. So, the only excitement on that warm, dewy morning was to help the two decide who was sleeping where, where their wardrobes would go, if Brian was going to be a weekend warrior or a full-timer.

Amelia shivered against the chill of the window AC unit. In her heart of hearts, Amelia loved Brian like a brother. All of the sisters did. And here they were, the perfect opportunity to bond the two menfolk, establish some common ground, but Megan had yet to make eye contact with her husband, and Brian was replying to their questions and prompts with one-word answers.

At Amelia's toast, Megan lifted her mug and smiled weakly. Michael raised his. Brian, thankfully, snapped to attention, clicked his phone off, shoved it in his pocket and dragged his mug to the table, settling in the open seat next to his wife.

Amelia sighed with relief when Brian raised his mug and let his face soften. "To new beginnings," he added.

It was painful. The tension. The effort. But it was a start. Amelia grinned at him and clinked mugs before lifting a brow at Megan.

"So," Michael interjected once they started in on the bagels, slowly making their way through the cardboard takeout jug of coffee. Megan had gone out to pick it up when she realized they had none. The Birch Bean

Company, the best coffee you could find on Lake Huron. "Brian," he went on.

Amelia sucked in a breath, excitement slicing through her trepidation. The anticipation of everything launched her on a rollercoaster. There was her sister and her brother-in-law, in battle gear against the monster that was divorce. Now, they sat within two feet of each other, sharing coffee from the same jug, dancing through the awkwardness of a very real and very raw reunion. Amelia felt at once like an actress in a great one-act and a director of an epic drama.

Brian looked up, chewing through a particularly over-sized bite of an everything bagel. "Mhm?" he asked, his eyebrows shooting up.

"Megan tells us you might be a startup guy. App development? Something like that?"

Brian swallowed the bite and dabbed his mouth with a paper napkin. "That's the dream," he replied easily, stealing a fast look at Megan who was busying herself with plucking crumbs from the space around her plate.

"And I guess Megan wants to start a business, too?" Michael pressed on.

Amelia paled. *That* part was a secret. Not even a secret, actually, it was a rumor. Something Kate mentioned in a sisterly gossip session after the group dinner out at the lighthouse. Megan was toying with a small-town business. Something to serve tourists and townies alike. It made Amelia itchy to think about. First there was Kate, with the bed-and-breakfast. The Heirloom Inn was doing well enough, since all Birch Harbor had in the way of accommodations was either the motel inland or a smattering of overpriced, under-cleaned vacation rentals. Second, there was Amelia herself, with the museum idea. Pretty soon, people were going to take notice. Amelia could see the headlines in the small-town paper. *In the wake of Nora Hannigan's death, her daughters move back to the lake and take over!*

Slicing her hand across her throat toward Michael, Amelia gave him a look, too. But the gestures were lost. He was too aloof. Hopefully, Brian was, too.

But Megan wasn't. "No," she answered. "Where did you hear that?" She eyed Amelia, who shrugged and shrank back behind her coffee mug.

Michael waved a helpless hand then saw his girlfriend cowering and snapped his mouth shut. After a beat, he answered quietly, "Maybe I misheard?" and joined Amelia in the retreat.

Megan glared at Amelia, but then she surprised them. "Well, actually, it was something I was kicking around. Not really a business, though. More like..." she glanced down at the table and pinched another crumb before her lips turned up at the edges. "A service."

Leaning in, Amelia had to look closer. Was Megan... blushing? The woman who wore only one color of nail polish? Who relied on black athleisure ensembles and asked her hairdresser for a *severe A-line*?

Amelia grinned. "A service? What service?" She glanced around the table, taking in Michael's expression, clueless but interested. Then Brian's, which she could only describe as alarmed. A good alarmed, though. A captivated alarmed.

"Yeah." Megan lifted her gaze and suddenly, Amelia was no longer the director. Or even an actress. She was in the audience. She and Michael both were.

What happened next was nothing short of inspiring.

Megan launched into an enthusiastic description of her dream come true. She even used that phrase: *dream come true.*

Something about seasonal mixers and tourists and locals and matchmaking all set inland on the Hannigan Field. White summery tents and lemonade. Hors d'oeuvres and three-piece jazz bands, or perhaps just a DJ.

The picture Megan painted was magical, but that's not what stunned Amelia into reverent silence.

It was that Megan only looked at Brian as she explained it all. Not once did she throw a side glance to Amelia. Not once did she break away to watch Michael's reaction. She kept her gaze unflinchingly on him. Like a challenge.

And it was that Brian, when Megan had wrapped up her *dream come true*, had reached across the table and found his wife's hand, squeezing it.

That's when Amelia knew that there would be no retreating to the townhome. No invitations for strangers to help keep the peace.

And it's when Amelia and Michael gently and giddily excused themselves.

Megan and Brian had, right in front of their faces, relit their candle. Through the so-called new beginning. The fresh start. The blank slate. Over boxed coffee and bagels and on the heels of a frigid undercurrent... the flame came in flashes, like a lightning bug. Quiet and invisible to others until *boom*, it buzzed to life, a miniature fire for all to see.

And Amelia knew that whatever her sister's *dream come true* was, exactly, she was going to be darn good at it.

10

KATE

"Let me get this straight." Kate pushed her fingertips into her temples. To her left stood Brian and Michael, their arms crossed over their chests like bodyguards. Across from her, seated at the farmhouse table in the kitchen of the Inn, sat Megan and Amelia, like children laying out their request for a pet, complete with an upkeep schedule and empty promises. "You were really serious?"

The question was directed at Megan, but both Megan and Amelia nodded their heads vigorously.

Clara sauntered into the room just then. She and Sarah had served breakfast on the back deck instead of in the parlor that morning. It was meant to be a dry-run for Labor Day weekend and the Inn-Warming Party. Sarah, in all likelihood, had meandered her way down to the beach. It seemed like at every turn, her new posse of local friends were waiting for her somewhere. As if she, this newcomer from the suburbs, had suddenly become Birch High Prom Queen.

Megan, Amelia, and Brian had crashed the rehearsal, though.

"And you're, what? Asking my permission?"

"No," Megan replied urgently. "We're telling you our plan. And asking for your *help*."

"I'll help. Sure, I'll help. But, I mean, how? I don't know the first thing about matchmaking. And I thought Amelia was busy." She frowned, not quite relishing her role as the perennial mother figure to her younger sisters.

"Labor Day weekend. That's when we will host our first mixer. The theme is 'Summer Lovin'.'"

"Like *Grease*," Amelia added.

Kate frowned. "It sounds like a teenie-bop thing. Not an adult mixer. I don't understand, Megan, I thought you were going to host, like, *events*. Like weddings and all that."

"Well, that's true. And I will. But it's going to be even bigger. It's going to be a boutique matchmaking service, sort of on the sly."

Kate shook her head. "I don't understand. *On the sly*? What does that mean?"

"I want the business to be based on finding a match. So, I'm going to set it around the premise of," Megan framed her hands out across an invisible billboard, "Single and Ready to Mingle." Her eyes glimmered with enthusiasm, and that coupled with Brian's mere presence snapped Kate out of her skepticism. She nodded slowly, taking it all in.

"So, your business is matchmaking," Kate began, wrapping her head around it, "and you'll host matchmaking events."

"And weddings," Amelia added.

Nodding again, Kate looked back toward the men. "Summer Love." She returned her attention to Megan. "Single and Ready to Mingle. 'Summer Lovin'.' A mixer."

Megan prodded her along by cycling her hand. "If we have it Labor Day, then we can draw in visitors and sort of, I don't know, pair them up with locals. Like you and I talked about!"

Clara eased into the open chair by the door, and Kate felt her eyes on her. A challenge. A test of the woman's kindness. Of her warmth and generosity.

There was nothing Kate could say. Nothing she could do that wouldn't squash Megan's dreams. So, instead, she stepped outside of her role as mom and inside of her role as sister. The role she knew best. The one she was relegated to and now trapped in.

Because returning to Birch Harbor and living in her childhood home had changed where she thought Nora's death would take them.

The truth, in all its newly revealed glory, was still dormant. There was no chance to be a grieving daughter. Or a small-town sister. No chance to be a lakeside innkeeper.

And there was most certainly no chance to be a scorned mother with a wounded heart and open arms. Now, it wasn't just the tenuous fibers of their family that was at stake.

It was much more. It was the Hannigan tradition. It was a Birch Harbor reputation, forged decades back, when the house on the harbor was more than a family home. It was a settlement. A dare to the community, suggesting that there was more to the little Lake Huron community than budding storefronts and blossoming eateries. There *would* be more. There would be descendants. And pain. And the preservation of the past in the face of the reality of the present.

Kate Hannigan wasn't Megan's mother, there to bring her down to reality. She wasn't Clara's mother, either. She couldn't be. Not if she wanted the focus to land squarely on the great success that these women could be.

She was their sister. Their equal.

And now, their business partner.

"Let's do it," Kate said. "A bed-and-breakfast. A museum. And, an event service."

"Matchmaking service," Megan added, smiling from ear to ear.

"*Boutique* matchmaking service," Kate corrected.

Megan shot up from her seat and started across the table. Kate thought she was coming in for a hug, but just as Kate also rose up, Megan reached her arms out beyond her, to Brian.

Grinning at the surprising exchange, Kate looked at Clara first. Her smile fell a little, but she reached her hand across the table, and Clara accepted it. It was only in those moments when Matt wasn't around that Clara and Kate shared the quiet moments she was so desperate for. The silent acknowledgements and small smiles.

Then, Amelia slapped her hand down on the table. "I've got it!" she declared, her voice vibrating with life. "We could form a corporation!"

"True," Kate replied, squeezing and releasing Clara's hand then gesturing toward her. "Clara could offer tutoring services or something, right?" The attempt to pull the youngest into the grand scheme was just an inch too far. One shade too bright.

Clara shrugged meekly. "I can just help here. I don't mind. I'm so busy during the school year."

"Clara will be our link to the younger set. She knows all the twenty-something lingo. Social media and stuff. Right, Clar?" Megan added.

Nodding in reply, Clara glanced at Kate, who stood from the table and rounded to her, standing behind Clara and squeezing her shoulders. "Clara can do whatever she wants. After all, she's the only true local we've got on the team."

At that, Kate knew she'd struck the right chord. Clara twisted and smiled up at her. "True. You're practically tourists. All of you."

They laughed together, a freshness glowing around the kitchen.

Amelia broke into the merriment with her earlier idea. "See? Let's call ourselves an enterprise."

"That's not a bad idea," Michael added, mostly for effect. Kate suspected he knew it was a silly proposition.

Catching momentum, Amelia went on. "Hannigan Sisters Enterprises."

Megan and Brian chattered animatedly, immediately agreeable, it seemed. And Kate liked the idea of a little corporation, but Clara's muscles twitched beneath her palms. It wasn't quite right.

It wasn't quite true, but then the last thing that they needed now was to come under some other drama. Nora's memory depended on the maintenance of her secret. *Not* the revelation of it.

If they were going to be successful in business, then Clara would have to stay the youngest sister.

11

MEGAN

Megan knew two things.

One, that all of her sisters believed in her marriage.

Two, that one sister did not believe in *Summer Lovin'*.

That hint of a lack of support niggled at her brain, pushing her to ask herself the same thing. *Was this all a bad idea?*

So, she stayed ahead of the curve, finding fault wherever she could. "I don't like the name," Megan declared that afternoon at the lighthouse. It was true, too. The name was bad.

She and Brian had visited Hannigan Field in order to take photographs and measurements. They quickly realized that whatever it was Megan was about to roll out would take far more work than she realized. Especially when Brian, in passing, mused aloud about *building* on the field. She'd scoffed, reminding him they had about one month to set up, organize, and advertise the inaugural event. And what would they build?

His reply was simple enough. "Our dream home." She laughed at the idea when he suggested it, but now the prospect of a house and a business all in one location... with him... it was becoming a distraction.

"Hannigan Field?" Amelia asked between bites of watermelon.

Brian had agreed to help Michael mount a painting they'd come across in the cellar. The girls were left to brainstorm.

"Not that. I mean *Summer Lovin'*. First of all, what if we don't get our act together by September? Then, it won't be summer lovin'. And even if we do, it's more like *end*-of-summer."

"True," Amelia allowed.

"But even if we do, it's odd. I think it needs to be more... I don't know. More... enchanting. Not so garish."

"Garish." Amelia nodded and gnawed into another chunk, humming to herself as she chewed.

"Oh, Am." Megan dropped her wedge onto the plate and wiped her hands along a paper towel. "What am I thinking? How can we pull this off in *weeks*?"

"Well, I mean, what's the rush? Do you *have* to open in the summer? You could always wait."

"Until when?" Megan asked, mulling it over.

"Spring? You could go with *Spring Fever*." Amelia smiled to herself. The smug smile of a woman with a house-and-business-in-one, *and* a new boyfriend, *and* several side gigs. After a lifetime chasing roles and just a summer of settling into her new world, Amelia was losing perspective. Turning content, or something.

"*Spring*?" Megan felt a throb creep up from her clenched jaw and settle beside either eye. "That's months away. We'll have blasted through our savings by then."

"How?" Amelia asked. "What bills do you have?"

Megan rubbed beneath her eyebrows, massaging the hollow space and attempting to free herself of the growing headache. "The usual bills. I mean, we aren't just going to mooch off you or Kate. We'll have to pay rent for the bungalow. And Sarah is going to get sick of staying here. You're probably already sick of her yourself. We need to *buy* something, you know. And then there are insurance payments. Food. I mean, come on. We can't just *not* make money."

"True." Amelia sighed. "But I'm not sick of Sarah."

"Our arrangement now is temporary. If we really are making a go of staying here... then we have to bring in money. We have to have a home—a real one. Not a two-bedroom apartment while our daughter couch surfs across the shoreline."

"So, you need jobs," Amelia pointed out as though she'd not listened to one word Megan had said. "Is Brian moving forward with his app idea?"

"What app idea?" Megan spat back, sarcasm coating her throat. "It's dead in the water. I think he's even secretly applying to software companies in the city."

Amelia's eyes narrowed on the last available red bit on her rind. "Oh." She bit in, the crunch an obnoxious distraction from Megan's desperation.

"You can't really start a business without capital. We could use the savings if Brian is going to skip his app idea. But I can't tell him not to follow his dream if I'm following mine."

"Dreams, ha." Amelia took a long swig of her ice

water and set it down with finality. "You need more than a dream to find happiness, you know. Take it from someone who is intimately familiar."

Megan's face fell into a deep frown.

"Listen," Amelia said, pressing her hand over Megan's on the table, her voice softening. "Follow your dreams. Sure, just go for it. I mean, I'm a walking example of someone who did that. But I didn't do the work. And when I did do the work, I wasn't smart about it." Amelia let out a long sigh. "Megan, I bounced out of college when I was about to fail one class. I left each theater that didn't give me a role within a couple of years, and I only applied to the biggest ones. I took on bit parts by the time I got to New York, but then I turned to waiting tables because, well, it was easier than the other hard work. Learning to act was hard work. Memorizing pages and pages and sticking to a diet or whatever, it all seemed like hard work. And I didn't get a good routine going. So even though I stuck it out in New York, by that point I was working hard on waiting tables and keeping up my social life. But I wasn't working hard *or* smart. Your so-called *dream come true* is not going to slot into place because you willed it to. Just because you two *say* you're back together. Or you *say* Sarah's going to start her senior year here. You *say* you're going to do this and that. Stop *saying* and start doing. And do it smart. And work hard." Finishing her impromptu monologue, Amelia leaned back and smiled.

Megan leaned forward. "You know what? You're right." She pulled her hand out from Amelia's, twisted in her seat, and called across the beach toward the tower, where the men were. "Brian!"

He didn't appear immediately, and Megan figured he couldn't hear her. She called again and still no reply.

"What are you doing today?" she asked Amelia, suddenly inspired.

"Um. Working around here?" It came out like a question.

"Great," Megan answered. "I need you to call Party People, that rental place up the shoreline. Order three big tents for Saturday of Labor Day weekend."

"Now?" Amelia asked, bewildered.

"Now," Megan answered, wild.

Then, she took off toward the lighthouse, slogging through sand as thick as mud until she came upon the entrance.

Peering inside, she saw a painting, hung evenly on the far wall. It was a family portrait of the original Hannigan family. The ones who first moved to the lake and erected the house on the harbor.

Not the Actons.

Brian and Michael weren't on the ground floor. She looked up along the winding metal staircase and to the observation deck through a knot in the floor of it. Unable to see them, she neared the painting.

If they'd uncovered it in the cellar, then that meant that it somehow had made its way from the house on the harbor to the lighthouse, an unlikely journey for a painting that would have meant nothing to her Acton grandparents, who'd long ago written off Nora as being a salacious tramp who took their son for granted and saw to it that he ran away for good.

The presence of the painting meant something else. It

meant that Wendell himself had probably brought it there.

It meant that maybe, just maybe, no love was lost between Nora and Wendell. Maybe he wasn't angry. Maybe he didn't leave.

"I brought it over from the house." Amelia's voice loomed behind Megan, whose face fell.

"I thought you said you got it out of the cellar here?"

Amelia shook her head. "Not this one." Then she ascended the staircase. Megan followed.

As they squeezed through to the platform, they found Brian and Michael, hanging a smaller painting, also a portrait.

This one of just Grandpa and Grandma Acton.

"I wanted them to have a view," Amelia added as Megan stared at it.

"A view of what?" Megan asked.

"Of wherever their son is."

A chill tickled Megan's spine, but she chalked it up to her sister's weirdness. After all, Megan had things to do. Decisions to make. A life to rebuild. A life her own father had long ago chosen to abandon.

TWO DAYS LATER, things were in motion. Tents, tables, and chairs were reserved. Food and drinks had been ordered from the Harbor Deli. Adult beverages from The Bottle. All they had to do now was clear the field and start advertising.

Megan couldn't believe how simple it was to plan a big party. Surely, everything was made easier by Kate's adept ability to work the phone and Amelia's charm in situating them with the local distributors. Still, it felt a little too good to be true. So far.

With Brian, Matt, and Michael assigned to the field (lawn mowers, weed whackers, clippers, and a rented trailer in tow), it came time to make a big, in-town announcement and then start blasting social media with news of Birch Harbor's first summer mixer, the perfect evening out for singles, near and far.

"Where do I even start with this marketing crap?" Megan asked Kate that morning over mimosas on her back porch. "Where are *you* starting?"

"You mean with my Inn-Warming Party?" Kate lifted a manicured eyebrow. For all the grunt work she'd been at lately, it appeared to Megan that her older sister had aged in reverse. She'd taken on a new elegance. She got a haircut and added low lights to her blonde. When she wasn't in jeans and a white tee with paint smeared across the front, Kate wore crisp collared blouses and neat khaki shorts. Her tan legs stretched down into white boat shoes. She looked more and more like a female version of Matt, even. Glowing and happy.

"Well, yeah. How are you advertising the *Inn-Warming?*" Megan answered through a silly British accent, as if to mock Kate, who was too bubbly to notice.

"Okay, *so.*" Kate launched into a detailed overview. The Inn had social media pages and a website which was how she reached out to tourists. Locally, she had an advertisement in the bulletin at St. Rita's and even one in the newspaper. "But I let that one expire. Way too pricey."

"Hm." Megan sipped her drink and stared across the water, looking past Amelia and Sarah, spread like blobs on beach chairs near the waterline. "Do you want to know something weird Amelia did?"

"Amelia's always doing weird things."

"True," Megan allowed. "I'll tell you, anyway. She hung Grandma and Grandpa Acton's portrait up in the observation deck of the lighthouse."

"Where? Isn't the observation deck all windowpanes?"

"No. There's a little wall at the back. It's supposed to be a bulletin board or something for record keeping."

"That is weird," Kate agreed.

"She said she thought they could have a view of Wendell."

Kate lowered her glass and studied Megan. "A view of him? Does Amelia know something we don't?"

Megan shrugged. "No. She's just nutty, as far as I can tell. That's what I'm saying, though."

"Amelia!" Kate shouted down to the beach where Amelia's chestnut hair shook off the back of her chair and she twisted to gawk up at them.

"What!" her voice floated back.

Kate waved her hand to gesture her in.

Languidly, Amelia rolled off her chair and shielded her eyes as she looked up at the porch. "What!"

"Come here!"

Megan watched as Amelia gesticulated to Sarah then strode through the sand, drawing stares from a group of passersby. She could have been a model, rather than an actress.

"What?" she said again, cocking her hands on her waist as she took each porch step like she was in an aerobics video. Amelia was the only forty-something Megan knew who could pull off a bikini and not look indecent. It could be her athletic build (she'd dropped ten pounds since moving to the lake). Or her quirky nature. Probably a combination of the two.

"A picture of the Actons in the lighthouse? Why?" Kate accused.

Amelia shrugged and frowned. "So they could have a—"

"A view?" Kate answered for her. Then she leaned forward. "Have you and Michael unearthed something that we should know about? Did Dad escape to Heirloom Island or something?"

At that Amelia laughed, flopped into a seat next to them and poured herself a mimosa with one of the extra flutes. "Actually, that *is* my theory."

"Oh, please," Megan snorted. "If he were on the island, we'd have heard about it faster than if he were shore-side. Or in Detroit, for that matter."

Amelia took a long swig, then shook her head and came up for air. "Michael dug up the case reports." She placed her glass on the table with intention then looked at each of them.

Kate glanced at Megan then wrinkled her brow. "And?" she prodded.

A wide grin spread on Amelia's mouth, a smeary type of smile, lazy and loose. "Nothing. Hah. Come on, girls. Don't you think I would have *told* you if I knew something? *But,*" she went on with new emphasis. "None of the case reports indicate that they even searched the island."

Megan batted away the conversation, disinterested and growing irritated. "I shouldn't have said anything.

I've got to get rolling with marketing. While you're up here, tell me something, Am. Where do all the single people congregate in this town? Because I suspect St. Mary's and the Birch Bee daily circular aren't going to cut it if I want to hit my target number."

"And what is your target number?" Kate asked.

Carefully, slowly, Megan tested out her business plan. "For the first mixer, I'd like to draw in an even number close to or right at twenty. Fourteen being the minimum for what I think is successful. I've been studying *The Millionaire Matchmaker*, *The Bachelor* and *The Bachelorette*, *Blind Date*, and *Make Me a Match*. Twenty could be a lot for me to manage at first, but if I aim high, then at least I'll have that momentum.

Kate interrupted. "Tell me you're not basing your entire business model off of reality dating competitions."

"I'm not," Megan spat back. "Just listen." Kate and Amelia both set their elbows on the table and fell quiet, staring intently at their younger sister. "Okay, so I'm not going to pull any punches. I'll make it crystal clear it's a singles mixer. Not a *swingers* mixer, mind you. The idea is to show up if you're on the market. You can bring friends, whatever. More like speed dating, this way. You'll get a cute little name tag, a ticket for three drinks max, a personal introduction with one of the matchmakers—"

"What?" Amelia chimed in. "What do you mean a personal introduction with *one of the matchmakers*?"

Grinning, she replied, "Well, I'm like the head matchmaker. If I can get to know each attendee, I can mingle through the crowd and help facilitate love connections."

Kate smirked. "That doesn't sound like you, Megan. The mingling. The facilitation."

"You're right," Megan confessed. "I'll be stepping out of my comfort zone. It'll be hard. That's where you two come in. And Clara, too, if she's up to the task."

"She won't be," Amelia bemoaned. "She's not a joiner."

"Well, that's on her, then. Kate, I'll let you bug her about it." Kate took a sip of mimosa and murmured something vague about *trying*, so Megan went on. "Okay, so if you agree to be there, then perfect. We will start the night with a little convocation or something, to identify each of us in our roles. We wouldn't want to be mistaken for..."

"For a hot local single?" Amelia joked, laughing at herself maniacally.

Kate rolled her eyes, but Megan just nodded solemnly. "Right. It has to be professional but fun and flirty. That's the tone. Speaking of which," Megan paused and drank from her glass. "This is not a hook-up thing. I want to make that crystal clear. If we roll this out and people get wind that it's some free-for-all, then there's no longevity. Or, even if there *is* longevity, it's not what I'm going for. I want tasteful. I want seasonal. I want true love for these events. And that's why I'll also host showers and weddings. *True. Love.*" Megan stabbed a finger on the table for each word.

12

CLARA

"You want me to make social media pages for your business?" she asked Megan.

Clara had slept in late. Then, once she did get up, she stayed in bed reading for another hour before she slipped back into sleep. Finally, after eleven, she tore herself from her sheets and threw on a bathing suit, fully intending to spend the day at the lake, maybe on Heirloom Cove, where she could be alone. She'd spent the last several days in the suffocating company of her sisters, working on this, that, and the other in order to push forward their many projects.

Projects.

Clara was not much for projects, unlike the rest of her family. Her perfect day consisted of a good book, a long walk, and then a yummy dinner alongside a jigsaw puzzle. And, while she fully realized the need to start making that change she'd told herself she was going to make (no Miss Havisham-Hannigans here, thankyouverymuch!), change was a long game. Clara couldn't just dive into being personable and sociable and energetic all at once. What was more, she had to save *some* of her energy for the new school year which loomed ahead on the tails of the Inn-Warming party and the grand opening for Megan's thing. What was it called? A sizzler? A spritzer?

Mixer.

Right.

But it was noon now, and she'd had enough respite to ride her bike—oh yes, Clara wasn't all blankets and books at the cottage—all the way down to the house on the harbor. And there she was, munching on a croissant while both Kate and Megan had their laptops propped open on the kitchen island, pointed like lasers at Clara and turning her into some sort of tech go-to.

Megan replied, "Well, I can do some of it. But I need your help. You're young and hip, a little."

"A *little*?" Clara grunted. "If you don't think I'm a lot hip, then why would you want my help?"

Pushing out a sigh, Megan nudged the computer closer to Clara. "You *are* hip. And you've got a direct link to my primary target audience."

"Which is?" Clara pushed back.

It was Amelia who answered this time. "Your youth. Your station in life. You, Clara, are single and ready to mingle in Birch Harbor, Michigan. Are you not?"

"I am not." Clara took another bite of her croissant then chased it with a long pull of black coffee.

"Well," Megan navigated to a different account on her computer. "You are single. You do live in Birch Harbor. We just need to know about the mingling part, too. Okay? Surely, you've had crushes or an interest in someone.

Surely, a boy, or a man, has asked you out. You've gone on *dates*! Tell us, Clar. What is it like to date in your generation? What are you? Generation Y? A millennial?"

"I don't know what I am, and yes, I've been on dates. It's no different than you guys. Someone texts you or messages you, you make plans, you sit through an awkward dinner and contemplate drinking a second glass of wine, decide against it, leave, get home fast so you can unbutton your jeans and take a full breath, then swear you're never doing it again."

Amelia laughed, but Clara just shrugged, accepting her fate as the Guinea pig for Megan's science experiment. If she had one thing to cling to, it was that at least she was a sister. She was important. Even if she was the runty baby of the family, maybe that was better than the lonely single child of the mother who was just a tick too old to have children anymore. She perked up a little. "Okay, so the difference is..."

Megan immediately sensed the shift and squeezed Clara into her, a display of enthusiasm and affection Clara didn't realize the woman still possessed. It was refreshing. Like old times, when Clara was just a little girl and Megan was the closest in age—twelve years older, but still there. Around. Available for cuddles off and on and late-night cartoons. When Megan left, Clara was just six or so. It was a long stretch of time before she'd know her again outside of the weekend persona that sulked in and out of town on obligations alone.

Fortunately, being back in Birch Harbor for good had apparently changed Kate and Megan. Clara noticed this and was starting to cling to it. A bit of spirit returned. The good old days in the flesh.

"The difference is the online experience. That's how we meet these days. The in-person thing is for old people."

Megan pouted briefly then her lips spread into a thin line. She put on a thinking face. "That's not all bad. I mean, I did say it could be all ages. Maybe we'll have some young online people and older offline people. We just have to make sure we cater to everyone."

"If you're going to cater to people like me, you have to find us online. We don't read the bulletin board at the Village. Or the one in the market. We scroll. Scroll, stop, read. Scroll, scroll."

"Okay, right. That's why we're doing this." Megan pointed to the screen then gestured Clara to move her hands to the keyboard. "Work your magic, babe. There may be a second croissant in it for you if you can get me up and running by dinner."

Clara rolled her eyes, but her hands drifted to the computer and she flexed her fingers, hovering as she asked, "What's the business name?"

Megan faltered and bit down on her lip. "Okay, so I'm not sure yet. We nixed *Summer Lovin'*. And we're definitely doing this Labor Day weekend, so it's not going to be Spring Fever, either."

"Not the event. We'll get to that soon. I mean the business name. The entity. Your page can probably run ads or something to specific events or whatever."

"Oh, okay. So, like, the matchmaking business." Megan drummed her fingers against her chin. Clara saw they weren't painted black for the first time in forever. Deep, deep red. Almost black. But not black. A small smile pricked Clara's lips before her sister replied, "Megan's Matchmaking?"

"What happened to Hannigan Sisters Enterprises?" Amelia questioned.

"No."

Megan and Clara said it together. In tandem. They locked eyes. Clara frowned. "I don't like that name. It's too cliquey." She was proud to speak her mind, even if she wasn't being totally honest. She was being mostly honest, though. No matter her relationship, she didn't feel like she was one of the Hannigan Sisters. Especially if they had an enterprise. Call her jealous. Call her bitter, but there it was. She didn't like it.

"Yes, *that*," Megan said, pointing her gaze at Clara momentarily, "*Cliquey*. Ladies, this is my matchmaking company. It's not your lighthouse or your inn or your tutoring service or social media coaching service." She winked at Clara, who could have melted then and there.

For the first time in forever, Clara felt seen. Noticed. Considered. Maybe she wasn't biologically Megan's sister. Or Amelia's or Kate's. But if they were still her sisters, which really they were, she just found her favorite. And it was not Kate. No. No. No. She smiled back, in on the conspiracy now.

"Okay, so you need a matchmaking business name. *Or,*" Kate stretched the *or* out as far as it would go, "an events company name. Don't shy away from the idea of scaling your business."

"Can I just skip that step for now?" Megan asked over Clara's shoulder.

Clara shrugged, disappointed to disappoint her new sister. "Not really. But what we can do is set up a page for

now. You can change it later or add a new group or something. That way you can get the ball rolling. It could be
vague enough to cast a wide net, then you can set up the
event through the page."

"Okay, what about Birch Harbor Events and
Services?" Kate was trying hard.

"I'd go with something a tad more personal," Amelia
suggested.

"I think," Clara confessed, "that using Hannigan
might not be a bad idea. I mean, before she died, Mom—
I mean, *Nora*—really had quite the following around
town. People know the name. I just wouldn't do sisters.
Maybe just..."

"Okay, I've got it," Megan said, her hands spread open
wide across the air. "Hannigan Field. Boom."

Clara hesitated only a split second before typing the
phrase into the Business Name box.

Hannigan Field.

She liked it. She liked it for Megan. She liked it
enough that she just might have to help out. It would do
her some good to get away from the water, maybe. Dry off
in a field of grass at sunset. Like a mini staycation. A fresh
locale. Where she could test out this whole mingle idea.

"Love it," Amelia said.

"Same," Kate declared.

Megan added, "Clara, you inspired me. And now
you're making it happen for me, look at you, Clar." She
pointed to the screen and squeezed Clara's shoulder.

"Okay," Clara said at last. "What's the description of
the services you offer? Maybe a cute tagline or a hook?"

Flashes of Mercy's dad blazed through Clara's head.
And blips, small ones, of every time she saw a cute tourist

and immediately sized him up as unavailable only to keep her eye on him during a long weekend on the lake. That's how things went in Birch Harbor. You saw the same people over and again. And yet, where were all these matches? Where was the opportunity for romance in Birch Harbor? Maybe Megan was onto something after all. Clara wondered aloud, "What if your angle has to do with, like, location, you know?"

"Yeah." Megan's eyes widened and she nodded slowly. "I like that. Something like... *find love anywhere.*"

"Or," Clara offered carefully, typing the words as she said them, "Birch Harbor: come for the lake, stay for the love."

13

KATE

With three social media accounts established by supper and the men en route to join them, Kate felt frantic. They'd spent the whole day online which had her eyes burning. Bringing Clara in to help really woke Kate up to what she'd been lacking in her own "digital presences" and even online marketing.

More than ever, she realized that both Megan and the Heirloom Inn now needed someone who could work their websites. Someone a little more professional than Clara.

"Brian," Megan said on a sigh, when Kate asked about taking everything a step further. "He's a whiz. He could bang out a website in an hour if he had to."

"Is he joining us for dinner?" Kate asked.

Sarah answered from her station in a kitchen chair, curled up with her phone, ever the teenager. "Yep. He just texted me and asked if the other guys were coming."

Amelia chimed in. "Michael is."

"I'm not sure about Matt," Kate replied. "I invited him," she flicked a quick glance at Clara, who seemed to twitch. Maybe it was Kate's imagination. "But he's with Vivi."

"Yes!" Sarah cheered from her seat. "Please! Have him bring Vivi!"

Kate's stomach churned. "I don't know," she replied to her niece. "Could be a little complicated." Kate could feel heat from her youngest sister. Her... *daughter*.

"Actually," Clara began, "maybe that would be nice."

All eyes turned to the petite blonde who sat at the island, quiet and still. The master of the monitors. The queen of their marketing push.

"Huh?" The word fell out of Amelia heavily.

Clara shrugged. "We don't have to say anything. If Matt hasn't told her, then we don't have to say anything at all."

Sarah interjected. "So, let me get this straight. We're still keeping the secret? The Kate-Clara one?"

Kate let out a long sigh. The whole matter was a sore spot, still. Uncomfortable. Like an elephant in every room, and she was well aware that even though she was excited to reunite Matt and Clara, the latter wanted no part. Should they tear down those walls now? Or add another truss?

"It's up to Clara, I say," she pronounced as she crossed her arms over her chest and directed a gentle gaze on the young woman she'd longed to cuddle. To wrap up in a hug and inhale her scent and wonder what could be left of their beginning. Had the faulty adoption ruined everything? Surely not.

Clara cleared her throat. "What's the point of keeping

the secret? That's what I want to know. Maybe the world has a right to know."

"Do you *want* the world to know?" Megan asked. She had a point. If they knew one thing about Clara, it was her repulsion toward attention.

Swallowing audibly, Clara frowned. "I don't *want* them to know. I just... it seems like you are all just moving on, and I'm still sort of—" she pressed her palm to her head, wincing then finding her words and recovering. "I feel as if I'm stuck in the same place I always was. This limbo of relationships. Even growing up, when I *thought* Nora was my mother, well... I wasn't your sister." She glanced along the room, pausing at each face and holding Kate's gaze finally.

Kate crossed the floor and twisted Clara away from the computers, holding her shoulders. "You were always our sister. You were always Nora's daughter, too. Nothing will change that. And I bet Nora wouldn't want us to change that, honestly." Kate looked at the others. "Isn't that right?"

"Actually," Amelia answered, "despite the dramatic diary entry, I'm positive Mom would never want it to get out. It's a small town. What would that have done to her reputation? I mean, didn't she want to hide it forever? Wasn't that the whole point to begin with? The reason we spent a summer in Arizona? The reason Kate stayed at the cottage when she came back?"

A wisp of Clara's blonde hair loosed from her temple, and Kate caught it in her fingers, tucking it behind her ear then catching the girl's stare. "Sorry," she whispered. "I've just..." She lifted her gaze to the others, then squeezed Clara's shoulders. "I've waited to be your mom forever. But I guess I can do that without announcing it to the world, right?"

"So, we're keeping the secret?" Sarah prodded.

"It's what Mom would want," Amelia added.

Megan agreed.

But Kate bore her eyes into Clara's. "Clara Katherine Hannigan, what do *you* want?"

Clara bit down on her lower lip, her brows furrowing together as she crunched the thought in her brain. Kate realized it was a big question. Burdensome and riddled with implications. She opened her mouth to take it back and start over somehow, but Clara opened her mouth to answer.

"I don't want the eyes of Birch Harbor on me. Not now. Maybe never, but not now. I'm ready to come out of my shell a little bit. I see that," she glanced around them. "I do. But Mom took a lot of pains to build a life for herself here, one in which everything was perfect. Her house was perfect until she moved to the cottage which was perfect until she had no more energy or mental capacity. She wasn't a perfect mother, though. She just wanted everyone to see it in her. It doesn't matter anymore that she'd erected a façade. But we can definitely honor her memory by keeping it in place. As much as possible, and who cares about the truth? Even if it did get out," Clara twisted her head directly to Sarah. "Who will care? It's old news, right?"

Kate blinked. "So, then... lips sealed?" she mimed zipping her mouth closed and twisting a key at the center.

Clara shrugged. "For now, yes. We have enough on our plates. The Inn. The lighthouse. Megan's venture.

Even Amelia's search. I think if we can swoop down under the radar, that's a better idea than to draw in a crowd for the wrong reason."

Nodding, Kate pulled Clara into a hug. "Then that's the plan," she answered, her voice low. Then, louder. "We keep it secret. For now. Clara is the miles-younger sister. Sarah's *aunt* when school starts," she lifted an eye at Sarah then at Megan, who both nodded. Finally, she added, "And we get back to discussing how we will draw a crowd for the right reasons."

The others agreed in various tones, but Sarah piped up once more. "Can I be friends with Vivi?"

A disquiet pooled in Kate's stomach. There was no reason to keep the girls apart. It might help Sarah acclimate, after all. But Clara might be tossed right in the middle. She said as much to the group.

Clara, though, replied reasonably. "Actually, I think if we're upholding the status quo, then yes. Bring Vivi. She seems fun, anyway. She might even distract us from the whole drama, right?" Kate watched Clara and her niece share a warm look, and it was settled.

Matt and Vivi would join them for dinner. They'd ask Brian for tech support. Michael could keep playing lawyer and detective with Amelia. Everyone was going to be perfect. They could breathe easy and get back to living. Thriving. Building their new small-town businesses in the place they called home.

The only thing that could get in their way was their own internal family drama. But with that neatly stored in a symbolic hope chest, they were safe. Safe to move on.

14

MEGAN

By the time the weekend rolled around, Hannigan Field and its upcoming, as-of-yet unnamed, event was well underway. With Brian's expertise and Clara and Sarah's social media smarts, Megan had garnered over one hundred "followers" and even had a newspaper ad set for Saturday morning. What's more, she managed to submit a (somewhat last-minute) proposal to the town for a public event permit. Birch Harbor Town Council was big on permits. They had to be with such a transient summer population. Otherwise, any Tom, Dick, or Harry would set up a cherry-picking venture one month only to be gone the next. It was something admirable about the town, really. That they wanted endurance. Staying power. Megan felt proud to submit her request.

Operation Matchmaking Biz was coming together.

The idea of adjusting to her living situation in Birch Harbor, however, had flown out the window.

First, she'd crammed her life into the little room in

the Inn. Now, she was unpacking the bare essentials in Clara's old one-bedroom bungalow, aptly named for its cozy space. Brian, too, had started moving his clothes and personal effects from the townhome, which added a new cramp: that of sharing an apartment with the man Megan was so certain she'd fallen out of love with.

The added certainty that Megan would *not*, no, no, no, *not* stay in the bungalow long-term made the new move even worse. She felt like a vagrant with no end in sight. No final destination. Just waiting for a real home to appear out of the dust.

Though he had weeks left on his lease agreement near the city, Brian decided that he'd better start spending more time with Megan to help with the mixer. She agreed. Whole-heartedly, in fact.

When he was not around, she suspected Brian was working his rear off to secure his own providence. Though each time she asked about his app idea, he brushed her off. She knew Brian wasn't the sort to sit and wait for things to come to him. He was decisive and determined, and her biggest dread was that he was left to look for a better job in Detroit after all.

Especially since he ended up insisting that Megan take their savings and use it for her business plan.

She kicked back at the idea, initially. First, she argued that he'd already laid claim to it when he decided to pursue his own software development. When he said he could make do without, for the time being, she still protested. It wasn't hers to use. It was for emergencies only. She could make money elsewhere. She could ask her sisters for help. Again, after nothing stuck, she looped back to his original request for the money. He was going to follow his dream, right?

But Brian had said no to it all. He could seek investors, which would be better. And anyway, the Stevenson checking account could float them for a little while. Besides, he eventually came to admit, he had a secondary prospect.

Her worries over the whole thing escalated the evening prior, Friday night, when Brian showed up at the apartment, late, ready to stay over for the first time.

Initially, they fumbled. He came in with two pieces of luggage. One an overnight duffle, probably. The other a bigger suitcase, heavy and awkward. She'd opened the door and tried to help, but he shooed her off. Once Megan asked if he wanted to unpack, he'd just shaken his head, studying the apartment as if seeing it for the first time.

Later, they struggled to get the sofa bed pulled out. They struggled searching for an extra blanket. And pillow.

Then, once they gave up on the whole bed thing and each sat across from each other with a glass of water, the window AC unit working hard against the heavy humidity that only then had begun to fall off outside, Brian revealed that her suspicions were true. That he had an interview lined up with one of Detroit's biggest manufacturing companies for a software engineering position. Exactly the sort of job he'd been trained to do. The one he'd done forever. It wasn't forward movement on the app. It wasn't something closer to the lake. It was the usual. The disappointing history of his professional career.

It is what it is, Brian had growled through a sigh, and Megan, for the first time in their marriage, was unwilling to accept something so amorphous. She fought him on the point. Told him he could have the savings; that he had to take it and had to get to work right away on his *app*!

That's when he reminded her there was a whole different issue. He needed something to drive the tech. A pitchable, fundable idea that would serve a need, *remember, Megan?*

She scoffed, and they went to bed. Her in the bedroom with zero pillows and a quilt. Him in the living room with one pillow and no blanket.

The next morning, however, proved to be a small fresh start.

At the crack of dawn, as Megan was quietly standing in the kitchen, measuring half a cup of coffee grounds, a *thwap* slapped beyond the front door. Brian stirred awake; Megan glanced at him, nervous he'd be tired and cranky.

He wasn't though. He didn't roll back over and huddle under his pillow. He stretched up, yawned, scratched his head, and grinned at her.

"Morning," he grumbled softly.

She smiled back. "Good morning."

The last time they'd seen each other that early in the morning, he'd left the bed before she woke up. Now, the tables had turned. She caught him. His sleepy stubble along the jaw. A small twitch just before he stirred. He was at once boyish and manly when he slept, a funny juxtaposition to Megan. Sweet, even.

"What was that?" he looked toward the door. Megan

finished setting the coffee maker and strode past him, opening it and glancing out suspiciously. Just before she closed it, she looked down to see a thin, rubber-banded newspaper cutting a nostalgic image across their doormat.

Clara hadn't changed her subscription address yet. Funny girl, a twenty-something who read a real live physical newspaper each morning. She wasn't the scrolling young woman she'd spoken of when they were discussing how to matchmake people her age.

Megan bent over and scooped it up, holding it in the air like a trophy for Brian to admire.

Slapping it on her hand, she carried it to the table.

"That's good timing," Brian said as he pulled himself from the sofa bed and started to tuck the single sheet neatly beneath the mattress before folding it with one, smooth lift-and-push back into position.

"You mean my ad?" she asked, setting the paper down and moving to the fridge in search of eggs.

"Well, yeah," he answered, chuckling until it turned into a long yawn.

Megan was afraid to look, actually. Opting for nonchalance, she indicated the eighteen-pack in her hand. "Not sure why I didn't go with a dozen. How will we get through eighteen eggs when you don't even live here?" She laughed lightly, and he reached around her, brushing her shoulder with his arm.

"We can have Sarah over for breakfast. Maybe I can stay more often." He poured coffee and all but danced his way to the table. "We have to check this out." Grabbing the paper, he snapped off the rubber band and shook out the pages, thumbing through all the way to the classifieds. "Wait a minute, did you buy a classified space or a feature?"

She glanced over at him and took in the scene. Her husband at the little round table, a coffee mug in one hand and the paper in the other. Her, fretting over what to make for breakfast. The only thing missing was a messy, burpy little Sarah in her highchair, cooing along as her daddy whistled some rendition of a nursery rhyme that was never quite right.

Shaking the memory, Megan settled on scrambled eggs and toast. "Feature. That's why it was so expensive."

"Ah," he answered. No judgment. No finger-pointing or chiding about budget. A soft, reassuring *ah*.

Maybe things could change.

Brian kept searching, and Megan started the eggs then joined him, inches away from his back, glancing over his shoulder.

"There it is!" she cried just a touch too loud. He didn't flinch.

Instead, he flattened the paper, glanced back at her then leaned over. "Where?"

Growing more comfortable by the moment, she rested one hand on the back of his chair and with the other pointed a deep red fingernail to a small box along the seam.

Brian read aloud, his voice jaunty and charming.

"Come for the lake and stay for the love! Introducing to the public, Birch Harbor's inaugural sweet, small-town singles mixer. Open to a limited number of guests (local and visiting), this first-of-its-kind seasonal dating event takes place on Saturday, September 2. Bring a friend. Reserve your spot now. Learn more at hanniganfieldevents.com."

Megan grinned from ear to ear.

"Wow," Brian said. "That's a great ad."

"Thanks," she answered, not bothering to hide the flush that crept up her neck and settled on her cheeks. She didn't mind if Brian saw her like this, vulnerable and excited. It could be a good thing. It could take them back to the early days, just like the image of him sitting near baby Sarah, sipping coffee and reading the paper.

"I'm proud of you, Megs." Brian pushed away the paper and his mug, and pulled his seat out a little, unexpectedly taking her hand in his. "I think you're going to do great."

"We," she answered.

He frowned. "We?"

"Well, you're moving back here. You're helping me. Our divorce is... on hold?" It came out like a question. She waited for the answer.

"We," he replied. "Yes. *We.*" Then, he stood, hesitating just a minute as she looked up into his eyes, wondering if it was a kiss he had to offer. More?

Instead, Brian dropped her hand, slid his arms around her waist and pulled her into him, holding her there, soft and warm. And it was better. Better than a kiss. Better than more. It was enough.

Together, they were enough. For each other and for their marriage. And that was the moment that Megan *knew* the divorce was *not* on hold, in fact.

It was entirely over.

All that was left was a husband and his wife, and their new start in a little bungalow on Harbor Ave.

Whatever happened with his interview was irrelevant.

Whatever happened with the mixer was irrelevant. Because *together*, they would be just fine.

Better than fine, actually. He would be Brian, the college boy from Detroit City. She would be Megan. Megan Stevenson. The matchmaker who found love at the lake after all.

THAT SATURDAY PROVED to be the best one in Megan's recent history. In a long time, actually.

After breakfast and another dozen re-reads of her ad, she and Brian took off to the field, where they were meeting with Kate, the unofficial party coordinator.

Sarah showed up, too, with Amelia. And even Clara found her way there. They hung around half the day, marking off what would go where and documenting it on blank pages. Once the party blueprints were set, they broke for lunch, all of them, and headed to the Village for a tasting at the Harbor Deli.

After that, the whole group tromped down to The Bottle for a wine tasting, too. It felt like Megan and Brian were wedding planning all over again. It was fun and happy, and she didn't want it to end.

After the tastings, Kate had to get back to the Inn for the afternoon check-ins. Sarah left with her, but that time not to help. She'd planned a little girlfriend date with Vivi and some of the others. With her school registration solidified, she was more determined than ever to expand her social circle, admitting that she needed to add juniors and seniors to her new lakeside life. Freshmen were a good start, but they didn't have much in common.

Still, it was Vivi, the little private school girl from the island, who had the connections. She was some sort of social glue on the lake. A thing Megan only loosely understood. After all, when you had two older sisters, friendships weren't something you had to work on. You already had friends at home. The ones made at school were entirely expendable.

Having an only child, though, Megan could see how important it was to tend to new relationships. And, importantly, old ones too. This was not just a lesson Megan derived from her daughter's needs. It was one that would serve Megan well, too.

It occurred to her that young Clara was in Sarah's shoes once, and Clara didn't have that... She didn't have that urge to slip inside of a tightknit group of girls and stick there like her life depended on it. Megan wondered if it had to do with Clara's disposition or, worse, Nora's influence... or lack thereof.

Megan forced herself to shake the thought as she and Brian said their goodbyes to Kate, Sarah, and Clara.

Just before things wrapped up at The Bottle, Michael had called Amelia, asking to meet.

Unprepared to return to the apartment and be alone with Brian again... or, at least, too nervous, Megan suggested they grab an ice cream cone and get a table on the deck that overlooked the dock.

As if the day couldn't possibly be any more perfect, Amelia agreed and told Michael to meet them at the Ice Cream Shoppe. Megan's sweet Saturday plans continued to fall into place.

But then, as soon as the lawyer arrived, everything fell apart.

15

CLARA

K ate and Sarah strode ahead toward the Inn. Kate was on the verge of being late for her four-o'clock check-ins. Sarah needed to change into a bathing suit, which she conveniently toted around in her bag. All this meant that the rest of the evening could belong to Clara, if only she was willing to set aside the nagging guilt that came with having a busy, busy family. Always someone needing help. Always more to do.

As the other two walked faster to the Inn, Clara lagged behind, contemplating her opportunity to escape for a little break in the action.

Almost subconsciously, once they were through the Village and just above the dock, she hung back even more, walking more slowly, peering down toward the marina.

Her dawdling paid off as she caught sight of little Mercy Hennings, her all-time favorite student.

Just as Clara was about to call out to Mercy and wave

her in to catch up and wish the girl luck in her adventures at high school, her phone buzzed in her hand.

Glancing at the screen, Clara saw it was the school district. Odd. They *never* called. Not during summer, particularly. The last time Clara fielded a phone call from anyone at work was from her own principal a year ago when she had to have her evaluation rescheduled due to an emergency. *An emergency.*

Frowning, Clara waffled between letting it go to voicemail and answering.

The decision was made for her when, on the fourth ring, her name floated up from the marina.

"Miss Hannigan!"

By the time Clara looked back down at her phone, the caller had been pushed to her voicemail, and Clara tucked her device back into her linen shorts pocket.

"Mercy!" she opened her arms and drew the teenager into a warm hug. A quick look past proved that Mercy's father wasn't in sight. Clara forced a smile back on her face and decided to chat with the girl. It'd be a pleasant distraction from family matters and the impending message that was probably recording in her pocket in those very moments. "How's your summer going?" Clara asked.

Mercy beamed back. There was a distinct change about her. Gone was all the shyness and seriousness. The nerves and the thin line across her mouth. She grinned widely, displaying a full rack of braces that, somehow, complemented her pretty, clear face. Mercy was the type of teenager you read about in books or saw in television shows *based* on teenagers. Perfect in looks and just a tad clunky in mannerisms. During the school year, her awkwardness materialized in her anxiety about academics. Now, though, she seemed giddy. Borderline goofy, even.

Of all the junior high students Clara had taught in the past seven years, Mercy was both the most beautiful and the smartest. *And* the sweetest. It was as if all three qualities worked in tandem. And yet, within the walls of the junior high school building, her peers seemed immune to her many qualities, overlooking her for flashier, brighter, less perfect students. The ones who, well, actually ate their lunch in the cafeteria. The ones who went out for sports or choir or who had been part of the fabric of Birch Harbor for so long that they were naturally part of the crew.

Mercy was an implant. A transfer from the city. Wan and pale at the start of the year, it took all of nine months for her to grow the light tan that came with living on the lake, even if some of those months were spent inside, escaping the cold. Local teens lived on the beaches of Lake Huron, curating their social media posts like they were laying out on the white sands of some Mexican shore, all summery and colorful. This demanded, of course, that the kids stay on the water until the very last day of good temps and trek back out there the very first day that such temps returned.

Mercy hadn't been in those troops, though. Those marching lines of adolescents who made their way from school to the Village for a quick pop before heading to inherently designated sections of sand. The jocks had their section. The drama kids had theirs. Goths. Nerds. Loners-who-found-each-other, and so on. Initially, in the prior fall, and then again that spring, Clara knew that

Mercy earned her tan from helping her dad, Jake. Jake, the fresh-water-biologist-turned-marina-manager. She had not belonged to a section. She did not enjoy the comfort of an assigned rectangle of sand to run to when worldly pressures bore down.

Over the school year, it became evident that Jake was Mercy's best friend. Second to him, sadly, might just be Clara. Or one or two of the girls from the math club or creative writing club at the school who had earned Mercy's attention here and there, but still, for the course of the school year, she'd been largely alone (by choice), though not quite adrift. Secure in her dedication to her education, Mercy had even confessed to Clara that she feared high school. She feared the social circumstances. She feared everything she seemed to pooh-pooh in eighth grade and all the grades before.

And then, *bam.*

Come summer, Clara had started spotting her out and about, on the edge of a glowing group of girls—two older, one Mercy's age. All deeply tanned, white-blonde, and long-limbed. Like an army of Barbies, they skipped through the village, down the dock, along the beach together, a bizarrely elegant unit of youth.

Of course, the one Mercy's age was Vivi. Vivi, a stranger and a sister all in one, beautiful package. Clara could not wrap her head around how Mercy, who feared the social pressures of high school, had become entangled with Viviana Fiorillo, the Italian blonde with a deep summer tan and white hair. Vivi looked like no Italian Clara had ever known. Not that she'd known many. She sometimes wondered where that hair came from. Did

Matt Fiorillo just prefer blondes? Is that why he and Kate hit it off all those years ago?

Regardless, Mercy and Vivi's newfound friendship made no sense.

And, in fact, Clara had been meaning to question Mercy about it.

"It's been the best summer of my life," Mercy replied, gushing. "I made some friends, and all of a sudden it's cool to have a dad who works on the marina, and I get to register for classes this week!"

Clara smiled in reply and squeezed Mercy's shoulder. "I'm so happy for you. I've been curious about your new group. That girl, *Vivi*, is it? She's not from our school, right?" Clara baited her.

"Yes, Vivi is from St. Mary's on the Island." Mercy drew her finger off the shore toward the floating bit of land mass that hung like a mirage just east of Heirloom Cove. East of the Inn.

Playing along, Clara widened her eyes as if impressed. "I've heard good things about St. Mary's," she answered.

"She's super nice. And she's totally... connected." Mercy went on, adding in picture-perfect descriptions of afternoons where the girls lay out on the beach, lapping up ice cream and gossiping about nothing.

Clara's brain stuck on Mercy's transformed vocabulary. Her acquired tangle of hip terms, the words rolling off the girl's tongue like she was always a member of some untouchable clique. "And my niece," Clara added. "She's spent a little a time with you four, too?"

Mercy nodded with enthusiasm. "I can't believe you're, like, *related*," she said with nothing less than awe.

Cocking her head, Clara wasn't quite sure about the implication.

Then it hit her, like a cruel joke it hit her.

Sarah was beautiful.

As beautiful as Vivi or Mercy—though without the added effects of growing up lakeside. When taken as a pack, the beauty of the five girls all blurred together. Like roaming movie stars on vacation, except Sarah, even without those added effects, stood out from the pack. Her dark hair and piercing eyes and pale skin weren't, after all, the antithesis of what it meant to be a stunning lakeside teen. Those suburban Michigan features melded into a foil for the other four, turning them into one cohesive group.

Mercy's suggestion stung. Clara tugged at her yellow locks and became suddenly aware that her laissez-faire attitude about her looks might be visible to others. Minimal effort went into Clara's routine, but her sisters had always said she was pretty. Her mom had, too. Mostly, though, Clara had received compliments about her looks from her mother's friends, the country club set. The ones who admired her youth and her Kate-esque looks. As she aged, Clara took it for granted that those natural markers of beauty would need upkeep. Tending. All of this rolled into one big ball of realization and washed over Clara like a tidal wave.

What was worse was that she couldn't hide her shock. She couldn't hide her horror, and it was very likely that she looked, even to a young girl, like she was about to drown in the pain of the slight.

Mercy, more perceptive than rude, immediately recognized her error. Smart, too, she found a graceful way to change the subject, but it was too late. Clara was at the sea floor, pulling her way back to air. Alone.

Clara pressed her hand to her oversized pocket which had buzzed back to life in the nick of time. "Mercy, I'm so sorry. I have to be going."

"Oh," Mercy replied, her face falling. "I'm—well, okay, Miss Hannigan."

"Good luck at the high school next year," Clara added, mustering a smile and retrieving her phone.

And as Mercy wandered back down to the marina and toward her too-charmed life with her too-charmed friends in that too-charmed town, Clara stole one more look into the window of the little shack of an office. A face flashed inside then emerged when Mercy arrived. There, in his perfectly Birch Harbor khakis and white polo and boat shoes was Mercy's dad. And he was too-handsome, too.

At least, Clara thought to herself, the temptation of him would be gone. Mercy would move on to the upper school and far enough away that Clara could forget about her and the fantasy she'd drummed up in her mind. The fantasy that she would date Mercy's too-handsome dad and become a second mother to the most wonderful young lady she'd ever known. Clara knew that she'd have to kiss the dream goodbye.

And she knew that she'd have to find a new favorite student.

Pressing her phone to her ear, Clara picked her way back up to the house on the harbor. She had to press the device tightly against her head in order to make out the message. It was her principal, in fact, calling from the district office.

Clara could scant make out the words, but what she could hear sank like a lead weight to the pit of her stomach. Unease simmered along her insides as she pressed replay on the message.

After a garbled *hello* and a brief introduction specifying who, exactly, was calling (her boss), the last bit of the message knocked the wind out of Clara's chest.

"Give me a call. We need to discuss something."

16

KATE

"Who does that anymore?" Kate demanded, her nostrils flared, eyes wild. She'd flipped into full-on angry-parent mode.

Clara's face was pale, her eyebrows scrunched together high on her forehead. The expression seemed to freeze there, and Kate wasn't about to stand for it. An incompetent principal who didn't know the first thing about communication.

She repeated herself. "Who does the whole *we need to talk* thing? Who?"

The last of the new arrivals were safely upstairs in their rooms. Kate was chopping kiwi slices like a butcher gone mad. Clara had played the voicemail on speaker, her boss's barely audible demand echoing around the kitchen like the fuzzy soundtrack of a courtroom transcript.

Kate took a deep breath. Where her secondary anger was stemming from she didn't know. Was it that her motherly instincts kicked in? Was it a mean-girl side of her? Stress from planning the Inn-Warming and dealing with having all three sisters in town and missing her two boys who were too busy with college to even call or...

"Do you think they're going to fire me?"

"No," Kate spat back. "And if they do, we have Michael now." She shook her shoulders a little, twisted her hand around the knife and set into a fresh kiwi, peeling and slicing in quick form.

"Then what does she need to discuss?" Clara asked, apparently moved to action by the looming drama, because instead of sitting there helpless and hopeless, she took to filling glasses with ice for tea or lemonade.

The guests would be down and expect their early evening appetizers in just minutes. Kate set her knife on the towel by the cutting board. She wiped her forehead with the back of her hand then carried the kiwi skins to the disposal, churning them to bits with the loud motor —the appliance was a relic of the time Nora started modernizing the house. At last, she washed her hands and dried them on her apron and took another deep breath, this one more satisfying. Everything was now set for appetizers.

"Look, the only way you'll know is to call her back. And you better do it fast." Kate pointed to the clock. "It's nearly four-thirty. They may not hang around until five during the summer."

Clara nodded, massaged her neck with one hand and retrieved the phone from the table. "I'm sort of freaked out."

Kate strode to her and placed a firm hand on her shoulder. "It's probably nothing. Really, Clar. But it *is* a crappy way of saying nothing. You know? I mean really, everyone knows by now that you don't text or leave a message with '*We need to talk.*'" She scoffed. "Let's just chalk it up as an advantage for you. You know it's a rude thing to do. You're bigger than that. You can handle whatever silly little summer professional development demand or curriculum question she has." Clara's face remained unflinching. Kate sighed. "Listen, I'm sorry I got you even more worked up. I'm... I'm stressed. Here." She pulled out a chair at the table and pushed Clara down into it before taking her own seat. "Call her. Quickly. Before the guests come down." Kate glanced through the kitchen doorway, assuring they had privacy.

Swallowing audibly, Clara woke her phone and tapped away before bringing it to her ear.

Kate offered a small, encouraging smile, and Clara's face loosened somewhat.

From her close proximity, Kate could hear the principal answer.

"Hi, Clara," came a high, pinched voice. "Thanks for returning my call."

"Hello, yes. I'm happy to help. What was it you needed to discuss?" Clara flicked a worried look up at Kate, who nodded her on.

The woman launched into her reply, and Kate narrowed her gaze on the phone, but shuffling on the stairs tore her attention away. *Crap*. Appetizer hour.

She gestured to Clara to take off toward the parlor and sank immediately back into stress. She could stall the guests, or she could sit with Clara.

Kate mouthed to her little sister, "Want me to come?" Clara frowned deeply, shook her head and batted Kate away.

Taking another deep breath, Kate forced herself to give her attention to the line of guests who were ready for *Sip and Snack on the Deck*, as she called it in her brochure.

"Welcome, welcome!" Kate cheered to the tired-looking group as they funneled in and stood awkwardly around the kitchen island.

"I see some unfamiliar faces, so I bet you're the ones who went to go park the car while your wives checked you in," Kate joked. They chuckled politely.

She spoke to them as if she were addressing a much bigger audience—more than the seven people who stood, hands in pockets, taking in the scenery. That was the trick, though. Practice how you play. Dress for the job you want. All those business adages from her brief stint in real estate became useful once she started gaining more traction with the Heirloom Inn.

That weekend saw a fresh, full house. The second floor was completely booked, and even the room they reserved for themselves or other family was filled. This was a risk Kate took. One she had to, if she was ever going to get anywhere. It was one thing to fantasize about reserving a room for the shadows of hope that came with a big family... maybe one day Ben or Will would surprise her with a visit. They'd bring a girlfriend, maybe. Maybe one day Wendell Acton would sweep back into town, needing a place to dry his boots before he told them about his wild adventure around the world.

. . .

BUT MAYBES DIDN'T PAY the bills. Not the utilities. Not the food. Nothing.

So, without the permission of her sisters, Kate booked the Heirloom Inn clear up until Labor Day weekend. And that was that.

She began the Sip and Snack with a brief tour of the premises and a historical introduction of what was formerly called *the house on the harbor*, both to locals and to the Hannigan family. "The property was settled around the turn of the century," she went on, glancing back and winking. "As in *1900*, for those of you who might be wondering." Another ripple of chuckles.

"The Hannigans were a fierce bunch of settlers who'd made their way from Ellis Island looking for a place to call home. Something like what they knew back in Ireland. There aren't many shaggy green cliffs along the northern U.S., however," Kate added playfully. "Turns out the Great Lakes were good enough. Family lore has it that as that original Hannigan brood trekked north along the water, they stopped in a grove of birch trees that carried on for some miles across the land and up and down the lake. Once they stopped, though, Great Gran refused to go one step more." By this time in the story, Kate was standing with the small crowd at the back of the barn beneath a pretty thicket of birches. "Legend says that she walked down to the shore from here, eased herself onto the sand, pulled her little black boots from her aging feet, and slid them into the cool water."

Kate looked back at the group, clasped her hands in front of her waist. "And the rest is history."

The story was true. Or true as Kate knew it to be. It was the same precious memory she'd first heard from her own Hannigan grandparents back when she was a young child. Before everyone left for greener pastures. It was a little story that worked its way into a tragic half-memory for Kate. For, as her grandparents left and it was just Nora who remained, Kate always dreaded the day that no Hannigan woman would plop down on the beach and declare that she wasn't going anywhere.

Nora stayed on. Not at the house on the harbor, but in town.

Then, disappointing in some ways, to herself, Kate went and got married. To Paul. That's when she decided that if she couldn't stick around town, she'd at least follow in her mother's footsteps of keeping the Hannigan name, just as Nora had. Carry on the line. Defy tradition and stick to it all at once.

Once Kate moved away for good (or what *felt* like good), she began to worry. Worry that she may never come back.

"Was it always a bed-and-breakfast?" one of the guests asked as they picked their way through weedy sand and onto the green grass of the backyard.

Kate smiled, "No. It was only ever a family home."

"So, why commercialize?" the woman's husband asked. Perhaps he was well-meaning. Perhaps he had no clue of the weight of his words. The accusation dripping in his voice. That she was soulless. A sell-out. Something hideous. Someone who didn't value her family history.

Kate stopped at the foot of her porch and looked out to the lake, a gentle breeze billowing her gauzy blouse. At the end of her line of vision was Sarah and her little clique of friends. Vivi was there. They laughed and kicked at the water and Kate felt suddenly dizzy, like she was flying through time back to her own teenage years. Before Matt. Before Clara. Before everything changed.

And she wondered if she'd made a mistake. If there might have been another way to cling to the past. To keep the house and all its memories without calling out to looky-loo tourists like these to come tromp on her personal history and ask rude questions.

Then, she thought of Matt and his skillful way with fixing it up. She thought of her sisters branching out into their own ventures.

She thought of her mother, her mother who *loved* tourists, unlike every other local in Birch Harbor, and at last Kate replied in an even, soft voice. "You're right. This shore always belonged to us. It was always a bit of a fight between the town and the family and the locals who wander across the private beach down there." She pointed to Sarah and the girls and a throng of beach walkers, unwitting trespassers.

"What do you mean?" the man returned, his crotchety voice pressing on her nerves but pushing her closer and closer to some truth she never knew existed.

Kate frowned at him. "It came time to share."

WITH THE GUESTS meandering about the property and down to the beach, drinks and fruit kebabs in their hands, Kate slipped back inside and searched for Clara.

She was sitting quietly on the sofa. Just waiting, like a child in time-out.

"Clar," Kate said, lowering herself on the cushion next to her. "I'm so sorry I had to shoo you out. What happened with the call?" She searched Clara's eyes and saw hurt there, but Kate wasn't sure if it was from the bad timing of things or news of the call. "Clara, I said I'm sorry—"

"No," Clara replied, shaking her head. "It's not you. I know you're busy, it's the call." She let out a sigh. "It wasn't a good call. No professional development. No curriculum questions."

Kate's face twisted and she braced herself. "What was it?" she asked as she bit her lower lip.

Their whole affect had changed. Gone was the ire over the vague message. Gone was the frantic stress of prepping the appetizers.

"A parent complaint. A few parent complaints, actually." Clara's eyes welled up instantly. She looked like she'd been holding in the tears the whole time Kate was waxing poetic about Hannigan family history.

"*What?*" Kate gasped. "What *complaint?*"

Clara shook her head and a tear plunked from each eye, streaming down her cheeks synchronously. She wiped them off and sniffed, composing herself. "They questioned some of the grades I gave out. They accused me of being too hard on the kids. And, I guess they think I play favorites with the smart kids." She sniffled again, adding quietly, "One smart kid, to be exact."

Kate let out the breath she'd been holding. "Okay, so it's not that bad, then. You don't play favorites. I mean, come on. You're a professional, Clar. Is it Mercy? Is that who they mean?"

Kate knew about this Mercy child. Ethereal and brilliant, Clara's dream student. The little sister Clara never had.

The younger of the two now nodded. "But not just her. They said it's clear I have a preference for students who care about school."

At that, Kate belted out a laugh. "Are you kidding me? What teacher doesn't appreciate kids who like school? *Come on!* And don't the district leaders *want* you to hold those kids accountable? Prepare them for high school? Don't the parents want that, too?"

"Well, that's the good news." Clara's eyes dried up, and she seemed more placid. Still not pleased. Whatever the good news was may not actually be good news. Kate sensed this.

"What?" she asked.

"They're not firing me. I'm not in any *real* trouble," Clara replied, lifting her shoulders.

"Well, it would be ridiculous if they did," Kate answered, resting her hand on Clara's knee. "You're a great teacher. Surely this is all a misunderstanding. Or an overreaction."

"I held my ground," Clara replied, her impassive face turning to fire. "I told them I'm not there to be nice. I'm there to teach, and I won't lower my standards. I think small-town kids need that. They need a push. I said all that to her."

Kate leaned back at this sudden burst of confidence from Clara, meek, bookish Clara who trudged to school and home and tucked herself away to recover the energy she spent during her waking hours. "Clar, that's *great*. I'm so proud of you!"

"But I can't work at the middle school anymore," Clara added, her mouth turning to a pout and her face flushing with the admission. "They said I'm not suited for seventh or eighth grade. Not if I'm going to take that stance."

The roller coaster swooped Kate back up again. "Wow. So... you *are* fired?" She scratched her head, searching Clara's expression for clarity. An answer.

"They aren't firing me, no. They're transferring me," Clara replied, shrugging. "I'm going to the high school."

17

MEGAN

The four of them were in sun-bleached Adirondack chairs on a lower deck off of the Village. The warm sand taunted Megan. She'd love to wander off with her ice cream cone at her lips and Brian's hand in hers as they pushed through the beach and to the water, sinking in the surf together as the sun set.

But it wasn't a double date. Or a single date.

It was a doom's date.

"There might be a problem." A hardness etched itself across Michael's face. He looked nothing like Amelia's boyfriend and everything like a lawyer. An upset lawyer with bad news.

The double scoop of vanilla in Megan's hand started to drip down into the ridges of the waffle cone.

Still under the misbelief that his bad news didn't pertain to her, she licked away the sweet melted cream and flicked a glance to Amelia, who frowned in return.

"What is it?" Megan asked.

Amelia added, "Is it about Dad?"

Stunned at the word, Megan swallowed. She was sick of this poorly conceived search for a man who abandoned his daughters and his wife. She was sick of Amelia's obsession with it and her unwillingness to see how painful it was to dredge up those old memories.

For Megan, the word *Dad*, the name *Wendell* was synonymous with some of the darkest days of her life. The days she turned from sweet baby of the family to left-behind middle child. The days Nora's already scarce cuddles and attention evaporated, leaving Megan high and dry. And yet all those cuddles and all that attention would quickly turn up anew in a different locale—baby Clara's bassinet.

And there was no Daddy to fill the void of the already scarce cuddles and attention. No more walks on the beach, digging for twisty little shells and colorful beach rocks. No more off-the-cuff lessons about the differences between freshwater life and sea life or what it was like to grow up in a lighthouse or how much he *loved* Megan and her sisters.

A sob crawled up Megan's throat and she set her jaw, ignoring Amelia's question as best as she could.

Her appetite for dessert left her, and her hand lowered to her lap, the ice cream cone towering precariously as the sun crept downwards, dragging with it the heat of the late afternoon. The muggy air picked away at her treat, mottling the chunky mounds and forcing Megan to pad her fist with napkins, which Brian kept pushing her way, one by one like an ER nurse shoving gauze at the operating surgeon. Moments ticked by in slow measure as Michael answered.

In fact, the lawyer's bad news had nothing to do with Wendell. No, sirree. Nothing *at all.*

"The town council called an emergency meeting last night. I guess your proposal landed squarely on the mayor's desk, and the mayor was... well, he was none too pleased."

"What are you talking about? None too pleased with a new business?" It was Brian who responded, defensive and instantly irate.

Michael held up a hand. "They post videos from each session on their webpage. I watched the whole thing. You can, too. So—"

"Wait, why?" Amelia cut him off. "Why did you watch?"

He cleared his throat. "The secretary sent me an email stating my client's proposal would go into review for immediate consideration. She said it was a closed meeting, but that they'd upload minutes and the video this morning."

"Client?" Megan asked. "Are you talking about *me*?"

Megan was not Michael's official client. He just helped look over the proposal. Proofread it, really. She wasn't paying him.

Amelia flushed. "I asked Michael to help us on a more official level. Pro bono," she added quickly.

Blanching, Megan felt her ice cream cone grow soggy. She stared at it, unbelieving, until Brian's hand crossed her lap, took the thing, then left to toss it.

"So, what did they say?" she asked, her voice trembling on the verge... the verge of what she didn't know. Crushing disappointment? Anger? Sadness? The distinct realization that Brian's hug from that morning and the picture-perfect day was a wash. She'd have to start over?

Again, Michael cleared his throat then scooted to the edge of his Adirondack chair before steepling his hands. "They rejected your request for a permit. You can't host a mixer."

18

MEGAN

"I can do whatever I want," Megan protested, immediately feeling all of fifteen years old. She shook her head and flushed at her own petulance. "Sorry, it's just, I don't understand. They won't give me a permit? Can I still have a mixer?"

Michael shrugged. "As a small party, if you want. But not long term or on a regular basis. You can't serve beverages to a big group of people who are paying you. Not without that permit."

"Why did they deny it?" Megan asked. Brian had scooted forward to the edge of his chair and taken her hand. It was that single gesture that kept her from lunging out of her seat and pacing the Village like a lunatic. It kept her calm. Rational. He always did.

Michael replied, "The town didn't understand your business plan. They thought it could be more lascivious than what you're intending to do."

Megan's face turned to fire, the bit of reason fighting against illogic. "*What*? Las*civious*? As in... indecent?" Her eyes wild, she looked at Brian and Amelia who shared in her shock.

"They took it to be a swingers' event."

"What's a swingers' event?" Brian asked, lamely.

Megan took a deep, deep breath and counted to three. "A swingers' event *is* lascivious," she answered. "It's where lots of people just want to hook up. It's not even close to what we're doing. They had to be looking for a reason to deny the permit," she huffed.

Michael nodded. "I agree. You made it patently clear that you and your sisters would host a matchmaking gala where single people would show up to be paired off *individually* with other people. It's a huge stretch, what they said. A huge stretch."

Amelia ate the last nub of her ice cream cone, less affected by the news, but only just. The chestnut-haired sister was known to never lose her appetite. She was that sort of person—the sort who ate all the time and rarely gained an ounce. And when she did gain an ounce, she'd lose it by snapping her fingers. She clapped invisible crumbs from her hands and grabbed Megan's knee. "It's a plot," she said darkly.

"A plot?" Megan answered, bewildered.

"A political plot."

Brian scoffed, and Michael let out a long sigh, jumping in and taking on his girlfriend's wild theory. "I wouldn't go so far as to say political plot, but I agree that it makes no sense. They are looking for a reason. You're right, Megan."

"But why? Doesn't the town want to see new businesses come to the shore?" Amelia asked.

Michael shrugged. "Yes and no. Birch Harbor is notorious for denying small business permits. Kate had trouble, too, though not as much. It's hard to deny a bed-and-breakfast when she had little competition."

"There's no dating service in town," Megan pointed out. "I have no competition."

"You're right," Michael agreed again.

How could someone so... *agreeable* be so *useless*? She frowned at him before adding, "I wonder how Amelia will do when she proposes a *museum*?" Michael shrugged helplessly, and Megan felt bad for thinking so poorly of him. "I'm sorry," she managed without looking up from her hands. "I'm being rude. I just... I just don't *understand*."

Brian cut in, even-keeled. "Okay, so if there's no competition and if Megan's idea isn't some tacky hook-up service, then what reason could these people be looking for?" His face took on a pained expression. Pain for Megan, she thought. She offered him a small, grateful smile.

Michael cleared his throat for the millionth time, and Megan wanted to shove a cough drop his way she was so angry. But she counted to three again and waited for his answer, her face open, ready. He went on. "Honestly?" he asked.

Megan nodded.

"They didn't just mention the lascivious thing in the video. It wasn't even the mayor's main issue. It wasn't why he called the meeting."

"What do you mean it wasn't the mayor's main issue?" Brian asked.

"I mean," Michael went on, "the mayor called an emergency meeting to oversee the proposal, which perhaps could have to do with Megan's added request for expediency. Of course, he did appear agitated in the video, yes. But he isn't the one who came up with the question about what the business was, how it would function, or if it was appropriate. They didn't come to that conclusion, or rather, *assumption*, for a very long time. At least half an hour, if you can believe that."

"So, how did it all start?" Megan asked.

"It was a little hard to hear," he replied, shifting his gaze to Amelia. Megan had never seen the lawyer nervous. But that's exactly the expression that crossed his face. Nervousness.

"We can handle it," Megan urged him, her voice softening as guilt racked her for acting so ruthless. So angry. "Go on, Michael."

"Well, they reviewed town hearsay," he answered, leaning back on his chair, bracing his hands against his knees.

Brian asked, "What do you mean *town hearsay*? Do you mean they gossiped?" His tone took on a thick, incredulous effect. As though he was learning for the first time that all the stereotypes were true. Small towns really did have the type of drama you'd see on soap operas.

"Not exactly. The mayor was careful. He asked that they consent to discuss the proposing member's local reputation and that of her family. Her propensity for success among her peers."

Megan's jaw fell open. What reputation could she possibly have? She'd only been back for less than a month! She looked from Michael to Brian then back to her sister. "This is a joke. Right?"

Michael shook his head gravely. "No, I'm sorry, Megan."

"What reputation?" Amelia asked, speaking Megan's mind.

"Honestly? I think it has more to do with Nora's than with Megan's."

Megan leaned back in her chair, accepting his answer and running it through her memory.

After Wendell left, Nora shut down her social life. For a while, at least. Once Amelia was out of the house, things began to shift. By the time Megan left home, she'd experienced what she considered to be three distinct phases of her upbringing. Before. In the wake of. And just after.

Just after... maybe three or four years after Wendell left, and before Clara had started school, Nora started volunteering for local events. She lived at the country club. She went out for wine with her girlfriends. Those occasions were burned into Megan because she was Clara's designated babysitter, of course. And when Nora would return home, Megan always expected to find something out about her mother that she didn't want to know. She expected to peek down from her window to catch her mother kissing a stranger as he bid her good-night. She expected to witness her mother stumble off the sidewalk, cracking her high heel and her ankle in one tragically tipsy fall.

None of it happened though. It was like Megan was waiting for something bad, and there was nothing bad.

Until now. "Why didn't they like Nora?" she asked Michael, her sweaty palms open to the sky. Heat pooled on top of her head, bearing down on her and burning off brain cells, willing her away from reason or critical thinking. Willing her far away from her own estimations of her mother.

Michael returned her look, offering something between *Come on, Megan* and *I'm sorry, Megan*. He raised his hands, too. "Because she was *Nora*."

"What are you even talking about?" Amelia cut in, her voice slick with ire. "Mom was the Queen of Birch Harbor. I swear she even has a pageant sash with those exact words. She won it at some country club party."

"I loved your mom," Michael agreed, pressing his hand to his chest. His face was earnest now, but something dark stood beyond the sympathy in his eyes. Megan saw it. She saw he knew. He knew that Nora never recovered from her shame, her personal shame, the transferred shame of having a granddaughter much too young, and the ultimate shame of scaring off a good man.

Maybe there was more to it. Maybe she wasn't just ashamed of Wendell's abandonment. Maybe she genuinely didn't think he just up and left. Maybe she worried. Maybe she was scared. Of the truth. Of what could be. Maybe the woman was heartbroken. How could any of that relate to how the town council thought of her? And thought of her daughters?

What bearing did Nora's heartbreak have on her reputation? Didn't other people in town have sympathy? Deep sympathy for the woman? She wasn't some rowdy teenager, drifting from spring fling to summer romance at the snap of her fingers. That would be an easy heartbreak. The sort that others rolled their eyes at.

But to be heartbroken with four mouths to feed? The littlest a baby? Not even her own? With no family to help?

To be the last one from her own lineage stuck in a lake town, beating down the walls her ancestors constructed in some desperate effort to keep others out?

Nora couldn't take on that heartbreak. She had to push it off and survive.

Pushing it off, surviving, moving on... that's what most people managed to do. They'd come out of that part of their life battle-scarred and streetwise but hopeful, longing for some sweet fresh start. A new man. A happier time.

Maybe those were the smart ones. Or not.

But it wasn't Nora. Oh no. Nora clung to survival. She curated it, modeling every aspect of life after the need to belong and be good enough... or better. Not so better to build resentment, but just better enough that she drew the eye of the community. She wanted to be just better enough that people longed for her as she had longed for Wendell.

Nora never did move on. She was in survival mode for most of her life. And that was never a good place over a long term. No, it wasn't. Not for Nora Hannigan. Not for anyone.

Unfortunately for the mayor of Birch Harbor and his town council cronies, though, Megan Hannigan Stevenson was *not* in survival mode. She was in thrive mode. And whatever bone he had to pick with her or her family, he'd have to do it in person.

He wasn't getting the chance to weasel out underneath some *lascivious* claim. No way. He'd have to face Nora's daughters head on. Eye to eye.

"I want names, and I want an address," Megan said at

last, pulling out her phone on which to log the information.

"Pardon?" Michael asked, turning his head as if he didn't quite hear her.

"I want to know where town council meetings are held. I'm going to do my own emergency meeting. But first, I want to know who they are. You two have your own research project going on. Now I will. I want to learn everything about them. What they do for fun. Where they spend their time. What businesses they *have* sponsored. I'm going to win them over. *We* are." She flicked a glance at Brian, her mouth in a tight, thin line, the fight for her business sharing space in her heart with the fight for her marriage. "Right, Brian?"

He nodded, his eyes turning to lasers as he shifted his gaze to Michael. "Honestly, I think we should start with how the town council knew Nora."

Michael pulled out his phone, too, more prepared than Megan previously realized. "Fair enough," he answered. "They're public figures. You have a right to their names." He began reading through the list, beginning with the mayor and shuffling through vaguely familiar surnames until he stopped at the last one. A woman. Her first name meant nothing to Megan.

Judith.

But her last name meant *everything*.

A melia and Megan exchanged a look of shock. Surely this was the premise for some episode of *Knott's Landing* or even *Scooby Doo,* for goodness' sake.

"Is there any relation to—" Amelia began.

Michael held up a hand. "Honestly, I'm not sure. But we shouldn't speculate, anyway."

"Let's all just take a deep breath here," Amelia answered, as Megan sat, her mouth still agape. "All we have to do is contest the rejection. Once we confront them—the town council people—with a perfectly clear explanation of Megan's intentions, then they will have to overturn the decision. They will have to allow her to conduct business in Birch Harbor. No matter who they are or how we're connected."

Brian shifted in his seat. "I don't get it. Which one do you know?"

Megan finally let her mouth draw closed before she

opened it again to answer, acid in her words. "We *do not* know her."

"We kind of know her," Amelia added, a teasing half-smile creeping up her face.

Burning a glare at Amelia, Megan cut her hand through the air. "We do *not know* this woman."

"Well, we met her, though." Honestly, Amelia wasn't *trying* to be difficult. But, if they were going to accuse *Judith* of blackballing them, then Michael and Brian had to have all the information available. After all, it was becoming clearer and clearer that the menfolk were a little better able to see the situation objectively and without the screen of twisty small-town rumors.

"Who is she?" Brian asked again, clearly losing his patience.

"Judith," Amelia began, but she was cut off by Megan this time.

"Why didn't she fight Kate and the Inn? If these people are ready to double down on some opportunity to flash a grudge around for all to see, then why not start with the Heirloom Inn?"

"I don't think they have a grudge," Michael reasoned, his voice even. "We don't even know if there's a *connection*," he pled.

"If there was a connection, if this Judith person is who we think she is, then you're right, Megan," Amelia said. "She would have blocked Kate, too."

"Well," Michael interjected, passing his hand across his mouth. "Like I said, they *did* put some heat on Kate."

"So, you're saying the council *tried* to block her, too?" Amelia pressed.

"Tried, yes. But at the time Kate filed for her permit, things were a tad different."

"Different how?" Megan asked Michael. "That was less than two months ago."

He let out a long sigh and clasped his hands over one knee. "It's nothing you don't know. The history of the house on the harbor, I mean. It's been, well, *fraught*."

"Fraught with what?" Amelia asked, the heat of the sun dwindling now, as it sank closer to the edge of the lake.

"The town has always wanted that property to turn commercial. They wanted tax revenue. Ever since the original Hannigans settled it, you know. Well, maybe not *that* far back. But the powers that be here, the other settler families I mean, always wanted the Hannigans to sell out. At one point, according to my research, there was an offer of a purchase. Some big wigs inland, long before the marina had been established, offered to buy the house and turn it into the town hall. They had grand plans, it seems, to run a dock out of the back yard and convert that old barn into a boat house. They were going to expand south from the house on the harbor. They wanted it to be the center of life in Birch Harbor. They wanted it to be what the Village ended up becoming, complete with a marina and lots of boat traffic. It's where the town got its name. That hope for a harbor nestled inside of the birches." Michael smiled sadly.

"And our ancestors said no," Amelia guessed.

"Obviously," Megan added, but her voice was free of sarcasm or spite. She sounded just as sad as the whole story was.

"Is it so wrong that our family wanted to keep what was ours?" Amelia asked earnestly.

Michael began to shake his head, and then Brian chimed in. "Maybe that's what Michael is saying, though. When Kate announced to the town that she was opening the house to the public, it came as a relief. Maybe the descendants of the settlers that fought your ancestors... maybe they are somewhere amid the town council, and they put it down as a win in their book?"

Michael nodded solemnly. "That's exactly what happened. In fact, Mayor Van Holt had the final say. He had the final vote on Kate's Inn."

"Van Holt," Amelia whispered. "They were the ones. The other settlers. Remember Megan? Those stories Mom and Dad told us? And Grandma and Grandpa?"

Megan nodded silently. She appeared to remember. And Amelia could tell she was devastated.

Amelia could see in Megan's eyes that she thought she lost to Kate. She lost to a legacy hard won. And in the wake of it, her matchmaking business was irrelevant. A pain in someone's butt. Not a compromise or some dramatic betrayal to her own bloodline. Something far less tangled in the web of town history. Something much sillier with someone who had a much sillier bone to pick.

And that someone won.

"Wait a minute." Amelia held up her hand and glanced at Michael. "If this woman is who we think she is, then how can she be on the town council?"

The other three looked blankly back at her.

Amelia went on, darkly. "She doesn't even *live* here."

"Maybe there's not a connection after all," Megan whispered, but something inside Amelia told her not to believe that. Something told her that the Hannigan women's fate was written in the stars that hung above the harbor.

"You know what?" Amelia asked, pushing up from her chair and propping her hands on her hips.

The others' eyes followed her up, expectant.

She set her jaw on Megan. "We're going to talk to them. We'll confront them. After all, if Birch Harbor is hanging by a thread that's connected to this person, who, by the way doesn't even live here full-time, then maybe we turn the tables. We're contesting it. And we're going to win."

20

MEGAN

Naturally, they'd have to wait until Monday to schedule a meeting with the mayor.

This had given Megan and Brian the rest of the weekend to, well, just *be together*. It was a weird concept for them, and they tested the limits of their comfort in their reunion.

Sunday morning was fine. Breakfast at Heirloom Inn. Kate wanted to take advantage of everyone being around so she could perform a test run for her Inn-Warming menu. Eggs benedict, French toast, bacon, and fresh fruit. Traditional but exquisite. After that, Clara disappeared, claiming she needed to work on her classroom.

Sarah asked to go to the beach, as if she didn't go every single day. After ensuring she had sunscreen and a hat, Megan shooed her off, pleased that Birch Harbor had turned into such an easy home for the girl, despite her temporary stay at Amelia's.

Temporary.

Everything felt temporary. Their apartment. The

dream of opening a business. Even Brian's ambiguous promises that he would *find something* or *get something going soon!*

That was the point at which Megan leaned into Brian and whispered her first admission of regret.

"Maybe we've made a mistake." She leaned back and batted sad eyes up at him.

Brian, who'd been laughing—Megan couldn't remember the last time she'd seen Brian laughing so much. Full on laughing that curled his body in and reminded her of their early days at college. At parties and football games and during sweet evening walks on the campus when neither one had a care in the world, when a perfect future was the only possible thing that could lay ahead.

All things considered, their future had turned out pretty perfect. They had their health. They had a beautiful child.

So, how could either one have the right to be disappointed in *anything*? Irritated with *anything*? How could either one have wound up in that death-warmed-over state their marriage had slid into?

He stopped laughing and tore his attention away from Amelia, who'd been regaling them over some past rehearsal foible. Bending to Megan, he slipped his arm around her waist, and the heat of it made Megan want to drag him into the parlor and pull herself into his body and sob like a wretched wife.

"Can we talk somewhere?"

He didn't hesitate or frown, he didn't accuse her of being melodramatic or a downer or any of the things that she probably was. His face turned soft, and he tugged her away and out onto the back porch. It was better than the parlor in terms of scenery. In every aspect, probably.

Megan headed straight for the outdoor love seat with big, forgiving red cushions, and he followed, his hand in hers like they were teenagers escaping a party to have a private moment.

Except for the teenagers part, that's just what they were, really.

"I'm sorry," she stopped at the sofa. "I can go bring you a coffee or something?"

"No, no. Let's talk. Talk first, coffee second." He sat, never letting go of her hand and pulling her down next to him.

Megan laughed lightly. "Whatever happened to coffee first, talk second?"

Brian's eyes searched hers as he ignored her joke and landed squarely on whatever he saw deeper inside of her, the doubt and the worry, obviously. "You don't want to live here?"

When he put it like that, contextualized it for her, it rang false. She shook her head and looked away out to the lake. Shrieks from a group of kids splashing in the surf caught her attention.

Unsure how to test the waters of her fear, she changed the conversation, jutting her chin across the yard. "If she were still around, Nora would be charging out there and screaming at them."

"At the kids?" Brian asked.

Megan glanced back. He'd followed her gaze then returned his eyes to hers, still searching. Always searching lately. That whole weekend it seemed like every time she locked eyes with her husband, he was looking for something in her.

"Yes," Megan answered. "That whole area of beach is technically private."

"I thought no beach was private. Aren't they all just *naturally* public? I mean, that's like saying someone owns the water, too."

Shaking her head, she replied, "No, there are such things as private beaches. Hard to enforce. Hard to nail down. Nora was always fighting. It's like she was afraid of it. The beach, I mean, and what might happen. It wasn't territorial or anything. It was this obsessive, ongoing fear." She hesitated, a memory flicking to life like a tired Zippo lighter. "Yeah. I think she was afraid."

"What do you mean?"

Megan let out a sigh before entering the world of her past. "Before Dad left, they loved throwing parties together. Every single holiday they had some kind of party and if the weather was good enough, you can bet it was a beach party."

Images swirled in Megan's brain. Even at New Years, when the air was frigid and the ground frost-bitten, there would be adults swaying out into the backyard, pots and pans clanging in their hands above Megan and Amelia, who would squeal in the fun of it. The late night. The big people. Living in the heart of that was thrilling.

Her face fell. "One Fourth of July, after the party, Dad left."

"Wait, was this—" Brian started to ask.

Megan cut him off at the pass. "No. A different summer. Years before. I was almost too young to remember. But I do." She scrunched her face, dragging the memories with all her might. "Everyone was gone. Except us. Mom—*Nora*," Megan corrected herself, "was frantic. She was like, wigging out. '*Where's Wendell? Where's your father? Did you see him? Did he leave?*' She was begging us for information as if we knew. But we didn't."

Brian's grip on her hand tightened.

She went on, pointing to the water. "At one point, she ran out to the beach. I can remember that part very clearly." Megan's face softened like she was watching it now. Nora holding her gauzy shawl around her body, running awkwardly as mothers seem to, her feet kicking up sand with every divot until she was knee deep in the water screaming for him.

"Then," Megan returned her gaze to Brian, "he just, *reappeared*. At the back door."

Where have you been! Nora had screamed.

"Where was he?" Brian asked now, watching her intently. Suspiciously, even.

I thought you drowned! Nora had screamed, but that time, her scream was lighter. Happier. Tipsy and silly and they hugged and kissed in full view of the girls, none of whom thought they would ever recover from such a scare until they saw that kiss and knew it was safe to laugh too. To keep playing.

I thought you left us! Nora had cried out again, once the kissing was done, and the five of them shuffled back up the porch and inside, to bed.

I would never, Wendell had reassured all of his girls, patting each on the head and scooting them upstairs.

That night, Megan had slept well. She'd slept safely, knowing her parents were there. That they loved each other. That even though life could be hard in the house on the harbor where they were constantly fixing things and working on things and getting yelled at for playing too close to the water... she was safe. They were all safe.

Even if they were scared. The thing was, Megan had never put together what there was to fear. Was it losing Wendell? Was it the lake? Was it the threat of someone coming and taking something from them? The house on the harbor? The beach? She'd been stumped all through the years.

Megan glanced at their hands then back up. "He was going to the bathroom."

A small chuckle spilled out from Megan, and Brian laughed, too. "The *bathroom*? Didn't any of you check there?"

She shrugged. "Nora just jumped to the conclusion that something *awful* had happened. Like she was just waiting for something awful to happen. She lived like that. In fear, I think. Survival mode."

Brian's face hardened. "Well, *we* don't have to."

"What do you mean?" Megan answered, doing her best to shake the memory. The memory that should have turned into one of those funny stories that Amelia pulled out of her back pocket like a party trick. But when bad things actually *did* happen in your family, all those funny stories stayed stored.

"I mean we don't have to live in fear. We can stay here; we can take the risks we've decided to take. We can make this work."

Megan frowned. "*You* want to stay in Birch Harbor? You like it here?" It occurred to her just then that where Brian might want to live hadn't even been on her mind. Up to that point, she'd simply assumed he'd keep his townhome as long as he could no matter what happened. He'd break his promise and things would fall apart again because maybe he didn't want to be with her. Up to that point, Megan figured he was *outside* of their family, still.

But he wasn't. He was there, *inside* with her. They were still a unit. They were still one.

"I want to stay where *you* are," he answered softly. "And yes, I like Birch Harbor. I've always gotten along with your family, and now that Amelia has a decent boyfriend and Kate is, well, *happy*... it feels easy. It feels right."

"What about the applications? Your job interviews?" she asked.

Brian didn't glance away. He didn't push a hand through his hair and mutter. He held her gaze. "I work in tech, remember? I'll get something that allows me to work from home. Just like the last one. I'm not worried, Megan. I'm not scared. I'm... I'm excited." A floppy grin splayed across his mouth.

It was everything she needed to hear. That he wanted to be with her. At the lake. And that he *wasn't worried*. He was not scared.

Even though Megan still was. She was still worried that the council would block her dream and that she'd never do the thing she'd always wanted to do... But all of that mattered less when she had the security of a strong marriage. Or, at least, a marriage that was growing stronger by the day.

"Thanks," she whispered, smiling at him and leaning into his chest as he wrapped his arms around her, a warm, tight hug that she could live in.

"Megan?" Brian asked.

She swallowed. His tone shifted.

Leaning back as he released her from his hold, she simply blinked in response, waiting.

Then, she saw it. In his face and his mouth. His now trembling lips and his tensing jaw. The same pattern of quirks that coalesced on his face when they were in the middle of a heated argument that neither one wanted to have.

"Brian," she answered, her voice hardening with each syllable.

He returned his hands to her shoulders, looked so far into her eyes that she no longer saw the trembling lips or the twitching jaw. All she could see was the last twenty years. The house in the suburbs. The arguments. The makeup nights. The mean looks and soft apologies. She saw Sarah. She saw herself.

He closed his eyes briefly, and it all went away, and when he opened them again, she saw the present. And at the exact same time with the exact same rhythm, Brian and Megan said to each other something they hadn't said in a very long time. Not with any truth. Not with any meaning.

The best three words in the English language. The words that Megan clung to in her hopes and dreams. The words that drove her interest in becoming a real match-maker, a person who brings two people together.

I love you.

And maybe more than ever... they *meant* it.

21

KATE

Michael had secured an appointment with Van Holt's office for Monday afternoon.

Once Kate was in the loop on how the Birch Harbor Town Council had denied Megan's request for a permit, she morphed into a full-blown Mama Bear.

"I'm going with you," she told Megan, crossing her arms as she stood in the doorway of her room upstairs in the Inn.

Megan had come for breakfast after Brian left to break his lease agreement. Things were moving fast between Megan and Brian, and Kate wasn't about to let her little sister mess anything up again. Or, rather, she wasn't about to let the busybody cronies who made up a hodge-podge of a council mess anything up. Kate knew the stakes.

Her little sister was now begging Kate to stay out of it and let her handle everything. "Michael is coming with me. We don't need you, Kate. It'll look bad."

"What do you mean it will look bad? They approved my business request, right? We can leverage that," she reasoned, pushing past Megan and downstairs to grab her purse.

"I think it could complicate things," Megan added, rushing down after. "Too many cooks in the kitchen. *We* can handle it, Kate."

Kate turned at the door, her car keys in hand. The Inn was totally vacant until Wednesday. She'd already started the wash and cleaned the upstairs baths and downstairs bath. She could use a break. And Megan could use a hand. "Okay," she conceded. "I won't go in. But at least let me *drive* you there. Then, if you need me, I'll be right outside."

Megan stopped at the bottom step and pressed her hands together. "*Thank you*," she answered. "But we'll take *my* car."

THEY RODE TOGETHER IN SILENCE, Kate mentally ticking off items on her to-do list. When they had ordered food and drinks for Megan's matchmaking gala, Kate decided to hold off on her own preparations, but now they were cutting it close.

She needed to get a handle on how many people to expect. Partly, she'd been waiting to see if Megan's RSVP list hit the target number. If so, Kate would assume all of those guests would also come for the beach party.

Yes, beach party.

Of all things, the Inn-Warming had turned into a foppish *beach party*.

It was Amelia's idea, ever the sand-lover. She had said there was no point in hosting a party *on the lake* if you were going to bar everyone from walking to the beach.

Kate worried about liabilities. At that, Amelia simply pushed Michael onto the case. He told Kate that anyone could sue anyone for anything, but if she wanted to protect herself financially, she already had. When she formed her LLC for the Heirloom Inn, she was well enough set. One extra provision she could take, however, was to ask partygoers to sign a disclaimer. Plus, she could hire lifeguards if she was *that* worried.

Maybe she was. It all came down to how many would show up. And if she and Megan really were coordinating their efforts, and if Kate really intended to keep her party as an exclusive event, then, well, she had to know whether Megan was moving forward with the match-making gala. Anyway, Kate hoped she would. It was Megan's dream, after all.

Once they arrived outside the little dated building inland of Harbor Ave, a pang of guilt shot through Kate. Birch Harbor Town Hall could use a makeover. An over-haul. Then again, if they continued to cavort about the harbor like lords and ladies of the lake, it was safe to assume no voter would ever support tax dollars to go to that cause.

The council members needed a makeover before the building would get one.

That's when a lightbulb clicked. "Megan," she hissed, as Megan prepared to jump out.

"What?"

"Remember, you've got to play to their interests. How can your business benefit the town?"

"Tax revenue," Megan answered simply, grabbing her handbag.

Kate shook her finger. "Don't forget that. It brings in tourism *and* it provides a service to locals. It doesn't have to be seasonal, either. You, alone, could improve town infrastructure, town offices, and all that. Keep that in your pocket, okay? Don't let it get emotional. Don't mention Mom. Keep it about the business."

Megan nodded impatiently as she secured her purse strap and looked over to the building. Kate's eyes floated down the length of her little sister, taking in her red blouse (*power color!* Kate had said when she shoved the silk garment at Megan just half an hour earlier). Beneath it, crisp white, knee-length shorts gave way to tan wedges. "Megan, wait," Kate said.

"What? Quick!"

"Something's missing." Kate searched Megan but couldn't pin it down.

"I have five minutes, Kate." Megan whined as she smoothed her shirt and glanced toward the building again. As her hands moved down to the hem of the blouse, Kate caught them.

"Your fingernails." Kate pointed.

"My *what*?" Megan held her hands in front of her face, alarmed.

"You don't have your black polish on!" Kate's voice was loud. A little frantic.

"*Kate.*" Megan rolled her eyes, but they landed back on her uncharacteristically bare nails.

Kate reached for her purse. She could have sworn she had a deep burgundy in there, but as her hand crossed the console, she glanced down and saw a bottle of black. "You have one right here!" she screamed, laughing as she grabbed it and passed it to Megan who, in spite of herself, grinned, took it and started applying quick even strokes.

In moments, she was done and fanning her nails. "You're crazy," Megan said, blowing on her hands in between the quick batting.

"No." Kate shook her head. "I just know who you're about to deal with."

Megan's smile left her and she nodded somberly.

"Plus," Kate went on, "you were never meant for red nails. Matchmaking or not. You've got that brooding thing going on. It might work to your advantage. Add a little gravitas to your plea, a little somberness." She paused, then added, "And it's who you are. You've got to be yourself. Above everything. Otherwise, what's the point?"

Smiling once again, Megan left, and Kate sat, biting her own bare nails now, watching for any motion behind the tacky white blinds.

Michael's truck was already there, so she predicted that as soon as Megan stepped a foot inside, clutching the handle with care as to not smudge her parking lot manicure, she'd run into him.

Kate learned a lot about Michael that summer. How smart he was. How much he came to care for Amelia and, by extension, her family. She learned that he was a good man to have in these circumstances, and she trusted him to guide Megan.

Still, though, if they hadn't re-emerged within twenty minutes, Kate was going in. Smart lawyer or no smart lawyer.

It was her sister in there, after all. Her sister and a pack of wolves. And Kate wouldn't settle for a loss. She wouldn't let Megan settle either. So, she set the timer on her phone, leaned back, and kept her eyes on those white blinds.

22

AMELIA

Michael had told her not to come to the meeting with the mayor. It was best to keep things professional and on the up-and-up.

Still, it was impossible to sit around and wait. Amelia knew how badly Megan wanted Hannigan Field to blossom into a breeding ground for love. What was more, Amelia knew how awful small-town politics could be.

The minute she and Michael began cracking into Wendell Acton's disappearance, the ugly side of Birch Harbor reared its head. To be fair, it wasn't as bad as some locales. On her trek through America to find the perfect role, Amelia had done a few stints in much more corrupt, much darker communities, some small and some big. Those ones all had one thing in common: unmitigated greed.

Greed was less at stake in Birch Harbor. So much so, in fact, that the mayor and his council members were entirely comfortable with turning away new revenue streams.

At stake in Birch Harbor was something quirkier. Old fashioned, even.

Something so preciously small town that it sounded like it could be a plot line out of one of Megan's reality shows or Nora's old soaps.

What was that one thing that could bring Birch Harbor to its knees?

It had a reputation to uphold.

And in that way, in fact, the powers that be in the little lakeside town were a tad nefarious. They always had been, ever since the early days. The council members and the mayor didn't try to be evil, but everyone is a little bad. Everyone makes mistakes. Everyone has needs, and in the case of Birch Harbor, those needs came together at the local government level in an effort to maintain the image of an idyllic summer tourist trap. A pretty little township with happy-go-lucky residents. A safe place to live and visit.

Sometimes, curating such a vision meant you had to weed out anyone or anything that might get in the way and gum up the works. Tangle the fishing nets.

Of course, Van Holt and his folks up on Harbor Ave didn't flaunt their ill-will, but they still tended to it. Loosely, to be sure. Vaguely, even. Managing such perfection meant they had to actually act and make the proper concessions to preserve what beauty spread out before them.

Over the years, that's what each mayor was assigned to do. First and foremost: keep the place safe. Keep it pretty. So, they propped up a few useful older folks in positions of interest, like a craggy lighthouse keeper, looking out for the odd ship that floated down Lake

Huron decades back, wayward and lost and about to crash into the shoreline and ruin everything.

Amelia learned this through her careful study of the case surrounding the disappearance of her father, of course. After all, what could be worse for a tourist town's image than a missing local?

A dead one, of course.

Fortunately, *none* of the evidence Amelia uncovered so far indicated any sort of death for her father. At least, none that would have taken place in Birch Harbor. And in what reality would a mayor or a town council member have one of their citizens killed? It didn't happen. Period. Despite the fact that Amelia's education on the topic was limited to a thin stack of paperwork Michael managed to retrieve from the Birch Harbor Police Department's evidence room, she could suss out that a murder wasn't in the cards for the Hannigans.

Apart from that, she learned other things, too. Like, for example, that when the Actons pointed a finger at Nora, the police ran with it, questioning every Hannigan they could find. And, for example, when they had run into a dead end on the Hannigan tip, they stopped the inquiry altogether.

The town never cared about finding Wendell Acton. They cared how they would look in the greater Lake Huron media.

And that's exactly why Amelia now stood in front of a series of framed newspaper clippings.

Three front pages, each from a different month during the year of his search. They read like a brief, turbulent tale of a local family who'd fallen to pieces.

The first: *Local father and husband missing from lighthouse area.*

The article to follow charted his movements from the start of that summer through to August. It also, conveniently and hurtfully, incorporated the *suspicious* and *distinct* absence of his family during that summer.

The second: *Hannigan family implicated in disappearance of local man.*

That article offered brief, useless updates. They'd searched the whole of the town, on foot and by air, and reached the same conclusion as before. It was odd, but that's as much as they knew.

The last: *Wendell Acton left town. Case closed.*

This one was most maddening and came years later. Many years, in fact. The conclusion was sloppy and wrong and detailed a quickly abandoned search and few answers.

And it ended, inadvertently, with a hurtful, cruel question in the form of a supposedly unrelated article that took up a narrow strip of real estate further down on the page (that part, Amelia did *not* frame but instead hid from daylight).

It read: *How to nurture your marriage. Ten tips from local wives who get it right.*

Quoted in the article was a familiar name. The name of a woman who Megan was coming face to face with right as Amelia stood there, the slip of paper in her hand as she stood in front of the three framed pages.

Michael asked her not to frame the articles, and if she was going to, that she at least kept them hidden in a closet or the cellar.

But no, she refused and instead displayed them taste-fully (as tastefully as one could display such a tragedy) in the corner of the living room, just beyond the wood-burning stove and its little concrete platform. A safe reminder of why Amelia really returned to Birch Harbor: to see to some unfinished business.

For all of Amelia's adult life, she'd been searching. For a good part, a great role. Overnight success on the heels of a long haul. A contradiction, yes. But Amelia's efforts were never consistent enough to call anything she accomplished *earned* success. If it came, it would probably come as luck.

But once she was home, *home* home, she knew she was never searching for fame or money. She was actually just running.

And so, she turned her attention back to the lake. The house. The Bungalows, the field, the cottage, her sisters, and everything that made up her very full life. Her life in a town where, in fact, she was a little famous. And that's when she knew there was a different search that needed tending. One that lived in her heart.

And it's why, even after her sisters pooh-poohed her efforts, she let them. She let them so that they could have peace and she could have space to *keep searching*.

In the meantime? Well, the meantime was very good to Amelia. The meantime was filled with those things that a woman wouldn't find in a misguided trip around the globe. It was filled with her first real love. Career satisfaction. Contentedness. Pure, boring, simple, *fulfilling* contentedness.

She looked back down at the fluff piece.

Local wives who get it right.

She saw the absence of Nora's name. Poor, maligned Nora. Queen of Birch Harbor.

Mainly, she saw Judith's name.

Judith Carmichael.

23

MEGAN

"With all due respect, Mayor Van Holt, what I'm proposing is something akin to a speed dating service. I can assure you every aspect of the events will be decent. It's a business Birch Harbor will be proud to sponsor."

Even as the words spilled from her lips, Megan didn't recognize them.

All due respect?

I can assure you?

Who had she become? It appeared that gone was the loser housewife who couldn't even land an online gig as a social media rep.

"Sponsor?" Judith Carmichael dipped her pointy chin to her microphone. "This has nothing to do with sponsorship or even endorsement. You merely applied for a special events permit."

It was ridiculous that Van Holt had called in the council for the meeting. It put Megan on the spot and might have sent her into a tailspin. Fortunately, she was surprising even herself and performing as well as she could.

She turned her gaze on Judith, and prickly heat climbed up her spine, activating another onslaught of reasoning. "Excuse my terminology, Councilwoman Carmichael, but surely you understand that I mean Birch Harbor will be proud to champion my small local business and support my efforts to move back home and contribute to society here. To the economy, too." She flashed a phony smile at the woman, a secret message meant to say *I know who you are. I know what you're doing!*

It might have worked, except one of the less spiteful —and less clever—council members chimed in. "I think it's an interesting idea," the man added, his accent so thickly Michigander that it even stood out to Megan as notable. "But I still don't fully understand it, Miss Hannigan."

"Mrs. Stevenson," Megan corrected robotically.

"Stevenson?" Mayor Van Holt answered. "I thought you were—"

Megan flicked a glance to him then to Michael, who cleared his throat. "Megan's married name is Stevenson. I thought we indicated that on the permit application?" He glanced nervously at Megan then back to the board. "Hannigan Field was left to her in her parents' will."

"Don't you mean her *mother's* will?" Judith Carmichael slid her readers down from her artificially slight nose and snaked her head around the slender neck of the microphone. She looked nothing like the lost woman Megan had met earlier in the summer. Then, introduced to Megan and her sisters as Gene

Carmichael's wife, she came across as little more than a wide-eyed tourist.

A question formed in Megan's throat, and she knew she couldn't continue her request without asking it first. "May I ask you something?" Megan interjected, her tone as deferent as she could make it in the face of the snotty remark and against the confused backdrop of her name on the permit.

Judith Carmichael's eyes narrowed and she raised her chin.

Michael cleared his throat beside Megan, but she pressed on, opening her gaze to the whole of the board. "May I inquire as to each council member's term of service?"

"Irrelevant," Judith Carmichael snapped back.

But Mayor Van Holt raised a hand. "Excuse me, Miss Hannigan—or, Mrs. Stevenson, rather. Shouldn't we focus our attention and time on your request for an events permit?"

Michael cut in. "I think, Mayor Van Holt, what Mrs. Stevenson hopes to learn is the cause for such a severe response to her request."

Megan began to wonder if she was on trial for something, based on the way Michael was handling himself. She didn't question it however, and even softened as he went on. "As I hope the council can see, her business proposition is entirely above board. Many of you have heard about matchmaking websites? Perhaps even dating apps?" he prompted.

The quieter council members now murmured in easy agreement.

Judith Carmichael, naturally, spoke in response. "*That* would be different," she huffed.

"And it wouldn't draw revenue in the same way as a physical matchmaking *event*," Megan added, her nerves turning to raw steel as she held the woman's gaze.

Bristling and leaning back, Judith flapped a hand up like she was tired of listening to such *nonsense*. She didn't want to listen to reason, that much was obvious. She had a different motive. Something more sinister that Megan wasn't prepared to confront. Not entirely, at least.

"The issue remains," Van Holt added, "we aren't clear about how you'll organize this event. And in her concerns, Mrs. Carmichael brought up some good questions. Advertising and marketing might be a real issue here, Michael." He broke from his dry, professional demeanor, releasing them all from the little show and talking to Michael man-to-man, rather than mayor to civilian representative.

Megan let out a sigh and just shook her head, but Michael pressed his hand on her shoulder. "Mayor, is Mrs. Carmichael the only council member to bring forth concerns? I have to ask because her role, and forgive me for asserting myself here, Mrs. Carmichael, but her role is that of a *summer* representative rather than a long-time or even permanent resident. Her voice, er, Mrs. Carmichael," Michael now shifted his soft, even gaze to Judith, "*your* voice is an important one. But so, too, are those of the rest of the council." Michael waved his hand across the board. His implication was clear. He was accusing Judith of ramrodding the others into submission. It was a risky move.

Looks of surprise and even amusement crossed some of their faces.

"Well," the frumpy man who spoke earlier answered, "Judy—"

"Judith." Judith Carmichael lunged at the microphone to correct the poor guy.

"Ope, sorry Judith," he replied, ashamedly. "*Judith* mentioned a real problem we could have."

"And what's that?" Megan interjected, losing her patience with the motley bunch.

"Didn'tcha say, Judith, that this place is going to turn into Hannigan Harbor if we aren't careful?"

Megan's mouth fell open. As did half the board's, the mayor's, and Michael's. She turned her stare to Judith, who didn't so much as flinch at the accusation.

"I beg your pardon, Mrs. Carmichael, council...?" Michael cleared his throat and started in on what Megan hoped would be nothing short of a lambasting.

But Mayor Van Holt broke in, "Now, now. Let's all just calm down." His face reddened and the puffy skin around his neck seemed to swell as he leaned into his microphone. "First of all, *yes*, Judith did wonder about a... a *conflict of interest*, all right? All right. And that *did* become a question, in fact. And that question along with the confusion over what in the world you planned to do up on that field, well," he chuckled nervously, "we were all scratching our heads, all right?"

Megan lost her nerve. It vanished. Poof. Leveraging the Hannigan name had been a mistake.

But worse than that?

Perhaps she had a bum idea. Perhaps a matchmaking gala, a summer singles mixer... perhaps it was the wrong approach all together. Maybe they were right. Maybe it would all end then and there.

Michael started to answer, but she tugged his arm and whispered, "It's fine. They've said no."

Clearing his throat yet again, he gently shushed her and added one final, devastating remark. "Mayor, council members, if your denial of this permit hinges on Megan's ancestry, then I regret to inform you that I'll be filing a lawsuit. To hold an individual accountable for the sins of her father is nothing short of discrimination. And *that's* assuming Megan's parentage or familial ties are even questionable at all. They aren't. The Hannigan name is a good one. Kate continues to prove that in the growing success of the Heirloom Inn. Amelia will prove that with her museum. And even more, Nora Hannigan proved that by her charity and selflessness. I don't stand here today to lecture you on the facts, however." His face turned to the woman who sat on the mayor's righthand side. "What I stand here for is not only in defense of Mrs. Megan Stevenson and her family but also in the pursuit of supporting my own community. And so I'll say it again," he lifted a finger and flashes of Atticus Finch at a podium blinked through Megan's mind, "if Mrs. Carmichael's opinion has tainted this board, then I may be moved to take things a step further."

Megan flushed at Michael's threat, but watching Judith Carmichael's face blanch and crumple was well worth the dramatic gesture.

"I'm not *tainting* anyone's opinion," she spat back. "I merely suggested that what with that bed-and-breakfast and talk of some lighthouse exhibit and the fact that your mother owns half the town, well don't you think it's smart for us to be conservative and diligent? Don'tcha think it's not a smart idea to... to just *rubber stamp* any old proposal that crosses our desk?" She was inflamed now, and no one could stop her. Megan held back and waited for this woman, this woman who'd embedded herself so quickly in local life, to short circuit. Judith did not short circuit, however. She had more to say. More revelations. "When I was on the town council at Heirloom Island, we had a similar problem where one family dominated the economy. It's the very reason I moved inland."

"Then why are you *here*? If you were so set against small-town politics, why strongarm your way into Birch Harbor?" Megan couldn't help it. She unleashed the question like a missile.

But Judith just smirked. "My husband lived here when he was younger, which I know *you* know, Miss Hannigan. And after we moved, he kept visiting, and I felt it was important that if he—*we*—were going to continue to be a part of Birch Harbor's society that it was my duty to help make it the *best* that it could be." She drew her fist across her chest in a little show of might, but Megan wasn't convinced.

Behind the woman's words was the truth. There was something more. A familiarity there. A fear that Megan recognized in her own mother for so many years.

Judith Carmichael wasn't protecting Birch Harbor.

She was protecting her jealous heart.

24

KATE

Kate's timer went off and still no sign of Megan or Michael.

Without a second thought, she unbuckled herself and punched the door open, treading with a purpose in through the door and directly to the secretary.

"Hi." She flashed a perfunctory smile. "I'm a party to the proceedings with the town council and Megan Stevenson. I'd like to join their meeting, please."

Her mouth hanging open for a moment too long, the woman then twittered for some moments, alternating between juggling the phone and flapping through scattered paperwork. "Um," she came up with at last, "I think it's a closed meeting."

Kate licked her lips then jabbed a hand into her purse. She reached for her wallet, drawn to the only silly thing she could think of.

Her freshly minted business card.

She slapped it down on the desk and tapped a finger

on the white space. "Katherine Hannigan of the Heirloom Inn."

Thrown off again, the woman peered at the card through her glasses then suspiciously up at Kate, confused no doubt, but also... maybe... intimidated? Kate wasn't above using coercion to get in that room and help her sister.

The secretary pulled the card closer in and frowned deeply. "There's no Stevenson here that I'm aware. But Hannigan, yes." She bit her lip and tugged her readers from her nose.

"Stevenson, yes," Kate asserted. "Megan *Hannigan* Stevenson. My sister and business partner. I'm a little late, sorry. They *are* expecting me, however." Kate pressed her lips in a line, willing away the white lie into the ether. She just needed into those doors so she could help sort things out.

But the woman behind the desk was proving to be more sentinel than secretary. She rose and pushed the white rectangle back to Kate. "I'll just go see."

Then, as the woman turned to go toward the nearest wooden door, it creaked open, Michael's hand pressed against it as Megan appeared. Kate searched her expression for a look of triumph but didn't see it.

Megan wiggled the back of her hand at Kate as the three of them moved to the waiting area just feet away from the reception desk. "They didn't work."

"What do you mean?" Kate asked, frowning and ignoring the secretary who made a light harrumph sound as she returned to her swivel chair.

"My black nails. They didn't work." A sad smirk curled Megan's lip, and Michael let out a long sigh.

"They said we could reapply if we clarify the event, but—"

"But what?" Kate asked, looking at Megan.

"But Judith Carmichael doesn't want us doing business here," Megan answered.

Michael and Kate exchanged a glance, and Kate looked back at the secretary before grabbing Megan around the shoulders and directing her outside into the late afternoon sun.

Once they were near the SUV, Kate studied Megan harder. "Why doesn't Judith Carmichael want *us* doing business here? I already *am*."

Megan just shrugged.

"*Why?*" Kate repeated, now directing her question to Michael.

"Why do you *think*?" Megan replied. "Clearly there's something there. She must have known about Nora."

"What could she possibly know?" Kate's eyes widened and she flashed a glance up at Michael, who stood lamely, hands in his pockets.

Megan shrugged again.

"Okay, then how?" Kate asked, acid churning along her insides and a pit opening at the bottom of her stomach. They'd only just agreed to keep everything quiet, and as far as she could tell, her sisters and Michael, Matt, and Brian had done just that.

"Gene," Kate murmured to herself.

Michael cleared his throat. "Pardon?"

"Gene. Of course he told his wife about his past."

"And you think she held a grudge? Over an accidental pregnancy?" Megan pushed her fingers to her temples and twisted toward the SUV. "Let's go. I need to get back to the apartment and lie down. I'm not feeling well."

They bid goodbye to Michael whose disappointment was palpable. Before he left, he promised to print and start on a new application for Megan, who thanked him.

Once they were in the vehicle, moving down the green-lined road back toward the harbor, Kate mused to Megan, working out what Judith's problem was. "She isn't even a townie. She's a summer person. And anyway, it's not like Gene and Nora's secret baby returned to Birch Harbor and nudged her way back into their lives. Liesel wants nothing to do with us. She gave us the lighthouse, for goodness' sake!"

Megan kept her eyes ahead on the road. "I know. It's obviously some jealousy thing. Some hang-up with us, but I don't get it. She was *so* awful in there, too. Just... just evil acting. Like a caricature. A stereotype of the little shrew who wiggles her way onto a town council and then elbows out the competition like her life depends on it."

Kate crossed her arms. "Something probably *does* depend on it."

"On what?" Megan asked.

"Judith is holding your permit hostage for a *reason*, I'm sure. I doubt she's totally crazy. If you get the permit and start the business, then that must threaten something that belongs to her. We just have to find out what." Even as she said it, the answer formed in her mind, flitting between two distinct possibilities. Two things that Judith Carmichael veritably owned and that any woman, not just Judith, would be reluctant to give up without a fight. It was all so obvious. Something Kate ought to have thought of had she known Judith boasted some kitschy sort of summer representative seat on the council.

At first, she considered the possibility that Judith was quite like Nora, a queen reigning over the lake from on high, her powers of party-hosting and charity-organizing at stake with this family of sisters moving back in and starting to take over. But Judith was not enough of a local for that to warrant her takedown on Megan.

It wasn't about losing Birch Harbor.

It was far more personal. Something against the Hannigans, specifically.

In the driver's seat, Megan gasped. "What if she has a matchmaking business she wants to open! Maybe *she's* my competition." A smile crept over Megan's face as she looked at Kate. "I'm *joking*. I think she's just a jealous sort of person."

"No," Kate replied. She wasn't smiling. She wasn't laughing. Kate knew exactly what belonged to Judith. She knew exactly why Megan was a threat. And Amelia, and even Kate, herself, who was safe before the first two returned to the fold.

"It's not quite jealousy. And it's not a business she's worried about losing," Kate said darkly. "It's her husband."

25

CLARA

Kate called an emergency family meeting at the Inn.

They sat at a new wooden table on the backyard grass. It was the first time Clara had ever sat at a table on the grass in the backyard there at the house on the harbor. Nora had always preferred the porch for eating or drinking or spending any sort of time outside, but Kate was well into preparations for the Inn-Warming Beach Party Bonanza, or whatever she planned to officially call it. They had even gotten some online interest and phone calls. Enough that Kate invested in two big, round, rustic tables for either side of the sidewalk that cut through the lawn. Half a dozen matching wooden chairs sat around each table, all delivered with the tables that very morning.

The emergency meeting took place at the southern side of the yard, two boxes of pizza consuming much of the tabletop real estate.

Beneath her, Clara's chair sank an inch into the earth,

rendering her even shorter and less able to properly reach across into the nearest box for a second slice once she'd finished the first.

Adding more pressure to the big drama at hand was the fact that Megan's singles' soiree had also picked up favorable notice from potential clients. The newspaper ad released an onslaught of interest, and Clara had announced, just as soon as she arrived, that she'd gotten a slew of text messages throughout the day from locals, people Clara didn't even think knew she existed. She'd unwittingly become some sort of middleman between Birch Harbor people and her new business-owner sister.

"They're asking when and where and what and all the things you outlined in that ad. They seem excited."

Megan simply wilted at the news. Clara felt bad for her sister. Almost as bad as she felt for herself now that she was in the throes of packing up her entire classroom —thankfully, Amelia spent the morning helping—and moving to a new building. That would be the easy part, too. Next came curriculum adoption and development. Training. More changes. More new, right when she thought she'd mastered the old. Compounding it all was that she still hadn't had the motivation or time to really spend on the cottage.

The porch screen door slapped behind them, and Clara twisted around to see Brian, hands in his pockets, pained look on his face, as he skipped down the three steps and over to the table, grabbing the empty chair beside Megan and greeting her first before the others.

They were now complete. Kate, Matt, Amelia, Michael, Megan, Brian, and Clara. Well, complete except for Sarah, who had grabbed her slice and taken off to a beach party down south, at the bottom edge of Heirloom Cove. She'd already gotten the spiel. Keep family business private. Have fun. Be home by eleven. Yada. Yada.

Clara was growing both more fascinated and less fascinated with her niece-cousin. More fascinated in her social life and how everything would materialize come September, when the two would see each other in a new context, beneath the buzzing fluorescent lights in the halls of Birch Harbor High. Less fascinated in their ambiguous relationship. Clara couldn't pin down if she was Sarah's peer or her mentor or what, and even though she was trying to overcome the whole Miss Havisham dis, it had set them apart. On separate journeys, somehow.

"That's great, Megs," Amelia replied to Clara as she passed a two-liter bottle of pop around the table.

"What's great?" Brian asked. "Is there good news? Is that the emergency?"

Megan had told the others that she'd only been vague with Brian, indicating simply that he needed to come straight to Heirloom Inn once he got back to town. She couldn't tell him about Judith. Couldn't bear to.

Clara felt like a bystander among all the others, everyone a solid twelve years her senior, she was like the runt, the sixth grader who stumbled his way to the edge of a fight between eighth graders, scared but entranced by the ring of chanting pubescents and their bizarre, violent ritual.

Matt chimed in, trying, it appeared, to be helpful. Helpful Matt. Easygoing Matt. Fiorillo family golden boy. Tanned islander. Handsome single dad who would give the shirt off his back to a stranger. The man who abandoned Clara.

She looked out to the lake as he spoke. "Clara here says that the ad for the singles' party is bringing in lots of attention." She felt his eyes on her, but she kept her gaze on the glimmering water, looking through the searing sunlight as it blasted her irises.

Why did she always have to sit facing the sun? Why didn't she bring her sunglasses?

"Let's adjust the umbrella," Matt added, apparently aware of her discomfort. Helpful as ever. He stood and cranked the canopy so it dipped down and offered shade on Clara's forehead. If she sat a little higher in her seat, it would cover her eyes. She'd be able to see again without squinting, whether she was looking at the lake or making eye contact with her family.

She tried to smile at Matt in appreciation, but surely it came out more like a grimace, so instead she murmured, "Thanks."

The conversation moved on. Clara let out a sigh and then, reasonably, with a can-do attitude, and by sheer will of forcing away the grimace, she sat taller in her seat.

"That's not even half the story, and it's not why I asked you to come," Megan continued before diving into a full-on review of the meeting with the council members. She spared no details, but even so, Kate jumped in, verifying certain facts and adding her own commentary.

Finally, when the group had it all, the full story on how Megan would never get to start her dream business, Clara realized that she had something to contribute. A small little secret that probably wouldn't matter, but it would at least be a way to slip inside their world.

"I know Judith."

Silence fell across the table. Sounds from the beach

carried up and bolstered Clara's courage. "Carmichael. I know Judith Carmichael."

"How?" Megan asked.

"Well, even before you introduced us at the marina," Clara nodded toward Amelia, reminding them all of that day when they inadvertently reunited with Gene and Judith, who then were putting on the tourist act, "I knew about them from around town. People talked about Mr. Carmichael, the old principal. I was too young to have him as my principal, remember? He retired before I started high school. But Judith, well, I've seen her at education conferences inland. She ran a few, even, and led the professional development sessions. I never talked to her, though. Or even met her, actually."

"She was a principal, too?" Kate asked.

"She was definitely a teacher. And then maybe she got a promotion at one point and became someone in charge." Clara shook her head. "At least, she used to teach and lead professional development. I don't know if she still does. That was all on Heirloom Island, actually. The only reason I remember it is because someone else pointed her out when I considered leaving Birch Harbor. It was a few years ago. Right after I started. I thought I might leave and go to Drummond Island or something, and the person I was with said that St. Mary's could be hiring. They told me that Judith woman used to work there and it was a great school. I even put my application in. I didn't get a call, though." Her voice trailed off as the memory flooded her brain.

"Wait a minute," Matt jumped in. "I would know her if she taught at St. Mary's."

"Not if she met Gene and got married before you

moved there," Kate pointed out. "Or even if she quit teaching before you had Vivi."

"True," he admitted, slumping back, *useless for the first time in his life, probably*, Clara thought to herself, suppressing a small grin.

"They wouldn't have been married until *recently*," Amelia speculated. "He wasn't with her when he was our principal."

"Right, but he was already gone when I started high school," Clara reminded them. "So maybe she lived on the island even as recently as ten years ago, in which case Matt should be familiar with her."

Matt shrugged. "What was her maiden name?"

Amelia's eyes flashed. "That article!" She swatted at Michael's arm, but he looked more lost than ever. "Michael, that article we found! It was the ten-year anniversary of Dad's disappearance. Her name was *definitely* Carmichael, so they were married by oh-two. Two-thousand-two!"

Scratching his head, Matt just shrugged. "I'm more of a Birch Harbor guy than an islander."

"What article?" Kate asked.

"In our research about Dad, we found three newspaper articles. The ones I framed." She gave a pleading look at Michael whose expression turned to playful exasperation.

"The ones you insisted on hanging up?" he asked her, smiling.

"Yes," Amelia went on excitedly. "The first two were from the early nineties, right after he left. The third was exactly ten years later, remember? When they officially closed the case?"

No one seemed to remember, or at least if they did, they kept mum to allow Amelia to continue on her rambling path towards some overstated revelation.

"When they closed the case, Judith Carmichael was featured in the newspaper. She wrote a snotty little piece on good wives or something. How to keep your man happy—that sort of inane thing."

"So?" Clara asked, enthralled (for the first time ever) about Wendell Acton. She stole a glance at Matt, and for a brief moment, they locked eyes.

Something welled deep inside of Clara. Some pain or hope. A sharp tug that moved her, throbbed along the inside of her skin and made her look at him differently. Not with more comfort, but with less.

Clara never knew Wendell. So, in that way, it shouldn't have been a shock to meet her *real* father so many years later, after never having one to begin with.

What made the reunion worse, in fact, wasn't that Matt had let her go so easily... it was that he was right there under her nose that whole time. And she was under his, too. He *knew* about her, and he never came to her.

And even more than that, he had a daughter the same age as Mercy, Jake's Mercy. And this could very well mean that Clara's own dad was the same age as—if not younger than—the man she had a crush on.

She swallowed and glanced away, unable to hold his gaze. Unable to stand the lure of getting to know him. Letting him in. Letting herself in, too. What if the only reason he was around was for Kate? What if Clara was a pest to him? What if he never wanted to know her? Then she'd have not one, but *two* dads who disappeared. Maybe, at least, they'd find Wendell.

She forced her gaze back to the others and mentally returned to the present issue. Judith. Oddball interloper who might have been a carbon copy of Nora. Really, she might.

Amelia's hands flew up at Clara's implication that the newspaper article was irrelevant. "So? So! *So*, it was weird!" Amelia cried back. "It was weird as all hell."

"Why would she write for the Birch Bee if she didn't even live here back then? She doesn't even live here *now*. Why? *Why* does this woman *care* so much?" Megan was pleading now, her fists balled up on the table, pounding lightly. "This jealous old—"

"Birch Bee." A thought arrested Clara, and she shot it back at Megan, cutting her off at the pass. "Maybe she wrote for the Birch Bee regularly. It covers Island news, too. Anyway, Heirloom Island is an extension of Birch Harbor. And if Judith was a teacher there, then she probably felt like even more part of our community." Clara glanced around, but she was met with a variety of expressions, none affirming.

She went on. "Okay, so I don't know her *well*, but I know she was a teacher or at least *in* education *and* affiliated with St. Mary's. Maybe that's how she met Gene. Through education."

Megan closed her eyes and pressed her fingers, painted black again, over her eyelids. Once she opened them again, she offered Clara a sad smile. "Thanks, Clar. But I don't know how that's going to help me change her mind. I don't think she cares because she lives a stone's throw from the Inn. I think she cares about something else entirely. And anyway, even if we did know what she was so desperate to protect, we can't change the town's mind, for that matter, either. I just need to take Michael's advice. Update the application. Give it another go and, in the meantime, look for something else."

"You're joking, right?" Though the sun had sunk degrees lower, it no longer hit Clara's eyes. She was perched high on the edge of her seat with one leg tucked beneath her, leaning in, her second piece of pizza untouched.

Megan frowned back. "Joking? How could I be joking? If I can't get a permit, what's the point? I'm not going to host one mixer and call it a success. The point of the permit is to establish myself as a business here. These events have to be *regular*. Until I can get the town to back me—"

"Yes, we *do* know." Kate's voice cut in loudly. "We do know why she cares. I know what Judith is protecting, and we know what she's afraid to lose. It's not Birch Harbor. It never was. Megan and I already discussed this."

All heads turned to Kate, and Clara sank back half an inch. The sun blasted across her vision, blinding her momentarily until she leaned forward, adjusted her seat at an angle, and then again perched high, anxious to learn the truth. Anxious to be involved in all the drama, and anxious to find her place in it.

For the first time in forever, Clara was part of the family. A silly, runty, peripheral part, but a part.

And she found herself desperate to know: why was Judith Carmichael, her grandmother's ex-boyfriend's current wife, keeping Clara's *aunt* from opening shop?

Or, put another way, what did this summer visitor have against the Hannigan sisters?

Kate held her palms up. "Gene."

Clara frowned immediately and all but scoffed. "Well, she doesn't need to worry. We aren't interested."

Megan chortled and added, "That's what *I* said."

But Kate shook her head slowly, as if what she was about to say next was the sole reason she drew everyone together. "It's not us Judith Carmichael is worried about. It's Nora."

26

AMELIA

"Well we have good news for ol' Judith, then," Megan replied to Kate, her tone thick with sarcasm. "Nora's dead."

"Wait," Amelia's eyes widened. "Does Judith think... does she think Gene is *our* father?"

At her question, Kate visibly recoiled. "Ew, *no*. That's not what I mean at all." She paused thoughtfully. "Although... maybe she *doesn't* know about Clara. Maybe..." Kate gasped. "Maybe she *does* know about Liesel. Oh my God, that's it!"

"What's it?" Amelia cried in response; she was lost now. Her lame insertion about the article was useless. She didn't understand Judith Carmichael or Gene. She didn't understand what Clara's parentage or Wendell's disappearance had to do with any of it. She just wanted to eat her pizza, drink her margarita, and go back to the lighthouse and finish painting the bathroom.

Kate replied, "Judith Carmichael is worried that if all four of us are back here, in Birch Harbor, setting up businesses and living our lives, then maybe Liesel will come back, too. I never considered that. I mean, at town hall today I realized she was definitely jealous. That's so obvious. But I thought it was either about attention or maybe she was wary of Clara or maybe Judith was the type to use that secret against us. But no. That's not it. She must know about Liesel."

"She doesn't," Michael answered, clearing his throat.

They turned to him. "What?" Kate asked. "What do you mean?"

"She doesn't know. At least, Gene hasn't told her."

"How do *you* know?" Amelia asked, suspicious of her boyfriend. "That article was a total coincidence? Judith Carmichael doesn't know that Gene was madly in love with Mom?"

He shook his head. "Maybe she knew *that,* but I'm pretty sure that Judith doesn't know about Liesel. I can't go into details, but Gene had me plan his estate. Recently. *Very* recently." He swallowed audibly and shifted his gaze nervously to the water. "Like, I said, I can't go into details. But take my word for it. Gene Carmichael never told his wife about Liesel Hart."

THE REST of dinner was a humid, itchy, awkward affair. The pizza sat unfinished. Amelia gulped down her drink and told Michael to take her back to the lighthouse. Sarah was staying at a girlfriend's house that night, and Amelia realized what it was like to have a child. She was actually looking forward to having the place to herself and having Michael to herself and blocking out the secrets of the past and the confusion of the present. She just wanted to paint and daydream and rehearse her lines for her upcoming show.

And yet, as Michael was driving her home, slowly twisting along Birch Harbor Ave and past the newly manicured Hannigan Field, Amelia blurted out, "Do you think it'll work?"

He looked over at her from the driver's seat, his hand on her thigh, casual and light and distracted. "Do I think what will work?"

Amelia answered, "If Megan just sends in a new application with a clearer mission statement or whatever. Will it work? Will she change their minds?"

He let out a long breath. "The rest of the council is reasonable. Maybe they can persuade Judith Carmichael to be reasonable, too. Majority rules. They just need to speak up."

"What if they don't? What if they *agree* with her that there are too many Hannigan businesses? What if someone sues us?" Her mind was rushing ahead to her own looming business opening.

"Who would sue you? Why?" He asked the question like he was surprised, but Amelia knew he wasn't. She knew he was thinking similarly. She grabbed his hand in hers and tangled her fingers into his.

"They could say we're running a monopoly on the tourist industry here. They could say we have too many pots on the stove or whatever the expression is."

Michael chuckled. "You girls don't have a monopoly. You do own a lot of the town. At least, that might be how it seems to someone like Judith Carmichael, but we'll figure it out." He pushed air through his lips, then added softly, as an afterthought. "I should have used her married name."

"What?" Amelia asked.

He glanced her way, a guilty look slashing across his face. "I submitted the application under Megan Hannigan. I wasn't thinking when I did it, and she signed it without reading it."

"Her last name's Stevenson," Amelia answered, still bewildered. "But why does it matter? Do you think that error was an easy excuse for them to reject it?"

"No," he replied. "I think that error was the actual reason they rejected it. If they didn't know she was a Hannigan, maybe there wouldn't have been a meeting. Maybe she'd have gotten that rubber stamp. It's my damn fault," he muttered at last.

"Oh my God," Amelia hissed. "That's it!"

"What?" Michael asked. He'd just turned onto the little road toward the lighthouse. The sun was beginning to set, its bottom half blurring at the edge of the lake.

"Forget about updating the application. Print a new one. Leave it blank. I have an idea."

27

MEGAN

The emergency meeting had long dissipated.

Too loudly, Kate asked Matt to help her with something in the basement. Amelia and Michael had left half an hour earlier. Clara, as well.

Now alone together in the backyard, Brian and Megan vacillated between a beach walk and turning in early. Dread loomed over her at the prospect of returning to the muggy apartment where they would go their separate ways only to wake up and tiptoe around each other in the morning, still unsure how to conduct themselves in the face of their recent history.

"I don't want to walk the beach," Megan admitted at last. "Sarah's down there somewhere. I'll feel weird if we bump into her, and... oh, who am I kidding? I just feel weird in general. We're here in the same town as our daughter living separate lives from her, and—" Megan was drowning. Life had been picture-perfect just months before. *What happened?*

"We'll get there, Megs," Brian answered, as they watched the sun start to dip on the watery horizon.

"How? We are living on our savings with no job prospects. No *real* house."

"We have *acres* and *acres*," Brian answered, then quickly corrected himself. "Well, *you* have acres and acres."

"For the events I'm not allowed to host?" She smirked and took a long sip of her drink, licking her lips and clearing the last crystal of salt, instantly craving more of it.

"For whatever you want," Brian answered. "You could build a house there if you wanted to. *We* could."

Megan had considered that many times over, but how would she? With what money? With whose help? "I don't know," she answered. "Sounds like another pipe dream to me." She hated her attitude. She hated how things were going great with Brian, but things were going so horribly in the greater context of their lives. She dipped her chin and shook her head.

"You sound so deflated." His voice changed. Megan glanced up at him, and his face was darker. His features hard.

"What?" She frowned, a deep frown. An angry one.

"You're so damn deflated, Megan. You're doing the *woe-is-me* thing again, and I can't stand it."

Taken fully aback, Megan shook her head and began to reply that *No* she wasn't. She began to argue, but something stopped her. The familiarity of it. The horror of the same old, same old. The painful pattern.

"You're right."

Brian's face opened, and though he'd obviously been

ready and waiting to argue, he stopped, too, mid-head-shake. "I *am*?"

A small, sad smile pricked her lips, and Megan nodded. She had the power to stop. She had the power to reroute them. Why had she always been so averse to using it? "Yes. I don't know why I'm like that. It's like I immediately jump to feeling sorry for myself. Despite this—" she waved her hand out at their sunset beach view, "I'm sitting here feeling like some sort of victim. I'm ridiculous. How have you put up with me all these years? The lack of gratitude?" There was more there, more to be said. She could accuse him of not supporting her. She could accuse him of putting his career first.

But what good would it do? None, of course. They'd been down that road. Nagging and accusing and badgering had never done an ounce of good.

So, on a whim, she tried a new track. She tried, for once, taking responsibility for the one thing she was responsible for. Her attitude.

And, to her delight and surprise, he spit her words right back at her. "No, no, no. How have *you* put up with *me* all these years?" They exchanged a grin, and he reached out his hands and took hers, then held her gaze. "Megan, you've always wanted my sympathy, and I've never given it. You've wanted a job, and I never helped you get one. And all these years, you raised our daughter while I focused on my career. Woe *is* you, but shame on me."

She blinked, tears cresting over her lower lash line and confusion clouding her emotions. To feel pathetic or to feel grateful... it was a choice, it occurred to her. So, she chose the latter. The better. The productive and positive.

"Shame on us both," she answered. "But we can start over, right?"

"Right," Brian agreed. "What's so wrong with having a few pipe dreams, anyway? Maybe that's what we've been missing all these years, Meg. I mean look at us, we were on the verge of divorce and then *boom*, you started chasing your dream. I started chasing mine, and *look*, Meg. Things got a little better."

"Until today," Megan couldn't help but point out as she lifted an eyebrow and chuckled good-naturedly. It was hard to commit to the whole positive attitude thing. She was trying, though.

Brian shook his head. "That's the thing. We can't just give up because of one crotchety woman. You're going to let this *Judith Carmichael* crush your dreams?"

Megan shrugged, wiping off the wetness from her cheekbones.

"Well, I'm not," Brian said. "I won't let Judith Carmichael—or *anyone*—crush your dreams. I say we push forward with this. I'll start brainstorming app ideas and you go brainstorm ideas for getting that permit. Deal?"

Smiling, Megan swallowed down the last tear and nodded. "Deal."

"Let's go to the bungalow. We can put a movie on," Brian offered. "I'll leave the sofa intact. Unless you'd rather I open up the bed..." he winked at her, and Megan wanted with all of her soul to giggle and slip away with him like they were in college again, snuggling in a too-small pullout sofa after one too many drinks, the TV glowing against their skin in the heat of the night.

But she couldn't. There was another place they needed to be.

"Let's go to the field."

IN THE TIME it took to drive out to the farmland, the sun had melted halfway down the earth, by now drenching the southern part of the country in darkness.

They hopped out of Brian's truck and passed the little wooden sign, refinished the past week by Amelia, who was good at that sort of thing: sanding and staining and adding a little art to her projects.

Now, instead of just the words *Hannigan Field*, little insect shapes danced in buzzy circles at the upper right corner, glowing golden under splashes of varnish.

"Are those...?" Brian pointed at the sign and started to ask.

Megan nodded. "Yes. Cute, huh?"

He chuckled, then grabbed Megan's hand and led her to the dead center of the field. Around them were markers for where to put tents and tables, and Megan could easily picture what her soiree might look like. She could imagine something akin to one of her favorite reality shows, playing out in real life for her to partake in. She could picture clusters of nervous people, making small talk and introducing themselves and pointing to their nametags as they realized they had this, that, or the other in common.

She could picture it all, even in light of the day's letdowns.

"What if you change tactics?" Brian asked, as they

reclined together in the damp grass, his hands behind his head, hers clamped across her abdomen.

Even seventeen years after giving birth, any time Megan touched her stomach, she recalled her pregnancy with Sarah. It was the highlight of her life, growing a sweet baby and sharing the experience with a doting husband. Had they drifted so far from that?

"What do you mean?" she asked, breathing in fresh evening air and studying the milky clouds as they hung in the red dome above. West of Harbor Ave was, in some ways, a different world from Birch Harbor. It had a country feel. When they were kids, Megan and her sisters would sneak away on the weekends to hunt down errant raspberry bushes or go on a mission to find a local cherry orchard. Inevitably, they'd return home half covered in poison ivy rashes and miserable as Nora scrubbed them with rubbing alcohol and oatmeal with the hose behind the barn.

"I mean, what if, on your new application, you adjust the business description a little? Change it up?" He pushed up from the grass, bracing himself on his elbow as his eyes caught fire. "Megs, that's *it*!"

She twisted her head to him and frowned. "What?"

Brian grabbed Megan's hands and pulled her to a sitting position, crisscross applesauce. Giddiness rushed up her arms, tingling into goosebumps. She'd changed from her earlier outfit into a black jersey dress, the hem of which she now pushed into her lap with their entwined hands. "What?" she asked again.

"My *app*." Brian was beaming, his grip tightened around her fingers.

Megan's brain flickered to life. "Yes, your app..." she repeated, trying her best to read his mind.

"And your dating service," he added.

She bit her lower lip. "Okay, your app and my dating service. My dating *events*," she corrected, frowning now again, struggling to grasp his idea.

"Love on location. You used that idea, right? Remember? Well, add the tech component. You've got marketing, you've got an audience, you've got longevity... *Megan*, we can turn your business into a multi-media affair. A full-service dating platform. *Meet online and then safely in person at one of our events.*" His voice dropped down like a radio announcer.

Megan nodded slowly, her gears turning as she jumped into his brainstorm. "Love on location. Meet me at the marina. Find love in the field." She looked at him. "An app." They were rolling now, throwing out taglines and hooks and soundbites. "So, they use the app to learn about me—*us*—and our matchmaking business. They RSVP to our events. We host them here! Brian!" Megan cried, "This solves *everything*!"

"You're even using Judith's own idea! She cited dating apps, right? You said that, right?"

"Right," Megan agreed, more impressed that he was listening to her and had remembered what she said. Even as small a detail as that. "I love it all, Brian. We can add the app component. You have a project. We can do it together, monetize the app even. Whatever, we have it! We have it!" She was talking a mile a minute, and he was nodding along until they grabbed each other in a hug, their clothes wet from the grass, their limbs jittery and hearts pounding as the sun sank even deeper behind them.

Megan pulled back from the embrace and looked into Brian's eyes. She had no idea if it really would work. She had no idea how it would work or how it could improve or if it might worsen her business idea, but none of that mattered. She loved Brian so much, that none of it mattered. His gaze slipped down her face, and she mirrored him, each now staring at the other's mouth.

Brian leaned in first, and Megan followed, and just as their lips brushed, something vibrated from his thigh. Megan's eyes grew wide and she leaned back an inch and searched his lap.

He moaned and released her chin from his hand then reached into his front shorts pocket awkwardly, sliding two fingers in and wiggling out his phone. "I'm sorry," he muttered.

She began to grab the phone and chuck it off into the field, but he beat her to the punch, turning it off without so much as a quick peek.

"Where were we?" he returned his attention to Megan and slipped his hand beneath her hair. She knew she smelled like wet grass and margaritas, and he did, too. But mostly, she realized, as their lips met and he kissed her, slowly, languidly... mostly, she realized he smelled familiar. Like her husband. Like her home.

Maybe they *would* build a house on the field. Maybe they *could* have it all right here, and soon. In a year, maybe. Maybe it was okay if Sarah lived with Amelia or maybe she'd move into the bungalow with them, or maybe whatever quirky situation came to pass... maybe it was *okay*.

When they broke from the kiss, Megan felt new energy return to her. Passion for her project, especially now that she had a true business partner. A life partner. "So, what will we call it?"

"Marriage," he replied, a sly little smile wriggling on his mouth.

Megan laughed and fell backward onto the grass again, like a teenager on a summer night, newly in love.

"That's not what I was talking about," she replied, grinning from ear to ear, heat pooling in her chest as she brought her hands to it to slow her heartbeat.

Brian eased himself back down beside her, sliding his arm beneath her head as she snuggled into him.

"Hey, look!" he pointed above them into the almost entirely dark night sky just above their bodies.

She squinted, almost looking too far—into the stars—almost missing what was right in front of her eyes.

A pair of fireflies, buzzing in circles, glowing golden.

"Fireflies in the field," she whispered, and turned to him, her face centimeters from her husband's. "That's what we'll call it. Our business."

"I love it," he answered. "Fireflies in the field."

28

AMELIA

"We have an idea," Amelia said as soon as Megan's voice came on the line. "I've been calling you and Brian for half an hour. I left a million messages."

"I know," Megan answered. "We saw. Is everything okay? Is Sarah okay?"

Amelia shook her head. "Sarah's here. She came home early. She's fine. It's about the business. It's about Judith, I mean."

"Well, Brian and I had a great idea, too," Megan answered.

Amelia felt antsy. She was sitting at the little wooden kitchen table with Michael, a freshly printed special events application squarely in front of her and one of Michael's black felt-tip pens lined up on the right. She'd been sitting there since she'd left forty-seven messages for her sister or brother-in-law to call back. And now they had. And they had their own idea.

Hers was better. She knew it. She just had to convince

Michael to let them do it. "I'm going first," Amelia declared, breathless.

Megan answered, "No, I am. Listen, Am, we've *got* it!"

Amelia groaned. "Fine! Okay, fine. What's yours?" They were playful in that back-and-forth, and Amelia was reminded of their youth; little fights about what game was next: Barbies or House? Where they'd eat their PB&Js: the grass or the beach?

"*Fireflies in the Field*," Megan began, her voice all drama.

"Ooh!" Amelia punched the phone onto speaker and set it on the table for Michael to hear. She repeated Megan's words for his benefit and to test them on her tongue. "*Fireflies in the Field*. Has a ring to it." She raised her eyebrows to Michael and gave a nod of approval. He did the same, and Amelia added, "What does it mean?"

Megan laughed. "We just pulled up to the lighthouse. I'll come in and explain everything."

MICHAEL POURED four glasses of wine and by then, Sarah had wandered out from her room, her face still in full makeup and her outfit a fresh dress rather than jammies. Amelia smiled at the girl and asked Michael to whip her up a hot cocoa, but Sarah shook her head.

Megan and Brian started in on a parental inquisition, reminding Amelia just how lenient she'd probably been with the teenager.

"We thought you were home for the night?" Megan asked.

Sarah let out a sigh. "Well, no." She flicked a glance to

Amelia. "There's an after party on the north beach." She jutted a chin toward the front door, and Amelia was captivated by the seventeen-year-old's quick adoption of the local geography. It was like she'd always belonged there, at the lake. Amelia had fallen in love with Sarah. They were kindred spirits, free spirits, both of them.

Amelia started to say *have fun!* but she was cut off by Brian.

"An after party? An after party for a party?"

"Well, the earlier thing was a bonfire. It was, like, a low-key back-to-school event." Sarah braced one hand on her hip.

"Clara didn't say anything about a back-to-school event," Megan pointed out.

Amelia sank into her chair, growing more aware by degrees that she might be to blame for Sarah's newfound come-and-go habits. She hadn't quite been crystal clear with Megan about how she was supervising her niece.

"It's almost nine o'clock." Megan flashed her phone at her daughter.

Sarah, ever the smart alec, flashed her phone back at her mother. "You said be home by eleven."

Uncomfortable with their impasse, Amelia tried to enter the conversation. "How about you call us at ten to check in," she suggested.

Megan threw a sharp glance at Amelia but softened when Brian squeezed her shoulder. "Sarah," he said, his tone fatherly and even, sending Amelia into the past like a time machine. Brian was so much like Wendell that Amelia could maybe see why Megan had always been indifferent about the disappearance. As an adult, she'd barely seemed to give it a second thought. Now Amelia knew why. She had her Wendell. Right there in Brian.

"Dad?" Sarah replied, bordering on irreverence and defeat.

Brian glanced at Megan and something passed between them, though Amelia couldn't read it. Some sort of silent agreement. A compromise.

"Keep your phone on you and check in with us at ten. If we don't hear from you, we're coming to look for you." Megan added a curt nod, and Sarah pranced to them, all supplicating hugs and quick pecks on the cheek before a big smile splashed across her face. She threw a wave to Amelia, plucked her car keys from the side table, then bounded out the door and into Amelia's sedan—a recent find on some used car trading-and-selling app called FindWheels. Apps were taking over the world, and Amelia was fine with it. Convenience was key anymore.

Megan and Brian's attention turned to Amelia, who braced for impact.

"An after-party," Megan scoffed. "Remember those days?"

Amelia's shoulders relaxed and she grinned. "We were lucky. We had each other to look out for us."

A frown replaced Megan's smile. "Sarah didn't have that in the suburbs. She had a few friends, sure, but she didn't have a clique. Or a group. No sisters, obviously."

"It's a good thing, then," Amelia replied, staring out the window as headlights spilled across the lake and turned up the beachfront road toward the north shore. "She has more than friends here."

"Yeah," Megan agreed. "The girls seem nice. A little

young to be out on the beach at night. I'm surprised Matt lets his daughter sort of parade around—"

Amelia cut Megan off, "Vivi? She doesn't parade around; she owns this place. You should see her and the others. I mean really, no one is going to bother them. They scare people, I think." Amelia chuckled, but Megan twisted in her seat to look out the window.

"Don't worry," Amelia reassured her sister. "They are good girls. They're good friends, too."

"Vivi?" Megan asked.

"Paige and Vivi and the others, yes. And Vivi is more than Sarah's friend, technically," Amelia pointed out, but a shadow crossed Megan's face. She fell quiet. Amelia let it go, whatever it was. Sarah was safe. Birch Harbor girls *were* good ones. Most of them. The ones Sarah had found, at least.

"Okay, so what is your great idea?" Amelia took a long sip of her wine and leaned onto the table, all her attention back on Operation Fireflies.

Megan copied her, taking a drink and leaning forward. "It's an *app*. A dating app. Brian is going to start building a program, and we are going to use it in our business description." Megan's eyes flitted down to the page in front of Amelia, and she reached across and tapped it with a dark nail. "Judith Carmichael had the idea herself. If we make this into an app-based business with a live event component, then it's sturdier. You know?"

It was almost too perfect. Like Megan and Brian had found out Amelia's idea and played directly into it.

"Um, *wow*," she answered simply, looking back at Michael.

He cleared his throat. "Good thinking," he added and smiled at Amelia, allowing her to take the stage.

Megan leaned back. "It's a great plan. A great name, too. Judith can't say no if we reframe our whole business plan. We're showing the town that this is not just some one-off party. It's the real deal."

Amelia smiled again. "It's a gorgeous name. And you're right. They will have to take you seriously." She bit her lower lip, keeping down the scream that was building up in her throat. The sheer excitement that Megan and Brian's idea was going to work so perfectly with hers.

"But?" Megan asked, glancing at Brian, who covered her hand with his on top of Amelia's table. "What is it? You're holding back," she accused, her eyebrows furrowing.

Swallowing, Amelia pressed her fingers onto the printed application and swiveled it one hundred and eighty degrees then picked up the pen and pointed to the line she'd completed for her sister and brother-in-law.

She tapped the name she'd written there and lifted an eyebrow at Megan. "It looks like we were on the same page."

29

MEGAN

Michael did not submit the application for them this time. In fact, he was hesitant about the whole thing, crying foul over the ethics of submitting a new permits application for the same business but under a different name.

Megan and Amelia held his feet to the fire and spent the next morning with Michael in his office. There, he waded through paperwork, finally settling on the fact that no, what they were doing was *not* illegal. And so long as he wasn't representing or delivering the new application, it might be a little better received.

After they finished completing the new pages, Michael drove them to the house on the harbor where they explained everything to Kate and Clara and were left to sit waiting.

Brian didn't take long. All he had to do was drop the application with the town council's secretary then drive back to the harbor.

Soon enough, they were all back together, at the

kitchen island, each with a steaming mug of coffee.

The night before, Sarah had called at ten, as she promised, and then made it home by eleven, as she promised. Megan knew she was dependable and capable of making good choices, and she knew Sarah deserved to have a little fun and embed herself in the social circles of Birch Harbor. Even so, an undercurrent of fear ran along Megan's spine when Sarah didn't turn up for breakfast right away.

"She's sleeping in," Amelia had reminded Megan.

"I'd like her to be here for this," Megan complained.

"For what? You might not hear back about the permit for a few days."

"I know, but I want... I just want things to be perfect. I miss her, okay? I miss my daughter; there, I said it."

Kate squeezed Megan's shoulders, and Clara set her mug down. "I'll go get her and bring her. I agree. We should all be here. A big family breakfast. After all, the rest of the week is so hectic."

The chimes over the front door clanged to life, and Megan peered through the doorway. There was Sarah, and at her shoulder, the white-blonde Vivi and one of the other girls, an older one.

Matt was on a project inland, so it was a little odd to see his daughter in such a confusing context. Still, Megan reminded herself that Vivi was not in the loop on the family drama. She was simply there as Sarah's friend. Nothing more.

Sarah confirmed as much when she made delicate introductions. "Everyone, this is Vivi and Paige. Vivi and Paige, this is... *everyone*." Sarah giggled nervously, and the group waved hello to the girls.

Megan watched Kate as she scrambled awkwardly to set about getting plates for the girls and sending them outside.

"It's weird to have teenagers around again," Kate commented, once the girls, clad in their swimsuits with messy beach hair and bright tan lines, had taken their paper plates and flip-flopped down to the beach. Megan and the others carried their mugs through the back door, too, settling onto the porch.

"It's weird that Vivi runs with the older girls," Clara said once they eased into the cushiony patio set.

Megan nodded in agreement. "I thought the same thing." She stole a nervous glance at Brian, who was at the porch table in a conversation with Michael about forming an LLC for the app and filing for copyrights and trademarks and all the boring things that came with establishing a legitimate business. The things that Brian was good at and that Megan couldn't wrap her head around.

"Actually," Megan confessed, her voice lowering, "I first thought it was weird that *Sarah* was hanging out with *younger* girls." She gave a worried look to Kate, her oldest sister and wisest.

"No," Kate shook her head. "It seems weird because they are in high school, but that age gap shrinks over time. Look at us," she passed her hand around and then pointed right to Megan. "Megs, you're four years younger than me, and we were friends at that age."

Megan gave her a look. "You had a one-year-old even before I started high school."

It was the first joke.

The first one ever. No one had dared to make any

light remark about the Kate-Clara thing. It was still just that—a *thing*. Ambiguous and tender.

Megan ran her tongue between her lips and winced. "Sorry. It was supposed to be a joke."

Kate smiled, answering Megan as she studied Clara. "I wish I'd *had* her. But Clara wasn't mine back then."

Megan laughed nervously. "True, I guess she was *Mom's*."

"No," Kate answered, her eyes still on Clara. "She was *ours*."

A broad smile broke out across Clara's face, and Megan reached over the table and grabbed her little sister's hand and squeezed. Amelia added hers on top, and Kate added hers.

Amelia said, "Who cares who she belonged to? Who any of us belong to? We're sisters."

"We're *family*," Amelia added.

The moving moment was cut short by Brian, who all but yelped. "My phone!" he said. "It's ringing."

Megan's hand slipped from her sisters' and she stood and crossed to her husband, reading the unfamiliar numbers as they flashed across his screen. "Would they really call?" she asked.

"Only if it's bad news," Kate surmised.

"Answer it," Michael directed. "We'll find out."

"Brian Stevenson speaking," he said for all to hear. Megan reached to the screen and tapped the speaker, shushing the others with her finger.

"Brian, hi. This is Gene Carmichael."

30

MEGAN

Her mouth fell open, and when Megan glanced around the porch, she saw her sisters' had, too.

Brian looked at Megan, clearly unsure how to proceed. She nudged him.

"Hi, Mr. Carmichael. How can I help you?"

"I want to call and, um, well... I was hoping you won't mind if I insert myself into your private business here. Yours and your wife's, I mean."

Megan's eye grew wider now, and she shook her head then took the phone. "Mr. Carmichael, hello. This is Megan. Brian and I are here with my family. We have you on speaker."

"Oh," Gene Carmichael replied unevenly.

Michael cleared his throat and held a hand to Megan as if to bring her down. He was obviously distressed, but Megan waved him off, replied with a small, calm smile and stood with the device in her hand. "Mr. Carmichael,

I'm going to step away from my family for a moment. I'd love to talk to you personally, if you won't mind?"

Megan had never considered herself belligerent. She wasn't the sort to argue with the manager of Target over a coupon. But she didn't shy away from confrontation, either.

She first learned this about herself when she got a job as a summer camp counselor for Birch Kids Camp. A sweet little disabled boy had come one year, and as it became clearer and clearer to the teenaged Megan that he would continue to be left out of most of the activities, she went to the camp director and, well, gave him a piece of her mind. She cited discrimination and exclusion and threatened the poor twenty-something that if he didn't find a way to let the kid have fun, too, then she was quitting. That's the only card Megan thought she had to play, after all.

What she didn't know at the time was how serious a charge she was making. After a swift and misdirected reprimand for insubordination, things escalated beyond Megan's involvement. Other counselors supported her position and someone's mother got involved. It ended with a dramatic overhaul of the Kids Camp.

Megan had won.

Her anger had won justice for the boy, but it came with a small price. She was quickly deemed a hot head and ended up floundering to find another local job the next summer. And the next summer after that and then so forth right up until the present.

Walking now down toward the beach, she took Gene Carmichael off speaker and sucked in a deep breath. "Mr.

Carmichael, I'm sorry to barge in, but I assume that you're calling for me, really. Rather than Brian." She stopped at the sea wall and turned on a heel. "I can give the phone back to him in a moment, but I wanted to talk to you about—"

"No," he interrupted. "I did want to speak with you, but it was Brian's phone number I found on the application. Right beneath his name."

She closed her eyes and pressed a hand to her head. He'd seen the application. He'd seen their little scheme to subvert the process with a new application and a different requestor's name *and* a slightly different business plan.

Brian dropped off a special events permit request for an upstart app called Fireflies in the Field. They were hosting an inaugural event, and the founding company member *Brian Stevenson*, not Megan Hannigan, would run it. No conflict of interest. No Hannigan family monopoly. And no lascivious undertones. A family business with a plan for a highly successful smart phone application to draw in tourism and connect locals all in one, romantic, fell swoop. Conveniently, and under Amelia's direction, they did not make any mention of the previous application OR the fact that Megan and Brian were a team.

Still, with the new plan, there was no way the town council could, in good faith, turn them down. Not without a fight. The new application answered every last concern. This wasn't Madison Square Garden that Megan was trying to rent out for a weekend. It was her own property. And the party wasn't some Mardi Gras bender. It was a tasteful cocktail hour with hostesses and croissants and lemonade and *fireflies*, for goodness' sake.

But clearly, Judith Carmichael had been present when Brian dropped off the application. Clearly the secretary took it to her, musing in hushed whispers that something seemed fishy.

And clearly Gene was there, too.

"Oh," Megan replied, unmoored and pacing in short strides across a corner of the grass just inside the seawall. "Okay."

"You know, Megan, I owe you an apology. Your whole family, probably," Gene went on.

She stopped pacing. "For what?"

A sigh came through the line before he answered. "Frankly, I owe Nora an apology, mostly. I sort of terrorized her. For a long time."

"My mother? You... *terrorized* her?" Megan flipped around to glance at the others up on the porch. They were watching, and she turned back into the little corner and faced the marina. From that spot, she had such a clear view of the dock and the slips and the bobbing boats... she could hear everything... see *everything*. She wondered what that view had been for her mom. Her lonely mom with no husband and that big, looming house on the harbor.

"No, no. I don't mean *terrorize*, it's just that I was in love with Nora. I never stopped loving her. Not after the baby was born, not after the baby left, not after your mother married and had you girls. I still loved her when you and your sisters made your way up to the high school, and I had to see you in the halls, little versions of

Nora, floating about like lake fairies, reminding me of what I never had with her."

A hollow formed in Megan's stomach. "Um," she started to reply, but he went on.

"I know. I know how I sound. I sound like a crazy old man. But you should know that even though I couldn't move on, I finally did. I met Judith, and it was the best thing that could have happened for Nora, truly. It gave her an escape from me. She even came to tell me so."

Megan squinted across the water as a family deboarded and strode up the dock toward the marina office, bewildered about how to take the first step into Birch Harbor. *Where do we begin?* She imagined the mother saying to the handsome man who stood with an armful of life jackets.

"What do you mean?" Megan asked, narrowing her thoughts on the pitiful idea of Nora—powerful, guttural, steely-eyed Nora visiting Gene, the tourist who turned local. What? Did she offer some sort of congratulatory speech or kudos? A thank-you kiss—chaste but teasing? Megan put nothing past the woman.

"It wasn't so long ago when I started my relationship with Judith, you know. Right after I retired. You girls had all left town. Just the little one was still here."

"Clara," Megan offered, instantly regretting it. She didn't want to let this man in. Not to her personal life or her family's life. Despite all his help with figuring things out, he had a way of making her recoil. He didn't sit right with Megan.

"Clara, right." He paused. "Well, Nora must have had her eye on me. I was in and out of town, still figuring things out. Wondering what I was going to do without the school, without her, and I spent a lot of time at my folks'. On my houseboat. That's when I started bringing Judith around. Well, she'd *been* here, of course. But we really... *anyway*, I'm sorry. One night, Nora came down to my boat and told me she saw I had someone. She was happy for me, and she told me she expected to have the freedom I never gave her."

His voice grew pinched. Megan wondered if that's what it sounded like for an old man to cry. She wouldn't know.

Remaining quiet, she again twisted to glance up at her family. They still watched. The sounds of lake gulls and foot traffic and boat motors vied for Megan's attention. She pressed a hand to one ear, waiting for whatever he would say next.

"I'm sorry," Gene whispered through cracked syllables. "I shouldn't be so emotional."

He *was* crying. Megan softened, but only enough to prod him along. Get him to his point. "It's okay. I understand." She willed herself not to cry now. Her mother's death throbbed in her heart. A realization trickled in: there was so much more to Nora than an austere woman, dead set on making her way in the world. There was more than the hard work and the absenteeism from school events. There was much more there.

"It was the last time I spoke to your mother," Gene said. "And it was going to be a great conversation. I would have gotten closure. I could have apologized to her for being such a pest. For pining after her for too long. I could have said those things, and we could have maybe... it would have been better, I guess."

There was a *but* coming, and Megan braced for it. A

small burst of wind curled up from the water, sweet and bitter. It cleared her airways and she sucked in a long breath of it. "What happened, Mr. Carmichael?"

"Judith saw us."

31

KATE

"He said it wasn't anything nefarious," Megan relayed to them after the call had ended. As soon as they spied her lowering the phone and turning back to the porch, Kate and the others had beckoned her back up.

"So, what *happened*?" Amelia begged, wide-eyed.

Megan lifted her hands and dropped them. "Nothing, technically. He said nothing happened."

"Until now," Kate pointed out, her voice filled with the wisdom of a woman who had loved and lost and loved again. A woman with two grown sons who she missed with a mother's heartache. She put it all together even as Megan had started her reconstruction of the conversation.

Gene and Nora had shared a twilight conversation at the helm of his boat, and Judith found them there and saw the history in Nora's eyes and the affection in Gene's and she made up her mind.

She hated the Hannigans.

"It's so... *immature*," Clara added. "What grown woman gets jealous on a dime like that? I don't buy it."

Kate considered what she said. "You have a point, Clar, but some women are just like that. Viciously jealous. Unhinged, even."

"I don't think Judith is unhinged," Amelia said. "Let's be fair. Seems to me like Gene stirred the pot. I mean come on. If he all but stalked Mom for, what? *Decades?* Then it's fair to say he might have more of a hand in this than we know."

"Maybe," Megan allowed. "But it *does* answer the question of why Judith is blocking Brian and me."

"True," Kate agreed.

Clara shrugged. "True."

"Okay," Brian broke in. "So, we're dealing with a summer town rep who has a history of jealousy. What about the rest of the council? Does Judith Carmichael call *all* the shots? Is she Van Holt's long-lost sister or something? I mean where does the soap opera end?"

"We're going to find out right now," Megan answered.

Michael frowned. "What do you mean?"

Megan smiled at Kate then at the others. "Gene told me to come back to the town council building. They called another emergency meeting. Who's coming?"

THEY ALL WENT. Ridiculously. In Kate's SUV. They crammed in together and caravanned up Harbor Ave to the grimy old building that wilted into the grass.

Not ten minutes later, Megan and Brian stood there, hand-in-hand at the entrance to the building, facing the others, each of whom had found a little waiting spot. Clara perched nervously on a bench, Amelia and Michael huddled together under a leaning oak off to the side. Matt, who Kate had texted just before they left, had shown up, too. He stood behind Kate, a dutiful partner, his arms crossed in solidarity.

Kate looked at her sister and her sister's husband, the pair that almost *wasn't* and wondered why. How? How did Megan, her moody little sister, stumble into such a perfect marriage? And how had she let it almost slip away?

Of course, that was life. A wave on the ocean, ebbing out and flowing in along a rhythm that was dictated by a force beyond what they could control. Much like Kate's own shattered past.

It was a little funny how things turned out, how life pushed along, like a locomotive, making its perfunctory stops: college, marriage, kids. And then, perhaps surprising somehow, it carried her right back to Birch Harbor, depositing her at the depot as a tired traveler who'd seen the world and would be happy never to step foot on that train again.

There she was, with her sisters, back home. Kate was living in her mother's house and her mother's before her. She was planning the beach party of the century like some local socialite queen. Her mother would be proud of Kate.

And during all of it, Matt had waited for her. Not in the ways many men waited for their true loves, holding out, pining. After all, he, too, had built a life for himself, and a respectable one at that. They both had to, after all. How else could they have survived? But regardless of where they each had been in those interceding years, Matt had loved Kate since they were just kids. He was her first kiss. Her first everything. In some ways, their little story resembled Nora and Gene's. But Kate and Matt had one thing that Nora and Gene did not.

Kate loved him back.

Matt's love was exactly what she needed to find peace in Birch Harbor. And there was nothing wrong with it. There was nothing wrong with needing the love of your life, even if you had found another one to hold your heart in the meantime. Even if you had a whole other life in the interim.

Once Kate and Matt circled back to each other, everything settled into place like little grains of sand skittering into a safe, dry spot high up on the beach, never to be washed away by the surf.

Kate's dry landing place was there with Matt and her sisters. Birch Harbor was a cozy corner of the world where so many years ago she'd planted a seed. Now she was back, after building a whole garden elsewhere, and she was nurturing that long-abandoned seedling and finding in Birch Harbor what she always wondered about: a true and final sense of home. And that's exactly what she wanted for her sisters, too. It's what they needed. It's what Megan and Brian needed if they were going to make this work.

"Good luck, Megs." Kate smiled up at Megan and Brian as she draped either arm over her other two sisters and pulled them in. "No matter what happens in there, just remember, whatever happens in there, you're home now."

32

AMELIA

TWO WEEKS LATER.

"There she is," Amelia hissed to Megan from their perch at the corner of the backyard. She lifted her faux-crystal cup of lemonade toward the back door.

The Heirloom Inn-Warming Party was in full swing, and Amelia couldn't have pictured a more perfect event for Kate. For *them*.

The whole town seemed to meander up from the harbor, and Kate and Matt were furiously keeping food on trays and drinks refilled.

Earlier in the evening, after things had just begun to pick up, Ben and Will—Kate's sons—made a surprise appearance. Amelia had spent an hour chatting with them and their girlfriends, acting like a welcome wagon and inviting them to stay with her for the weekend. This was quite a point of contention, as Kate fretfully *insisted* she'd make room for them in the Inn—somehow, somewhere, even if it meant she slept in the parlor or kicked out another set of guests. That was when Amelia stepped in and declared she had space.

Sarah had niggled her way into the conversation. "They could stay with Clara," she'd offered, but Amelia had given her a sharp look. She was trying to take the whole Aunt thing more seriously.

"*You* can stay with Clara." Amelia chided Sarah. "She won't want these four crazies in there. I've got the second room *and* the futon. And lots of energy," Amelia had beamed at her sweet nephews and their girlfriends.

Sarah had rolled her eyes and wandered off to her girlfriends, crushed to be excluded, but oh well. Amelia knew how important it was to welcome Ben and Will into the Birch Harbor fold. After all, it had been the original plan, and with the Inn still under reno (the basement was so close to being ready), Amelia knew she had to protect her sisterly promise and be the perfect hostess.

When she saw Sarah later, she had grabbed her elbow and whispered, "Listen, girl, you're not a tourist anymore. You're a townie, now. You gotta act like one, okay?"

Sarah, charmed and intrigued, no doubt, threw Amelia a sidelong look and asked, "And what does that mean?"

"It means that when a tourist comes to town, you make room." She winked, and Sarah had just laughed and drifted back off, giggling and gossiping with the younger set. The next gen of Birch Harbor babes.

Presently, Megan squinted next to Amelia. "Where?"

"Look, right *there*." Amelia spun to face Megan and nodded her head behind her. "Literally coming out the back door."

"Oh," Megan answered, her eyes widening. "She's not with Gene, though."

"Just give it a minute," Amelia bet. "She's not the sort to trail behind her man, but he *is* the type to let her take the lead."

They were being a little mean. A little petty. And it wasn't a flattering look. Amelia swigged the last of her drink and cleared her throat. "I say we turn the tide. Are you with me?"

Megan frowned. "Turn the tide, *how*?"

"This is a housewarming. And it's *our* house," Amelia answered.

"*Inn*-warming," Megan corrected.

"Whatever. We have a chance to call a truce. Don't you want to do that? Might be good for business." Amelia wasn't only thinking of Fireflies in the Field. She was also thinking of her museum project. Her theater troupe. Her shows. She was thinking of all the things that the Hannigan women needed to protect now that they were back in the fold, back in Birch Harbor society. The protection could only come from doing exactly as Nora had learned to do: play nice. Even if it wasn't always sincere. Her mother's words trickled into her mind. *Fake it till you make it.* They had a new meaning now.

"True," Megan allowed. "All right, I'll follow your lead."

Amelia took in a full breath and started toward the porch where Judith was now standing, somewhat awkwardly, just as Gene came up behind her and snaked an arm around her waist.

Squeezing in and out of the clumps of guests, Amelia

and Megan made it halfway to the porch when Amelia looked up to see Judith and Gene were gone.

She searched the crowd on the porch and then combed the grass with her eyes, but nowhere did she see the sleek A-line or cheesy Hawaiian shirt.

"*Crap,*" she hissed.

"There you are," Michael's voice rose up behind her as his hands slipped around her hips and he pulled her into him.

Before she'd moved home, such a move might have lured Amelia into some stranger's fleeting life. Weeks with the wrong guy, too young to know she was too old for him.

Now, it was different. Michael's arms were strong and firm and safe. He'd had a glass of champagne, and it was enough to loosen him up, but not too much to render him useless.

"Hey," Amelia whispered as she slid her hand around his neck and twisted into his arms. "Can you do me a favor?"

"Anything for you," he murmured back before pecking her on the cheek and relaxing his grip back to a state of decency as he greeted Megan, a sheepish expression crossing his face.

"Can you look around and see if you can spot Judith or Gene?"

He raised up on the balls of his feet, which unnecessary at his height, and scanned the crowd, giving them a play-by-play.

"I see Sarah and her friends—" he paused and glanced down at Megan. "They are chatting up a group of shirtless boys on the sand."

Megan's face turned to alarm, and Michael chuckled. "I'm kidding. They *are* talking to some boys, but I recognize them from around here. Harmless, I think. Also, they're wearing shirts."

Megan rolled her eyes and slapped Michael's arm half-heartedly.

"Go on," Amelia said, bracing against him and trying to look above the throng of people.

He twisted around and searched the porch and in through the windows and doors. Floating tea lights and lines of tiki torches lit the whole area, but night was falling fast. "I see Kate and Matt in the kitchen window. It looks like... yep... they are kissing."

"Like, making out?" Amelia asked, surprised.

Again, Michael chuckled. "No, it was a quick kiss. Very discrete. Still," he tilted his head to her and winked.

"Oh, come on," Amelia replied, growing impatient.

"Okay," Michael continued, lifting his hand to shield his eyes as he pretended to look harder. "There's Clara, in the doorway. She's walking with that girl, Mercy, is it? And... she's... *smiling*... for once?"

Amelia play-punched him on the shoulder. "Enough with the snarky observations. Just find our targets."

"Fine, fine," he answered, swooping around to study the beach. "Ah-ha! Twelve o'clock and halfway down to the water." He pointed, and Amelia followed his finger to Judith and Gene, striding slowly through the sand, dodging an evening sand volleyball match.

"Thank you," Amelia pushed up and kissed him on the cheek, grabbed Megan's arm and took off down to the lake.

Once they were through the seawall and past the

danger of getting pegged in the heads with a volleyball, Amelia spotted Judith and Gene at the water's edge. "There," she pointed for Megan.

They were walking fast now, as if they were afraid Judith would slip into the water and leave forever.

Not before Amelia righted things. Not before they made peace.

"Mrs. Carmichael," Amelia called over the noise of the party behind them.

The woman turned her head, and when they locked eyes, for a brief moment, Amelia saw her mom. She shook the image and grabbed Megan's hand.

"Hello," Gene answered for the both of them. "Lovely party you girls have organized," he added. If Amelia didn't know any better, she'd say he nudged his wife toward them.

Amelia thanked him, then elbowed Megan.

Her sister took the cue, "Actually, I also wanted to thank you both again," she started, glancing quickly at Amelia, who nodded her on.

"Whatever for?" Judith asked, her voice louder than it needed to be. Amelia saw the plastic champagne flute in her hand, almost empty and dangling in the woman's bejeweled fingers.

"For granting my permit," Megan answered. Amelia squeezed her hand.

Judith lowered her plastic flute. "Oh, right." She took a step out of the surf, and Amelia looked down to see she was barefoot. Behind her, Gene was holding her sandals in his hand. He stood barefoot, too. Amelia felt awkward now, finding them like this, in some private moment, barefoot on the beach. She started to open her mouth to excuse them and head back in, but Judith took another step.

"I suppose I owe you an apology," Judith said when she was just inches away.

Amelia's mouth turned dry. "You do?"

Judith nodded, her lips a thin line.

Megan released Amelia's hand. "We accept."

Taken aback at her sister's bold response, Amelia tried to cut in, "No apology necessary. Things got a little conflicted with all of this." She tried to laugh and wave her hands around as if to reference the Inn-Warming party and everything else her sisters were doing that probably upset poor, old, jealous Judith.

"Yes," Judith asserted, her voice still oddly loud. "I'm sorry, Megan. And, Amelia, is it? I've been a little... *protective*. Of what, I'm not sure." She cackled. Oh, yes. Amelia knew a cackle when she heard it, and that woman was *cackling*.

"Judith," Gene said from behind, his voice a warning.

Judith shrank, but only just. "I'm sorry for holding your interests hostage, ladies. Truly. I want Birch Harbor to be the best it can be. Really, I do."

"Why?" Megan asked.

Judith blinked rapidly. Amelia bit her lower lip and winced.

"Why?" Judith echoed.

"Yes, why? You're an islander, right?"

"That's right," Judith answered, less assured now.

"What draws you here? What are you looking for?" Megan asked. "Why does our town matter to you so much?"

"Megan," Amelia hissed, grabbing her sister's elbow.

"No," Megan replied. "I don't mean it to be rude. But it's a fair question. If we are going to share Birch Harbor, then we should know about each other. And I'd like to know why, if you two live out of town and just spend the summer here... in your houseboat... why are you so much a part of this place?"

Gene cleared his throat and took a step forward, but Judith held her hand up, stopping him. She looked Megan up and down and licked her lips then answered, "My family settled Birch Harbor, too," she said at last. "My ancestors fought for this very parcel of land. They wanted to build the harbor right here. Where we stand."

Amelia blinked. "You grew up here?"

"No," Judith answered, her voice even. "I grew up on the Island. My grandparents were sort of castaways after all of the settlement issues from their parents. I always felt badly about that, you know? That they lost. And, well..." She looked as if she had more to say. Buckets more. But she stopped and smiled sadly. Then, she passed her plastic flute to Gene and reached each of her hands out to Megan and Amelia.

They glanced at each other briefly, then accepted the woman's chilly, bony grip. "I'm happy you girls found your way back here. Really, I am. I'm happy for all of you. I'm glad Gene, here, stepped in. I'm glad he knocked some sense into me."

And then, she squeezed their hands, released them, and went to Gene. He smiled at his wife, and everything felt finalized. Solved. *Good* and happy and sweet.

Judith and Gene started to walk off, north toward the harbor where their houseboat sat waiting. The little piece of something they owned. Maybe they'd go back to their second home on Heirloom. Maybe to their inland home down south or up north or wherever they lived.

Megan leaned into Amelia, and Amelia wrapped her sister in a hug.

But just as Judith and Gene crossed the invisible border between the Hannigan's private beach and the marina, Gene twisted around and looked at them.

Even though they made their truce with Judith, even though Megan and Amelia had her blessing... Amelia knew there was still something more. Something left.

She knew, for some reason, it had nothing to do with Nora.

And *everything* to do with Wendell.

33

MEGAN

The Inn-Warming party lasted well into Friday night, but come Saturday morning, Megan was up and at 'em, grabbing a quick bagel with Brian before they headed straight to the field to finalize the set-up.

The day was a hot one, with little cloud coverage. Thick humidity hung around them as everyone—Megan's sisters and their menfolk and even Sarah and a few of her girlfriends—worked together to get chairs positioned with their pretty fabric seat covers. They strung up lights and set long plastic folding tables with summery fabrics and accoutrements.

Amelia had been late to pitch in, showing up with Michael at last and murmuring something about a lead on the Wendell case.

But Megan didn't want to hear about it and squashed the conversation immediately. "He left. That's that. Save your investigation for any other day, *please*, Am," she begged her sister privately. "It's not about me. Or you. It's not about *Dad*. I just want this day to be about *us*. Our hard work together, and all the good things we're making happen here, okay?"

Though Amelia didn't apologize, she agreed, accepting that there was a time and place to continue the hunt and that Megan's very first Fireflies event was neither the time nor the place.

The food and drinks arrived just an hour before the mixer was set to begin. Megan agreed to let Clara oversee the buffet set-up so that she and Brian and the others could scurry home to get ready.

The plan was for the men to hang around on the edges. Kate had wondered if they'd be a distraction or appear single and therefore mislead the eligible bachelorettes, but Megan's research suggested otherwise. For the very first event, it needed to look well-attended. And with only twelve RSVPs, Megan didn't care if they put Brian and Matt out there to mingle and play along.

Still, it was a point of contention, so the agreement was for the sisters' dates to stay on the periphery, pitch in with anything and be warm bodies and helpful hands.

Amelia would be the official Mistress of Ceremonies, which was perfect. Kate wanted to man the food and drinks tables. Megan, for her part, was the Head Matchmaker in Charge. Megan and Sarah would run the registration table. After that, Megan planned to give a quick introduction to kick things off ahead of Amelia's welcome speech.

Sarah had her own event that night, an *actual* back-to-school bonfire, hosted by the school. Clara wasn't required to attend the bonfire, but indeed it was a point of conflict for her. Being the new teacher at the high school, she could make a first impression among some of her students and new colleagues. And usually, she'd have liked the chance to have a social event through her work.

But Megan knew Clara, and she knew that it was a lot to ask her to attend two big parties in one night, which was why she told Clara that, after the food and drinks were ready and Megan had returned, if she wanted to skip the Fireflies mixer, that was okay.

So, when Megan and Brian returned to the field, just fifteen minutes before kick-off, she was surprised to hear Clara say she'd be back soon.

"You *are* coming?" Megan asked her little sister, pinning her elegantly printed name tag onto her chiffon top.

When it had come time for Megan to plan an outfit for the evening, Amelia urged her to go with a pink sundress—something that said *romance*. Something pretty and light. But Megan had already had something in mind. A bright red blouse—Kate's on loan—and sleek black skinny jeans. On her feet, yellow-strapped wedges. Coincidentally, Brian had selected a similar ensemble: red button-down shirt and khaki slacks. Tan loafers. Together, they looked every bit the part of a business team whose company had something or other to do with *fireflies*.

"Yes," Clara answered. "I'll just run home to get changed and be back, a little late maybe, but I'll be here."

Megan couldn't help herself. "No school bonfire? You're choosing us for once?"

Clara, to her credit, didn't pale at the implication. Or pout. She simply smiled and replied, "Yes. That's exactly right."

JUST AS CLARA took off toward her car in the recently cleared lot they'd designated for parking, a stream of three unfamiliar vehicles rolled up the gravel lane.

Megan sucked in a breath and turned to find Brian.

It was time.

Kate, Amelia, Michael, and Matt were in position. Sarah and her friends were stalking the food table, and a few local acquaintances who Megan had reached out to were already there, sitting at tables and helping make the space look like it was filling fast.

They'd kept the chairs and tables sparse to begin with, so that when the first *real* guests gingerly made their way across the gravel drive and to the registration table, it appeared that the party was already in motion. Trucked-in planters with shaggy ferns and full-bodied pines in addition to heavy bouquets at the center and corners of each table, including the registration table, had been a worth-while investment. Since they'd positioned the event space centrally in the field, they needed to ensure it looked... *impressive*.

And it did.

Jaunty summer tunes throbbed from the DJ's speakers. The sun was dipping low enough that the summer heat had burned off enough to stave away discomfort.

"Hi!" Megan greeted, gesturing the incoming trio of women toward her table. "Welcome to Fireflies in the Field! I'm Megan, and this is my husband Brian."

The women introduced themselves and secured their nametags. Just as Megan nudged them towards the refreshments and was about to take a deep breath, sink into her chair at the table and send up a prayer that others would show, Brian tapped her on the shoulder.

"Megs, *look*."

He pointed toward Harbor Ave.

There was no such thing as rush hour traffic in Birch Harbor, Michigan. On the weekends, though, there would often be a steady stream of vehicles cresting the hill from the northwest en route to the lake.

Never, however... *never* in her life had Megan seen a full-blown traffic jam on that stretch of roadway.

"Are they—" she frowned, and the words fell away as Brian nodded his head.

A line of cars had built up at the entrance to the field, each waiting for a break in the oncoming traffic in order to turn in. Toward her event.

"Oh my goodness," Megan gasped.

Within half an hour, Megan and Brian—Sarah had long left to get ready for her own event—had registered over twenty-five people, crushing Megan's goal and pushing their resources to the very limit.

Once it seemed safe to say that they could get things started, Kate declared she'd be on standby to bring over more food.

Megan was glowing with the results. Some of the faces were even familiar. One of the town council members—the goofy man who couldn't quite keep up with the likes of Judith—was there. So, too, was an old high school friend of Amelia's.

Two people that Megan recalled from Nora's country club clique bee-lined for the beverage table.

A handsome man who she could have sworn she'd

either met or seen at the marina stood awkwardly at the edge of the dance floor, his hands in his pockets.

A gaggle of unfamiliar faces, tourists maybe, looking for a weekend date or a lifetime love—who was to say? The point was, they were giving Megan a chance. They were giving *each other* a chance.

A few of the guests had even attended the Inn-Warming the night before, which solidified the fact that Megan and Kate's paired marketing strategy could work.

"Okay," Megan whispered to Amelia as they stood at the edge of the food table. "People are chatting naturally, so I think we need to monitor the rhythm here. I'll do a super quick intro, then you can give the welcome address. Keep it under a minute. I think we save the activities for lulls."

"What about my directions?" Amelia asked. Megan had given her sister a set of directions to read that included an overview of a few party game activities. They planned on a rotation of sorts, but it was feeling unnecessary.

"This thing already has a heartbeat. Let's keep it to an outline." She grabbed Amelia's notecards and thumbed through, pointing along at each. "So, tell them that we'll open the evening with drinks and appetizers. Then they can mingle while we bob around and do a little digging— that can take the place of the formal interviews. You can mention that one of the hostesses might come by with some questions. After an hour or so, we'll start the party games, then we'll end the night with desserts and dancing."

"Should I mention that the questions are for our matchmaking profile?" Amelia asked.

Megan shook her head. "Keep it vague. The goal is to make this comfortable. Not awkward. People shouldn't feel like they are being set up. We'll only formalize the interviews if there's a dip in the momentum."

Amelia leaned away and gave Megan a look, but she brushed it off. She knew what she was doing. She'd trained her whole life for this (insomuch as she could)—watching her reality shows, playing matchmaker among her own friend circles wherever possible. And of course, Megan was a living success story. Proof that it was always better to let chemistry seep in rather than force it. Besides, there in the grass, beneath the glow of the soft string lights and against the steady beat of her personally curated *Summer Lovin'* soundtrack, love was officially in the air.

"What about the rules? Do I go over them? Do I talk about exchanging phone numbers?" Amelia asked again, and Megan studied her briefly.

"Are you nervous?" she asked.

Amelia shook her head. "No, no. Not nervous, but... I've never had, like, a main gig."

"A main gig?"

"Yeah," Amelia replied. "I'm going to be in the spotlight. Like, all eyes on me during a *monologue*. It's my moment."

Megan laughed and squeezed her sister's shoulder. "Just be you. Leave the rules to me. You've never been a rule-follower, anyway."

Amelia smiled and laughed, nodding her head and throwing her shoulders back. "Okay, I've got this."

"Just remember," Megan added, "our goal is to make

everyone feel like this is a safe spot to fall in love. And the only way they'll feel like that is if they like us."

"Don't they have to like each other, too?" Brian asked, slipping in between the two women and wrapping his arm around Megan's waist.

"Yeah," she admitted, "I suppose it will help if we make sure Mr. Town Council doesn't linger too long at the twenty-somethings' table." She lifted her wine glass toward the poor sitting ducks and laughed again. "Amelia, let's get started. I think we can actually do this."

"Go get 'em, girls," Brian said, sending her off with a quick kiss.

Megan snuck behind the DJ and asked for the mic. Amelia was at her side, clad in an off-the-shoulder pink dress and Bohemian flats. The pair of them up there may have come across as opposites. The serious one and the hippie. The pro and the am. But together, they were a team. And when Megan caught Kate's eye as she cleared her throat away from the mic, she saw there was just one person missing.

Clara.

She briefly scanned the crowd, smiling as the milling bodies paused and turned to her, the music drifting down to a minimal level.

"Good evening," Megan said into the microphone. She didn't see Clara, and after just a beat, forced herself on. "And welcome to the inaugural Fireflies in the Field mixer. My hope is that tonight will be your first and last time using our service," she winked blatantly as the crowd laughed. "But in truth, you'll always be welcome at our mixers. Maybe next time, you'll be dragging your best friend here. After all, only those who are in love can make the best matchmakers."

Low murmurs rippled against the night, and Megan smiled again. "If we didn't get to meet earlier, I'm Megan Stevenson, and this is my sister Amelia, our Mistress of Ceremonies. Before I give the mic over to her, I'd like to open the night with a brief toast." She held her glass up, and the group mirrored her. "To finding fireflies in Hannigan field."

The women in the crowd ahhed, and Amelia whispered a compliment to Megan then took the mic.

As she spoke, working off the cuff and without her notecards, Megan crept away and joined Kate at the buffet.

"Great job," Kate murmured. "And Amelia is knocking it out of the park, too." Kate held up a hand and waved as Amelia introduced her.

With a smile plastered across her face—even if she wanted to, she couldn't stop—Megan leaned over to Kate. "Where's Clara?"

"I haven't seen her return. I sent a quick text and no reply yet."

"Do you think she's going to the bonfire instead?" Megan asked, worried. Though why, she couldn't pin down.

Kate looked around and then shrugged. "If she is, she's missing out."

Breaking her grin to bite her lower lip, Megan asked, "Do you think it's going well?"

"Are you kidding?" Kate said. "It's adorable. People are having fun, and it's low pressure. That's the best way to move forward. Because, you know what? You're right," Kate pointed out.

"Right about what?"

"If you're successful, then you'll never see these people again. So, adding that little bit about this being more social than romantic, that was clever. I swear I think I saw a collective shoulder drop when you said that."

Megan smiled again. "Good, good. Well, that is the goal. We're here to set them up and have fun, and we hope they find love, but you know... it's more than that. It's a community thing, too. Our app is going to help drive the romance part of the business, but these events... they will be the heart and soul, you know?"

"Right," Kate replied, but her attention was drifting. "Then again, you might be surprised at how many people *do* pair off tonight."

"You think?" Megan asked, though Kate was smiling and staring off, her eyes glinting in the dusk on a new point of focus.

"Yes," Kate answered, lifting her chin to direct Megan's gaze toward the edge of the dance floor. "I think I see tonight's first pair of fireflies. Look over there."

But Megan didn't get a chance to see what Kate was pointing at, because right when Megan turned her face, someone grabbed her hand from behind and swung her around.

Brian.

"I have a surprise," he whispered, drawing her a few feet away from Kate and cupping her face in his hands.

Returning his mischievous grin, she asked, "What do you mean?"

He tugged something out of his back pocket. And that's when she saw it. Not the thing he was pulling out to show her, but his ring finger. On it, his wedding band. Her hand flew to her own white gold set, the square, modest solitaire, and she twisted it, her mind reeling over the fact that not once... not one single moment in the last several months had she even considered pulling it off of her finger. And not once did she ever notice that his was missing either.

A laugh climbed up her throat at their antics. Their foolish descent into filing for a divorce that was never meant to be. Their rush to sell the house. Everything hard that happened to them because of their decisions.

But then he frowned, the paper he'd withdrawn frozen in the air above them. "Why are you laughing at me?" he asked.

Megan's face softened, and she pressed her palm against his cheek and leaned into her husband, kissing him on the mouth, a sweet, soft kiss that smelled quite like home. When they broke, Megan squeezed her eyes shut then opened them again and answered him. "I'm laughing at *us*. How did we even get here?" She peeked up at his face as she finished the question.

He smiled, too. "Oh, you know. *Life*," he replied, his smile turning goofy and his eyebrows scrunching in the center. The wrinkles there were a reminder of all they'd been through. All their years together. He started to lift the paper again, but Megan had another question.

"Wait," she said. "Before you show me the surprise, I have another question." Her expression turned serious, and she swallowed.

"Okay," he answered, his tone dipping as his face hardened.

"Brian, how do we *stay* here?"

At that, his goofy grin returned in full force and he slapped the paper against his other hand. "That's what this is about."

He unfolded the packet and held it out so she could read.

Her eyes flashed across legalese, down to Brian's signature, then to another one. Beneath the latter a familiar name was printed. "It's a contract? With Matt Fiorillo?" She blinked and cocked her head around the pages.

"I got that job I applied for," he answered. "I can telecommute. I can work from here and also build our app. We're safe, Megan. We don't have to worry about how to fund your business or where we're going to host Sarah's graduation party next summer or where she'll stay when she visits from college. It might be a hard year,"—he was rambling now—"but I talked to Amelia, and she said we can move into the two-bedroom bungalow come September. That way Sarah will be with us while we build, and anyway, *Megan*, we have the *future*. We can make it work. If we put in the effort, we can make everything *work*."

Still confused, she shook her head, squinting back at the pages then searching his face. "You took another job? What about your dream? And what is this?" she raised her hand to the pages, and he dropped them.

"Megan, my dream wasn't building an app. My dream was having the freedom to be with you and Sarah. My dream was *us*."

She smiled, still tentative, still confused.

He lifted the papers again but waved them around,

and Megan's eyes flitted from his enthusiastic gesturing to the warm lights in the backdrop. The happy people dancing. Her sisters. And then her eyes fell back on her husband, who explained himself. "I hired Matt. This place is going to be more than a field of dreams for your mixers or a business front for our dating app."

Megan started to put it together, her face going slack at the realization. "Are you saying...?" she started as she let her mouth fall open in disbelief.

Brian nodded urgently. "We break ground in one week. *Megan*," he lifted her chin with his free hand and searched her eyes. "Hannigan Field is going to be our home."

She began to say something, but he held a gentle finger against her lips. "*That* is how we are going to stay here, Megan."

His eyes twinkled, and Megan smiled. She swallowed down the urge to cry and instead fell into Brian, squeezing him and breathing him in and knowing with every bit of her being that he meant exactly what she wanted him to mean. Home in Birch Harbor, home in Hannigan Field, had drawn them together. But it was the hard work... the time together both in town and on that forgotten plot of land inland from the lake—away from the others but still near her sisters... it was Brian and Megan's combined efforts and their dedication as a pair, as a *team*, that would *keep them there*, together.

"Birch Harbor," came a voice behind them as they broke away from a second kiss, this one even better than the first.

Megan turned to see Amelia and Michael passing behind them, en route to the dance floor.

"What?" she asked her sister.

Amelia winked. "Come for the lake, stay for the love."

Megan rolled her eyes and laughed, but Amelia and Michael went off toward the dance floor, a song from *Grease* blaring from the speakers.

"I said no *Summer Lovin'*!" Megan called after Amelia, laughing again.

Amelia twisted in Michael's arms as they hit the parquet floor and lifted a hand. "Look around you, Sis!" She waved across the field. "It's too late!"

Megan followed Amelia's gesture and took it all in. Her vision had come to life, but more than that, other things had fallen into place too. Romance for each of them, even her. Tourists and locals intermingling and sharing the little harbor town together, as one. Her eyes flitted across the dance floor and past the buffet and landed squarely on a distant couple.

"See?" Kate said, catching Megan's gaze as she joined Brian and Megan. "What did I tell you?"

Megan found Brian's hand and squeezed it, a smile curling across her lips as she watched the sun set behind her baby sister.

34

CLARA

Clara had arrived later than she planned. She'd been hung up at the cottage, searching desperately for something perfect to wear. She felt drawn to white, and though she herself didn't own a white dress, she had the distinct memory that her mother had some such frock. A light, gauzy sundress that would no doubt fit Clara. It was one characteristic the two women shared: their slight stature.

Rummaging frantically through Nora's closet, which still sat untouched, she came up empty.

Nearly sweating after a quick, hot shower and a blow out, she had one more option: the cottage basement. Clara hadn't recently ventured into the cottage basement. It was a small, cramped, damp space, mildewy and forgotten. When she and her sisters had previously started their search for some of Nora's more notable belongings, even the items from her will, Clara willfully kept the basement out of their search radius but was surprised that her sisters didn't push her to look there.

When they'd come across Nora's diary in the junk drawer in the kitchen, the search was deemed irrelevant and put on hold. After, once other matters came to the forefront that summer, Clara continued to keep mum about the basement.

It scared her a little, after all.

But now, with this sudden urge to look as pretty as her sisters, she managed to push the fear aside, grabbed a flashlight from the laundry room, and forged into the bowels of her inheritance.

Bypassing the single dead lightbulb that hung at the top of the staircase, she shone the light down the steps and around the floor, recognizing some old furniture and little else.

It was a generally barren space, surprisingly. Still, Clara had a distinct recollection of bringing down boxes of Nora's old clothes not long ago. It was her assignment in the wake of the diagnosis—the first step in clearing out Nora's possessions when they all realized the end would be near.

Sure enough, as she made her way down, she found the boxes, pushed up against an old bureau.

Clara set the flashlight on a dusty little side table facing the boxes, the bureau and the back corner of the basement. She flipped open their dry rot lids and started digging through, pulling outdated underclothes (even a lacey negligee, purchased in the eighties, no doubt) from the one and moving on to the other to find heavy winter coats, reeking of mothballs but folded quite orderly.

About to give up and go with the orange tunic she usually wore on the first day of school, Clara stood and started for the flashlight. That's when she saw it. A third box, wedged between the bureau and the wall, the top taped shut.

"Ah-ha," she huffed to herself, victorious. She *knew* that cute white dress was down here. It had to be in the last box. Had to.

Stepping beyond the first two boxes, she pulled herself closer to the third.

And that's when she saw the *other* thing.

The thing she was tasked with finding. The big thing.

Nora's hope chest, hidden behind the bureau, there the entire time. She really hadn't looked that hard for it, had she? She really was afraid.

Clara bit down on her lip. She was at a crossroads now. Skip the mixer and tear into the chest? Save the chest for later and dash off to keep her promise to Megan?

It was no competition. She had to go. She had to find that dress and go.

So, Clara pinned the hope chest to her mental to-do list, ripped off the tape on the third box, combed through until she found a folded stack of white garments, and jogged back upstairs.

The hope chest could wait. Nora could wait.

The present was more important.

And, for the first time in forever, the future was tickling Clara's heart. For the first time in *forever* Clara knew that she could hold her mother in her heart but go after something that she wanted first.

∾

NOT AN HOUR LATER, Clara had parked her little car in the

newly graveled lot and made her way, embarrassingly late, to the field.

The scene was something out of a woodland fairytale. Lights twinkled in the dusky night sky, and upbeat love songs spilled from the speakers. She was proud of Megan.

Smoothing her mother's dress and slightly nervous that other people would be able tell that it was still a little damp from a quick rinse and dry, she swallowed and picked her way through the short grass, her sandal straps rubbing fresh blisters into her ankles.

Clara wasn't unfamiliar with looking *nice*. She did it every day of the school year, fixing her hair and adding a little mascara. Ironing her polos and khakis or shift dresses and applying a dab of perfume on special days, like parent-teacher conferences.

But tonight she went above and beyond, and she was worried she didn't quite pull it off.

In addition to the gauzy knee-length garment, she wore a push-up bra she'd forgotten she had. She added smokey eyeshadow above her lashes and rubbed a pinkish gloss across her lips. Peachy blush felt heavy on her cheeks, even though she used a light hand, and she'd backcombed her hair at the crown of her head, smoothing it and mussing it and fussing with it until it fell back to its usual blonde wisps anyway.

All in all, Clara wondered if she came across as trying too hard.

She bit her lower lip, tasted the gloss and shuddered a little. A voice interrupted her nervous approach to the party.

"Miss Hannigan?"

Clara faltered at the greeting, and her eyes adjusted to

what, or *who*, was striding toward her from the party. Not her sisters or Brian or Matt. Or Michael-the-Lawyer.

It was him.

"Mr. *Hennings*?"

"Jake," he corrected, smirking as he held a drink casually in one hand, his other hand shoved in khaki shorts pockets.

She pointed to herself. "Clara."

"Clara," he replied, a grin forming across his mouth. "I thought you might be here."

Her breath hitched in her chest, and she wasn't quite sure how to reply. Quickly, she glanced beyond him and around the party. It was packed, with bodies moving on the dance floor, some huddling in small circles at the buffet and some relaxing languidly at the tables. Megan had pulled it off.

Clara smiled, then returned her gaze to him, still uncertain what to say. Then it dawned on her. "Oh, right. Hannigan Field. You probably know my sisters were hosting it, and—"

"No," he answered, his smile slipping.

"No?" Clara asked, squeezing her clutch against her abdomen.

"Well, Mercy said you were—"

Clara sucked the insides of her cheeks through her teeth and inhaled sharply. Could her students see into her heart? Could they see everything she was and wasn't and how she longed for companionship? Could Mercy— sweet Mercy with her new friend group and a bright future full of dates and bonfires and bliss... did that girl tell her dad something? Something that even Clara didn't know?

"Did she say I was single?" Clara blurted out.

Mr. Hennings—*Jake*—laughed nervously. "Oops," he admitted. "I'm not always sure what I'm supposed to share or what's a secret."

"It's no secret," Clara replied, growing more comfortable now that she had crossed an invisible threshold of some kind. She let out her breath.

He grinned again and threw his head over one shoulder. "Let's get you a drink."

Clara looked past him to the refreshments and saw Kate watching, grinning from ear to ear. Megan and Brian were there, too, huddled together intimately, in their own little world of marriage and business. A perfect reunion.

Clara felt herself flush but managed a quiet "Okay," and followed Jake.

They passed by the two meddling women, though he didn't seem to notice.

"*You look amazing!*" Kate hissed as Clara locked eyes quickly with her sister.

Megan nodded and gave her a discrete thumbs up around Brian's back, and Clara beamed in return, her heart pounding hard in her chest.

"Do you need any help?" she squeaked out to Megan as she hesitated a moment there.

"Yes," Megan replied, amusement curling her lips.

Clara came to a complete stop, her eyes flashing to Jake who was slowly making his way closer to the beverage table.

"Oh, I'm sorry. Okay." Defeat filled her voice and she flicked her gaze back and forth from Kate to Megan to Jake.

Megan rested a hand on Clara's shoulder and pulled

her closer. "I need your help right now," she said, her eyes narrowing.

Clara's heart sank. Jake still hadn't noticed she was stalled. "Okay. With what?" she replied meekly to her sister.

Megan exchanged a look with Kate, who answered on both their behalves.

"Clara, we need you to go sneak away with that sexy marina guy and have some fun for once, got it?"

Flushing deeper now, Clara's eyes grew wide and she couldn't suppress the smile prickling at the corners of her mouth. Her sisters giggled, but Clara didn't care. She loved it. She loved them. A spike of adrenaline coursed through her veins, and all she could do in reply was nod and force herself to keep walking.

After allowing Matt—always helpful Matt whose gaze she still refused to meet—to pour her a lemonade, Clara and Jake made their way to two empty Adirondack chairs out past the dance floor.

It was back-up seating that Megan had Michael and Matt situate on the off-chance the event drew in a bigger crowd. Clara smiled at the faint bit of hope and how, indeed, they were the only available (and private) seats in the whole field. Her heart grew full that the tides had changed so much over the summer. From the loss of their mother in May to Kate's return home, to the big secret, all the way to Amelia's search for truth and Megan's search for happiness.

Through so much of it, Clara had often felt like a footnote. Sure, she was embedded in the upheaval; she was the initiator of it all, in a small, unwitting way—her very birth had thrust the family down a whole different road. Some might even suggest she was the problem with the Hannigans, though not by any fault of her own.

But lately, things were different. She was around more, helping her sisters and finding joy in the work. So long as she could have her down time here and there, her soul had grown degrees more complete with each passing day.

And now, there she was, talking to an impossibly handsome man at her sister's impossibly gorgeous mixer on an impossibly perfect Michigan summer night.

She took a sip of her lemonade, studied the glass for a moment, then perched a little higher on the edge of her chair, mirroring Jake's position. They faced each other at an angle, their knees just inches apart.

"Mercy was mortified that I was coming to this thing," he confessed, looking at her from the corner of his eye.

"Oh?" she answered. "Well," she hesitated before laughing lightly. "I suppose that makes sense."

He laughed too. "What do you mean?"

"She's a teenage girl. She lost her mom..." Clara glanced up, nervous that she'd overstepped, but though Jake's face had turned solemn, his expression was still soft. There was still a light in his eyes. "I'm so sorry," Clara added with a whisper.

"It's okay," he answered, his voice low, too. "Time has helped us. Both Mercy and me, but you're right."

Clara's heart sank. "I am?"

"Mercy has struggled a lot with that."

Swallowing her hope like a horse pill, all Clara could do now was nod along. Then, something occurred to her. "You know," she began, tentative.

His mouth pressed into a thin line and he leaned a little closer.

She went on. "That's something she and I have in common, I suppose." By and large, it was the truth. After all, it wasn't Kate who raised Clara. It wasn't Kate who had changed her diapers, fed her in the wee hours of the morning. Kate didn't register her for school and help her go shopping and get her hair cut and send her to time-out when the easy thing to do would be to indulge the baby of the family. It was Nora. Nora never remarried. Nora never dated. Nora stuck by Clara, bringing her up to work hard and be charitable and kind and even despite all the things that Nora failed at as a mother... she was still just that. She was Clara's mother.

"That's true," Jake agreed, a sad smile forming across his mouth. He dropped his head. "It's too bad Mercy won't have you for her teacher anymore."

Clara cleared her throat. "You haven't heard?"

"No," he answered, frowning and shifting on his chair, inching closer to her. "Heard what?"

"The school transferred me. I'm going to teach at the high school now."

"Oh, wow! That's great. That's really great. Mercy will be thrilled. Does she know? Is there a chance she could have you?"

Clara chuckled at the barrage of questions, and he grinned foolishly.

"I'm sure she does," she answered, her face brightening at the reality of her big change.

Previously, she'd dreaded the move. Now, maybe, she ought to embrace it. Maybe more could come from looping with Mercy and her cohorts. After all, it would mean another shot at a parent-teacher conference with Jake, wouldn't it?

"She'd have told me," he answered. "We talk about everything."

"Oh." Clara twisted the plastic cup in her hand and bit her lower lip. *What else had they talked about?* Could she have revealed that Clara had no other teacher friends? That she ate canned turkey for lunch and once gave Mercy a *C* for a reading assignment? Clara blinked away the anxiety. "Was she excited for the bonfire tonight?"

Jake, aloof to Clara's inner turmoil, nodded and his expression brightened. "Very. She's found a group of girls and made new friends. I'm so happy for her. The last couple years... well, you know."

"Yes," Clara agreed. "She's sort of... above it all, though, isn't she? The cliquey middle school stuff and the silliness of her fellow teenagers?" Clara tried to laugh lightly, and he smiled, nodding his head for a moment.

"Not above it," he replied, his face twisting in thought. "Just outside of it. It used to worry me that she preferred her own company. Now, I realize I should maybe worry about her being on the beach all day and every night." He grinned and eased back, taking a sip of his drink.

"It's hard to find a balance," she offered, thinking as much of her own struggle with that as she was of Mercy's struggle. The struggle to be social. The struggle not to crawl inside of herself.

"I have a hard time with finding that, too," Jake admitted.

"You do?" Clara frowned. "You seem so..." she faltered to finish her sentence, but he waited, not correcting her, not cutting her off. He waited, his face open, his eyes soft. It occurred to Clara the only thing she could say in that moment was the truth. She had his attention. Why squander it? "You seem so happy," she whispered. And he did. He was the opposite of someone struggling to figure out who they were and what they wanted. Each time she'd spied him at the marina, he was smiling and laughing, cracking jokes with tourists and deck hands, boaters and employees from the Village. His effortless polos and khaki shorts... his boat shoes and his dark tan and white teeth... what was there to balance?

"I am happy," he replied, running a hand through his hair. "But some things are missing from my life, you know?" As he said it, he licked his lips and lowered his eyes to her mouth.

The music slowed down to a dull pulse, and Clara sensed a shift in the night—both away from them at the party and there, in the little clearing where they sat, their knees touching, her heart pounding.

The conversation had grown heavy like the air, splitting away from talk of his daughter and her career, and settling between them like a sprig of mistletoe. Balance. Happiness. Whatever it was that was... *missing*. It was probably the same thing Clara had been missing.

She'd only just arrived at the party, and her goal was just that: to arrive at the party. Whatever happened after her arrival—whether it be helping with the cheesy matchmaking interviews or clearing the tables—she just meant to get out of the house and have a little fun.

And now, just twenty minutes in, she was sitting with a man in an angled set of red chairs, flashes of fireflies— lightning bugs, *real* ones!—sparking to life around them.

Though awkward and uncomfortable, Clara couldn't tear her eyes from Jake. She couldn't search for her sisters, for their approval. She couldn't study the event to ensure it was going as well as Megan had wanted it to. She didn't need too, though, because Fireflies in the Field was turning out to be exactly what Megan wanted it to be. What all of the sisters wanted it to be.

There, on the brink of finding something—be it summer love or a two-way crush or whatever in the world Jake Hennings was missing in his life and for some unknown reason was implying that he had *found* in *her*... Clara was happy. Giddy happy. In spite of herself, her lack of balance, her inner fears and her outer struggles... Clara Hannigan was happy. And no matter where things might go with that widowed man, who was broken like her, she knew that Labor Day Weekend and all of its Hannigan family drama wasn't the end of summer.

It was the beginning of Clara's life.

And just as she was about to prompt him and ask what it was? What was missing? Mr. Jake Hennings leaned across the small space of field beneath them, rested a hand on the white fabric she'd tucked over her trembling knees, and kissed her.

35

SARAH

Somehow, despite visiting the lake several times during the summer over the course of her life, Sarah Stevenson had never once been to a bonfire on the beach. She felt like the star of a nineties movie or something, standing there with a red Solo cup in one hand (just pop! Don't freak, Mom!) as a tall blaze threw off sparks and heat.

She wouldn't *be* the star if it weren't for her status as Senior New Girl. Typically, people who emerged at a new high school their senior year had something wrong with them. They were army brats or flunkies.

But everyone knew Sarah Stevenson had nothing wrong with her. She was Miss Hannigan's niece, that's how. And even though good ol' Aunt Clara had a reputation as a hard you-know-what, she also had a reputation as the pretty teacher. It was enough to lay the groundwork for Sarah to also be pretty, apparently, because that's why the tentacles of Birch Harbor High's girl society slithered their way around her and dragged her under the water with them.

"Sarah!" Vivi squealed as she stumble-tripped through the sand. Little Mercy was at her side, shrinking smaller by the minute in the glow of the fire and against the loud crowd of the pep rally that raged nearby. "We've been looking *everywhere* for you," she droned dramatically.

Sarah held back her eye roll at the younger pair and flicked a glance to her closer friends, Paige and Chloe. They caught on and tilted their heads synchronously.

There was nothing *wrong* with Vivi. In fact, she was a total threat. A perfect incoming freshman with Baywatch looks and a hot dad. She'd gone to St. Mary's on the Island. Literally, there was *nothing* wrong with her. But Sarah didn't need freshmen friends. Not as the Senior New Girl, especially.

The night had worn on slowly. It began with a rocky performance courtesy of the Birch Harbor Marching Band, then faded into burgers and s'mores at the grill, then recharged with the current pep rally. In between each little event, most of the kids wandered around, braving to walk along the water despite the principal and football coach blowing a whistle every time one of the students came within four yards of the shoreline.

Now, Vivi and Mercy had found Sarah again. She was happy to be a mentor to the girls, but it was getting a little silly. Sarah was even starting to feel embarrassed to be seen with them all over the place.

She plastered a smile across her mouth and greeted the two littluns. "Hi Viviana. Hi Mercy. Are you two having fun?"

"Totally. Lots of hot guys. Lots of fun," Vivi replied. "I heard there's an after party at your aunt's place," she went on conspiratorially.

Sarah did a double take. "A *what*?"

"Yeah, my dad said we could hang out on the beach there." She threw a pointed finger south across the harbor and to the dimly lit house that hung along Heirloom Cove.

Sarah returned her gaze to Vivi. "Really? I haven't heard about it."

"Well, I mean, my dad says we are always welcome to hang out there, you know?"

The marching band had long packed and left. The blazing fire grew stronger, though, to the beat of someone's Bluetooth speaker as its scratchy bass boomed across the sand. Sarah peered around. The school chaperones were still there. The football players and half the volleyball team, all designated in painted crop tops, were still there, too.

"It doesn't look like any of them are headed over to the cove," Sarah pointed out and glanced back at Paige and Chloe, who just shrugged.

"I'm out," Paige replied. "We've got Mass at eight."

"Same," Chloe chimed in, squeezing Sarah's shoulders and waving to Vivi and Mercy.

Sarah crossed her arms over her chest. "I see. You two just want to come hang out at the house on the harbor."

"It's called the Heirloom Inn now," Vivi corrected. "Right, Merc?"

The smaller girl shrugged.

Sarah shook her head. "Whatever. Let's go." It was better to keep the peace when it came to a delicate relationship like the one she had with Vivi. Even Sarah's superiority as a senior wouldn't grant her protection from the likes of a girl such as Viviana Fiorillo.

They checked out with the chaperones and walked down the beach, through the Village with its Saturday night crowds, and across the marina.

Small talk was the only option. If Sarah could bore the girls to death, then maybe they'd finally call their folks to come pick them up and she could get back to the lighthouse and go to sleep. The next week was a big one. Her dad had spilled the beans that they'd all be moving into the two-bedroom at The Bungalows. Sarah was neither excited for this nor disappointed about it. She missed being with her parents, but it'd feel weird to live in an apartment, even if it was a nice one or a family-owned one or whatever. Still, she had the distinct sense that such a home might set her at some kind of disadvantage somehow. It was another reason to keep mum about the whole Clara-Kate thing that her aunts and mom kept dredging up. No point in drawing any negative attention. Not now. Not for the start of the school year. Not when she had so much else on her plate mentally.

"So, what's it like having a dad who works at the marina?" she asked Mercy.

Mercy just shrugged again. "Cool, I guess. We go out on the lake all the time."

"He's got a great boat," Vivi added, nudging Mercy with her shoulder.

"What do you do? Ski?"

"Um, not always. Lots of time we just look for stuff," she answered.

Sarah slowed down. They were approaching the

private beach behind Heirloom Inn, and she wanted to suss out if any of the guests were on the back porch. As the oldest, it was her job to ensure they weren't acting like hooligans or trespassers. She tugged her phone from her back pocket and quickly tapped out a text to the group chat with her mom and aunts. *At the Inn with Vivi and Mercy FYI.*

"Oh, yeah?" Sarah replied. "What kind of stuff?"

"Animals, like different sorts of fish and stuff. Sometimes other things. Like," Mercy's energy ramped up a notch. "Did you know there have been, like, *dozens* of shipwrecks on Lake Huron? My dad was just telling me about that the other day when we found this old pop can that looked like it was from the seventies or something. It was just floating out there in the water, all rusty and old. My dad thinks it probably came up from some shipwreck, but he's still studying the lake. He knows more about Lake Michigan and Lake Superior."

"Wow, cool," Sarah replied, vaguely interested as she confirmed visually that no one was on the back porch. "Okay, we can hang on the porch. I'm too tired to walk the beach anymore." She hated to shut Mercy down just as the girl was warming up, but it was getting late, and Sarah was getting bored.

The other two followed her up through the low gate at the seawall until they made it to the porch, settling into the sofa and cushioned chairs as Sarah dragged her phone out again and began thumbing through social media.

Vivi and Mercy started chatting about a particularly cute boy they'd noticed at the bonfire, but a new text popped up on Sarah's phone. *On our way there. Fireflies was great!*

It was her mom. Sarah silently cursed herself for not asking how it went first. *Yay! Way to go, MOM!*

Her eyes flitted up to the girls, and she let out a sigh. "Looks like you were right."

"Right about what?" Vivi's eyes flashed at the affirmation.

"An after-party. Here. Except it won't be high school kids. It's my aunts and their dates, sorry to tell you." She pouted her lips and cocked her head.

"Oh, right. I keep *forgetting* you're like related to half of Birch Harbor," Vivi replied, clearly picking up on Sarah's attitude.

Sarah let out a sigh. "Yeah, I guess. Look, sorry I'm being a little... edgy. I'm just exhausted. We've had a lot going on and—"

She was cut off by voices through the window above their heads.

Vivi's face lit up conspiratorially and she crouched lower on the sofa, drawing a finger to her lips.

36

KATE

They spilled in through the front door, all giggles and stage whispers. Kate and Megan left the boys in the front yard where they'd gotten immediately distracted by some side conversation about the *new build*.

Megan was glowing from the success of the evening and all but drooling over her prospective house project.

"Can you even *believe* it, Kate?" she asked as they made it safely into the kitchen where they could talk a little louder, since they weren't directly beneath the guest rooms. "A house. In the *field*. *Our* field, Kate!"

Kate smiled at her little sister, so overcome with happiness for her that her cheeks hurt. "It's going to be perfect. You know that? Absolutely perfect."

Megan let out a contented sigh then looked through the window. "Where are the girls?" she looked down at the phone. "Sarah said they were going to hang out here."

Kate twisted around and craned her neck toward the hall. "Were they in the parlor?"

Megan tapped away on her phone. "I'll ask. They'd *better* not be down at the beach." She walked to the far window, the one behind the kitchen table that looked past the porch and down to the beach. Kate followed her and peered out through the dark glass.

The beach was lit well enough by the dock lights that they could be sure the girls weren't there. Or if they were, they were in the water. She shuddered.

"Do you remember that story?" Kate asked Megan. "The one about that great aunt Mom had?"

Megan's eyes grew wide. "Yes. The one who drowned ages ago. Just out there." Megan pointed her finger. There was no sadness to come of this revelation. Megan didn't know the aunt. But it was one of those Hannigan stories that splashed through generations, a modern-day cautionary tale akin to Little Red Riding Hood or Goldilocks.

Kate let out a sigh. "People think Mom was possessive of the beach. But she wasn't. She didn't care if tourists lounged in the backyard, but she didn't want them walking on her beach. Not where..."

Megan shook her head and threw the door open, calling loudly across the dark night for her daughter. Kate joined her, stepping onto the porch in time to hear, "Sorry!"

Three little heads peered around the door. Sarah, Vivi, and little Mercy Hennings.

"Girls," Kate chided. "You scared us to death!"

Megan added, "That was freaky. I instantly thought you had drowned or something."

"I know, I know. Sorry, Mom," Sarah replied, unfolding herself from the seat that had been hidden beneath the kitchen sink window. "I'm ready to go home."

Kate hooked a finger to Vivi and Mercy. "You two come on in. Vivi, your dad is just out front."

It was the first time Kate had ever addressed Vivi in that way. Like, almost, a stepmom. And as she watched the pretty blonde traipse lithely through the kitchen and out down the hall, she saw something else. She saw what she had lost. Raising a daughter. Whispering over popcorn with a teenager, rearing up the woman who might one day become her very best friend.

She saw it all in Vivi.

And she wondered if maybe... just *maybe* there could be a chance that she might have that yet.

37

MEGAN

The three of them loaded up into the SUV like old times. Brian in the driver's seat, Megan in the passenger, and Sarah in the center of the bench in the second row.

They rehashed the night together, Sarah and Megan trading highlights. It turned out Sarah's new best friends were Paige and Chloe, which reassured Megan.

Still, she asked as delicately as she could, "So, what's up with Vivi and Mercy?"

"What do you mean?" Sarah replied through a yawn as she fell against her seatback.

"Are you, sort of, I don't know, connecting with them?"

Sarah groaned. "*Mom.*"

"Sorry!" Megan's hands flew up in self-defense and she and Brian shared a knowing look. "I'm just wondering."

"I get it. Vivi is technically... what? My cousin by

marriage or something? Half cousin? Whatever, but *no*. She's a *freshman*."

"Well, let me share my highlight of the night," Megan interjected, twisting in her seat to share a bit of gossip with her daughter. "Did you know that I made a match tonight?"

Sarah rolled her eyes. "Ew, Mom. Look, I'm super happy that you two are getting back together or whatever, but just... *ew*."

Megan and Brian laughed together, and she replied, "No, no. Not your dad and me. I mean Aunt Clara."

"I don't know if you had much of a hand in that," Brian cut in.

But Megan lifted her palm. "I provided the event, did I not?"

"True," he bobbed his head from shoulder to shoulder.

"Then there you have it. Being a matchmaker isn't about assigning boyfriends and girlfriends. It's about greasing the wheels. Oiling the pot. Sprinkling a little magic." She turned and winked at Sarah. "Anyway, guess who else showed up?"

"Who?" Sarah asked, her interest clearly piqued by the small-town juice.

"Mercy Hennings' *dad*!" Megan revealed.

Sarah didn't react at first. Then, after a moment, when Megan turned again, about to explain who he was and how he hit it off with Clara, Sarah opened her mouth.

"What if Clara's her teacher next year?"

"Aunt Clara," Brian corrected in the rearview mirror.

"What if she's *your* teacher?" Megan pointed out. "That's how it is in Birch Harbor." She let out a happy sigh and shook her head, returning her gaze to the view of the lake as they coasted down Harbor Ave.

From the back seat, Sarah spoke again. This time her voice had lost its edge, and if Megan didn't know any better, she thought she detected a little trepidation in her otherwise self-assured daughter. "Mom, couldn't that, I don't know, be a *problem*?"

"Couldn't *what* be a problem, Sarah?" Megan asked, her adrenaline slowing as she unfastened her seatbelt to walk Sarah inside.

Sarah grabbed her things and popped out of the second seat, joining her mother in the cool night breeze as they strode through the darkness toward Amelia's front door. "If my *cousin* is my teacher, I mean," Sarah answered, turning to Megan on the front porch.

Megan took a deep breath and let it out, reaching her hand to tuck a strand of her daughter's hair behind her ears. Sarah reminded Megan of herself. Bold, dark, and typically serious. "Sarah, as far as this town knows, Clara is your *aunt* and we are one, nice big happy family. You have nothing to worry about." She flicked a glance to the inky water of the lake. "Except for drowning. But don't worry. Birch Harbor High is inland. Away from the water and away from all that drama. Everything is going to be *fine*."

EPILOGUE

Amelia

Amelia sat at the table, the article clutched in her hands. Michael was tired of mulling it over, but she still had a desperate urge to reach out to this woman. This insufferable islander who was hell-bent on making sure everything was *not* fine for the Hannigans.

But then she got a text. From Clara. A reply to her earlier question.

Yes. She went to St. Mary's. With Mom. I found the year-book. It was in the hope chest...in the cottage.

CONTINUE THE SAGA

Find out what happens next in *Cottage by the Creek*.

Ready for a change of scenery? Order Elizabeth Bromke's standalone novel *The Summer Society*.

ALSO BY ELIZABETH BROMKE

Birch Harbor

Hickory Grove

Maplewood

The Summer Society

ABOUT THE AUTHOR

Elizabeth Bromke writes women's fiction and small-town romance. When she's not reading or writing, she's working on a puzzle with her son and husband or taking long walks with her golden retriever, Winnie.

Elizabeth graduated from the University of Arizona where she studied English, theater, and Spanish. She now lives in the mountains with her family and among a chatty variety of woodland creatures. Learn more by visiting her website at elizabethbromke.com.

Made in the USA
Middletown, DE
14 August 2020